Praise for *The Lies They Tell*

"This was a little bit *Gatsby*, a little bit *The Girl on the Train*, and I loved every minute of it. Throughout the absolutely propulsive storyline, I found myself resisting the urge to devour the book in one sitting. Every single character, from the mysterious, simmering Tristan to the smart-mouthed, charismatic Reese, and Pearl, with her quiet bravery and grit, is written with precision and complexity, while the coastal Maine setting is a character in itself, vividly evoked and lovingly portrayed."

**—Jessie Ann Foley, author of *Neighborhood Girls*
and Michael L. Printz Honor Book *The Carnival at Bray***

"Gillian French combines class struggles, family drama, and, of course, murder, like an alchemist, creating something greater than its parts. This book lingers in the best way possible."

**—Lamar Giles, Edgar Award finalist
and author of *Fake ID* and *Endangered***

"French describes in unflinching, haunting prose the social inequities and rugged, often treacherous landscape that define the 'real' Maine. An excellent teen mystery that reveals far more than 'whodunnit.'"

—Maria Padian, author of *Wrecked*

"With haunting, gorgeous prose, *The Lies They Tell* is a masterful mystery that will transport you to the dark coast of Maine, where big secrets lurk in small towns. Privileged summer families, murder, intoxicating boys, and a fierce heroine converge in this novel perfect for fans of *We Were Liars* and *One of Us Is Lying*."

—Shannon M. Parker, author of *The Girl Who Fell* and *Rattled Bones*

"Gorgeously written, chilling, and twisty, *The Lies They Tell* kept me guessing until the very end. Small-town mystery at its best."

—Carlie Sorosiak, author of *If Birds Fly Back* and *Wild Blue Wonder*

"*The Lies They Tell* kept me guessing until the final pages. Readers will root for Pearl as she navigates an undercurrent of darkness and deception to solve a mystery and save her father's reputation. A strong heroine, a satisfying conclusion—this is one of the best YA novels I've read all year."

—Paula Stokes, author of *Liars, Inc.*

Also by Gillian French

Grit

THE

LIES

GILLIAN FRENCH

THEY

An Imprint of HarperCollins*Publishers*

TELL

HarperTeen is an imprint of HarperCollins Publishers.

The Lies They Tell
Copyright © 2018 by Gillian French
All rights reserved. Printed in the United States of America.
No part of this book may be used or reproduced in any manner
whatsoever without written permission except in the case of brief
quotations embodied in critical articles and reviews. For information
address HarperCollins Children's Books, a division of HarperCollins
Publishers, 195 Broadway, New York, NY 10007.
www.epicreads.com

Library of Congress Control Number: 2018933335
ISBN 978-0-06-264258-5

Typography by Erin Fitzsimmons
18 19 20 21 22   PC/LSCH   10 9 8 7 6 5 4 3 2 1
❖
First Edition

For Jeremy

ONE

THE LAST NIGHT the Garrisons set foot inside the Tenney's Harbor Country Club, the windows were laced with snow. The weather report called for six to eight inches by morning, and three already lay crisp and untouched across the western expanse of lawn beyond the glass. The Garrisons would have their white Christmas. Mother Nature wouldn't dare disappoint.

Pearl had the distinction of waiting on them. She was a small, spare girl with dark hair worn in a pixie cut and an odd cast to her eyes, which, upon closer examination, were two different colors, brown and blue. She said good evening and handed them a wine and spirits list while they looked through her, registering nothing, clueless that her dad had worked for them for nearly three years now and was, in fact, huddled beside a space heater in their gatehouse at this very moment, watching the Celtics on her tablet.

David Garrison ordered a scotch and water, his wife, Sloane, a white wine. Joseph, their youngest child at ten, frowned at the list and said, "I'll have a beer," which earned a laugh from his sister, Cassidy, and a "*Hush*" from his mother.

Tristan Garrison was absent; Pearl noted it as surely as everyone else in the dining room. Whispers had been circulating around the club for a week: the Garrisons were opening their Tenney's Harbor home for the holidays, a first. Now one of their remarkable children was missing.

When Pearl returned with drinks and bread, Lou Pulaski, occasional golfing partner of David, came over to the table and clapped David's shoulder. "Back in the great white north, eh? Damned glad to see ya. Where's your oldest tonight?"

David's jaw flexed as he shook out his napkin. "He stayed home."

"What—back in Greenwich?"

A pause. "No."

Pearl flicked her gaze at Sloane. She was looking down. So were the kids. Lou chuckled uneasily and lurched onto other topics, but for Pearl's part, she was glad to take their orders and fade away.

When she reached the kitchen, one of the swinging doors

was propped open, and a sparkly ball of evergreen dangled above it. A kissing ball. Some of the busboys stood around, grinning and waiting.

She spun on her heel and ran straight into Reese, who steadied her, his eyes a little bloodshot from the Christmas cheer he'd been into before their shift began. "Watch it, Haskins," he said.

"You watch it." She'd been watching him all night—somebody had to—as he chattered, joked, spilled pinot noir on table linens, produced origami geese from cocktail napkins for little kids, and flirted with ladies old enough to be his grandmother. Buzzed or not, he'd crush her in tips; he always did.

Behind them, Indigo Conner said, "You guys," in a soft singsong, tapping the kissing ball, making it sway.

The chant began: "Do it, do it." Pearl held her tray in front of her like a shield. "I've killed men for less."

Reese smiled, shrugged, and stepped aside. As Pearl turned, he caught her face in both hands and laid one on her.

She closed her eyes, leaning in, tasting the hint of rum eggnog still on his breath. His fingertips slid up her temples into her hair. People were whooping and whistling, and when the moment finally broke and he let go, she staggered, as if the kiss itself had been holding her up.

Reese went into the kitchen without a backward glance, busboys pounding his back and ruffling his hair. Pearl wiped her mouth, then smoothed her club blouse and tie with hands that felt palsied and weak. When she looked up, Indigo was watching her.

The girl smiled a little as she passed, grazing Pearl's arm hard enough to let her know she was there. "Everything you hoped for, sweetie?"

Pearl stared, a blush of volcanic proportions rolling up from her collar. She saw her next move so clearly: grabbing a handful of Indigo's thick, curly ponytail, taking her down into one of the tables, china and crystal exploding around them, her own fists a pummeling blur.

In reality, her face burned and her eyes filled as she made for the patio doors. Damned if she'd let Indigo see her cry.

Outside in the dark, Pearl hit the clapboards and sank into a crouch, savoring the sting of the wind. Ten seconds. She could afford a ten-second meltdown. Then chin up, back to work, before that little Nazi Meriwether came out here to see who was wasting club time.

Fifteen minutes later, face washed, cowlick combed down, Pearl delivered the Garrisons' entrées. She thought she sensed Cassidy studying her eyes, but that was nothing new. She hoped they didn't still look weepy. From the direction of the kitchen, a faint cheer went up as the busboys caught more victims. "Can I get anyone any—?"

"No." David's tone was clipped. He didn't look at her as he sawed into his roast duckling. Pearl gave a half bow and departed, careful to skirt Indigo and Reese in case the urge to tackle came on her again.

The Garrisons ate. Onstage, Steve Mills, who performed cocktail piano standards at the baby grand every weekend, launched into "Merry Christmas, Baby." Once the Garrisons had scraped their bowls of crème brûlée clean, Steve said into the mic, "Good to see some of our snowbird members, the Garrisons, joining us tonight on this Christmas Eve-Eve." A flourish over the ivories. "Maybe you folks can help me convince Cassidy Garrison to come on up here and play a little something in the spirit of the season?"

A momentary hush as people turned to look at the Garrisons. Asking a piano prodigy like seventeen-year-old Cassidy to "play a little something" felt like asking da Vinci to join in a game of Pictionary. Some reluctant applause followed.

Sloane whispered to her daughter. From where Pearl stood by the Christmas tree, it looked like she squeezed Cassidy's knee under the table. Placidly, Cassidy pushed her chair back and walked up the risers to the stage as everyone clapped again, relieved.

Slender and erect, Cassidy sat, shook her hair back, placed her fingers on the keys. She may as well have been carved from ivory, cool and flawless beneath the recessed lighting, long pale hair streaming down the back of her midnight-blue dress. She didn't look like any seventeen-year-old Pearl had ever seen, and Pearl had just turned eighteen last month.

"Gloria in Excelsis Deo" unfolded from Cassidy's fingertips. She sang in Latin in a clear, glass-bell voice, words that Pearl couldn't understand, but felt anyway. They made her eyes sting again, this time not unpleasantly, as she stood back among the twinkling lights and German blown-glass bulbs, witnessing what nobody knew would be Cassidy Garrison's swan song.

The room didn't breathe until the last note faded into the eaves. This time, the applause was thunderous. People stood. Cassidy said "Thank you" softly into the mic and returned to her family, who waited, unmoved by yet another command performance from the girl who'd brought down the Boston Symphony Hall at age eight.

The Garrisons left soon after that, shrugging on coats made from cashmere and the finest wool, Joseph laughing once, audibly, before the lobby doors closed between them and the night.

Gradually, the evening ended, members signing credit slips and wishing one another a merry Christmas on their way to the coat check. When Pearl went to the kitchen to put in a final dessert order, the kissing ball was gone and the doors were shut; the help was hangdog, meeting no one's eyes. Meriwether had been here. The fun had been sucked from the premises like sunlight into a black hole.

At closing, Pearl waited by her car to make sure Reese

was okay to drive. Ski cap on, hands tucked into the pockets of her Carhartt coat, she shifted from foot to foot, watching the back door.

When Reese came out, he was leaning on Indigo, much of his face lost in the thick faux-fur collar of her coat. Whatever he whispered in her ear made her laugh. Unaware of Pearl in the dark, they passed his car in favor of Indigo's old Skylark.

Pearl sank into her driver's seat, working her lips over her teeth, the familiar resentment back again, eating away at her. She started her engine when Indigo started hers.

She followed them down Harbor Road, the ocean a massive, brooding presence to her left. She kept her distance, watching the silhouettes of their heads in the headlight beams. The Skylark fishtailed lazily. Leave it to Indigo to drive on summer tires year-round. She was nineteen, living on her own, doing whatever she damn well pleased.

Pearl lived on Abbott Street, Reese on Ocean Avenue, but they wouldn't turn in there, she was certain. She stayed on them until the stop sign, where the Skylark went into a slow spin, swinging into Main Street and stalling out in the path of a plow truck. The horn bellowed. Pearl reached out as if to catch them, her lips parting without sound.

The Skylark rumbled, gunned, and reversed into the opposite lane, dodging the plow by what looked like no more than a foot. It sat cockeyed for a few beats; then the tires spun, and it drove on.

Pearl released a shuddery breath. Knowing those two, they were laughing right now. *Look what we almost did. Look how close we came.*

Or maybe they were laughing at her. Maybe they'd known she was there all along, stalking them through a nor'easter with her heart pounding, nose running, clothes full of the smell of roasting duck, only to confirm what she already knew: they were going back to Indigo's apartment, to her bed, and what they did there would be more than Pearl had ever done with anyone, because the only person she'd ever wanted to do it with was Reese.

She went home to the silent little house on Abbott. She showered, left a light on for Dad, who wouldn't be back until four a.m., then curled up under the covers, staring at the wall. She'd never been so sick of herself. She wanted to wriggle out of her skin and kick it away like a clammy bathing suit, somehow erase the memory of kissing Reese back, right in front of everybody, the perfect, desperate fool.

Sleep shunned her until almost midnight. Outside Pearl's window, snow continued to fall.

At the same time, on the other side of Tenney's Harbor, the Garrisons were burning in their beds.

TWO

Six Months Later

THE BOYS HAD been in the sun—tennis, maybe, or just back from the yacht club. Their brows were damp, postures loose, recuperating. They sat around the table like young guys do, taking up a lot of room, unconcerned by the stares they drew from members and waitstaff alike, lips moving in whispered conversation.

Pearl watched them, breathing shallowly, feeling panic, exhilaration. He never sat in her section. Now here he was with his entourage, the boys of summer, owning the place.

She gathered three menus and went to them, playing the part. "Can I start you gentlemen off with some drinks?" Her voice sounded stiff, an octave higher than usual.

If Tristan Garrison knew her, he gave no sign. That was the way with summer people; they were perfectly comfortable not knowing the locals who prepared their food, changed their sheets, or those, apparently, who were drowning in the undertow of their personal tragedy. "Water, please." His voice was quiet, dismissive. He did not look at her.

Tristan's fair skin bore the touch of late June sunshine, but he'd grown thin since winter, still leanly muscled from the racquetball court and hours on the treadmill. Pearl knew the raised veins on his forearms, the faint frown line between his brows that hadn't smoothed even with the arrival of his wingmen. She studied him whenever he came into the dining room, gripped by the physical and emotional recoil she—and most everyone else—felt in his presence. Alone. He was so alone, even in a room full of people, and maybe in that they shared some kinship.

"Iced coffee. Cream, sugar, shot of espresso. Don't put too much ice in it." The boy across from her sat tipped back in his chair, his white tank top contrasting against his deep brown skin, designer ball cap cocked at an angle. The club had done away with the gentlemen-must-wear-a-jacket-and-tie policy long before Pearl began working here, but there was still a certain dress code to be maintained, and Akil Malhotra was way below par. Pearl knew him by sight. Everybody knew the Indian kid who'd stolen the golf cart last summer.

The boy on the left was one of the Spencer grandchildren.

He had the look: shaggily blond, deeply tanned from living at the family compound in North Carolina the rest of the year. He smiled at her, his gaze moving from her face to her breasts and back again. "Surprise me." A faint southern accent, honeying every other word.

She blinked. "Very good." One more quick glance at Tristan before she left.

She took orders at two more tables, meeting Reese's gaze on her way to the kitchen; he was waiting on Mimi Montgomery-Hines and her friends, a tableful of elderly ladies who wore ropes of beads and big hats and bright lipstick, like an inverted version of a little girls' dress-up tea party. Mimi adored Reese; the maître d's knew to seat her in section three without being told. Reese dropped Pearl a wink without breaking his stream of banter, and the sun-washed room rang with women's laughter.

The bar was unmanned, so she grabbed a bottle of San Pellegrino from the cooler herself. Tristan always drank San Pellegrino. Someone's fingers stole over the back of her neck, and she smiled, knowing it was Reese.

"Hiya, twinkle toes." He went around the bar, took the lid off the blender, and dumped in ice, lime juice, triple sec, tequila.

"You'd better get out of there before Chas comes back."

"Hey, he's taking a whiz, my table needs drinks. You think I don't know how to make a margarita?" He put a swizzle stick in his teeth, commenced chewing. "C'mon, c'mon, what do you need?"

"Iced coffee: cream, sugar, espresso. And I've got a guy who wants me to surprise him."

"Slap on some pasties and come out singing, 'Happy Birthday, Mr. President.' Works every time." He pulled the coffee pitcher out of the fridge and poured.

"You know from experience, huh." She waited as he gave the blender a blast. "Isn't it kind of early in the day for those?"

"Haskins. What have we learned about the rich?"

She sighed. "That it's socially acceptable for them to drink more in a day than we do in a week."

"Right. And since it's now"—he checked an invisible watch—"just a hair past noon, Mimi and her cronies need a pick-me-up so they can make it till cocktail hour. Salt some glasses for me."

Looking over her shoulder (you never knew when Meriwether might decide to do a walk-through, attending to her assistant managerial duties with grim fervor), she went to him and ran a lime wedge around the edge of the margarita glasses, dipping them in coarse salt. Being this close to Reese O'Shaughnessy was like standing beside high-tension power lines. She felt the energy thrumming through his wiry, not-quite-six-foot frame, and the abruptness of his movements, careless, sloppy, but still getting the job done. His auburn hair fell into his eyes, and she put her hands in her pockets to resist smoothing it back. Friends didn't stroke each other's hair. She was pretty sure that was in the manual somewhere.

"Who let the Prince of Darkness out?" Indigo's low voice made Pearl turn. The girl leaned on the bar, one hip angled out, watching Tristan. She somehow managed to make the uniform of green-and-gold-striped tie, white blouse, and black slacks look like sex on wheels, as if it had been specifically tailored to her. Pearl's size-small blouse hung loosely, and she had to wear a belt to keep the slacks from slipping down her nonexistent curves. "Looks like the posse's back in town." Indigo turned her cool gaze on Pearl. "Lucky you."

Reese filled the glasses. "Bet he leaves a killer tip. Buh-bum-bum." Indigo and Pearl made identical sounds of disgust. "Jesus. Warn me before you go all highbrow, girls. Indy, what do you need?"

"I'm still waiting for my surprise." Pearl hoped she sounded light and breezy.

Reese mixed cola and grenadine, garnished with a maraschino cherry. "Roy Rogers. Unless he's ninety, he's never heard of it."

Pearl loaded her tray and left, straining to hear what was said in her wake. Indigo: "Pitcher of mimosas and a sex on the beach. Just make it," before Reese could say anything. Possibly a good sign. Those two were notoriously on-again, off-again, though they'd never been officially on, and if they were off now, Pearl doubted she'd be notified.

She set the glasses down in front of the boys. The Spencer grandson bit into the cherry immediately. Tristan didn't glance up at her; he had his phone out. "Have you decided?" she said. Tristan continued with the touch screen, letting the other boys order before him. Whatever he chose, she knew he wouldn't eat it.

When she turned to go, Pearl paused to let the maître d' lead a party of two past her. The couple spoke in low tones, casting looks Tristan's way. He seemed unaware, or maybe he was used to it by now, his new normal. Pariah.

Tristan had always garnered stares, but originally it was because he was a Garrison, a National Merit Scholar, already a first-string lacrosse star in his freshman year at Yale. Tall, strikingly dark-eyed, brown hair carefully maintained to a half inch above his collar. Now his hair was longer, ignored, his style off-the-rack, though he possessed more personal wealth than most of the members would ever know, which was no small statement. It seemed everyone felt fascination-meets-revulsion in Tristan Garrison's presence, followed by *but the police cleared him; they let him go, didn't they?* Somehow, it wasn't a comfort. Not at all.

When Pearl brought the boys their entrées, the Spencer grandson said, "Well, damn. You're amazing. How'd you remember all that?" as she set his plate in front of him, a Reuben on panini bread, spicy mustard and dill spears on the side.

"I can read without moving my lips, too. You'd be surprised." She bit the inside of her cheek. She could almost hear Reese say, *Your filter, Haskins. It's broken.*

Instead of looking embarrassed, Spencer grinned, lopsided and guileless. "If that's an invitation to get to know you better, I'm up for it."

She cleared her throat. "Would anyone like another drink?"

Akil snorted. "Burn."

"She's just doing her job." Spencer's ease was unshakable as he held up his glass. "This is great, by the way. What's in it?"

"Roy Rogers." She tucked the collapsible stand and tray under her arm. "Enjoy."

She snuck a peek back. He'd turned all the way around in his chair to watch her go. Heat creeping into her cheeks, she did a little bobbing and weaving to lose herself in the crowd.

Chas was back behind the bar, hopefully none the wiser that the underage waitstaff had been at the helm, and Reese was at Mimi's table, which at that moment exploded with hooting laughter. Hard to tell what was going on, exactly, but Reese had a cocktail umbrella tucked behind his ear, and everyone's glasses were almost empty. Pearl studied Mimi, a small, plump woman in a purple linen short set, her gray hair curled under her chin. Mimi was one of the only club members who'd kept Dad on as a caretaker after what happened to the Garrisons; she'd simply called from Texas around the end of April to ask him to open the cottage for her and slap on a new coat of paint while he was at it. It was the first work Dad had gotten in almost a month, the first paycheck they'd seen other than Pearl's in two weeks.

The boys ate quickly, economically, no time wasted in conversation. When Pearl returned, Tristan had angled himself toward the door, rubbing absently at his left arm. "Can I get you gentlemen anything else?" she said.

"Yeah." Spencer leaned forward. "Your number." It had to be the oldest pickup line in the history of food service. Akil groaned, tugging his hat low.

Pearl withdrew the check from her apron pocket and set it on the table, patting it lightly. "Have a pleasant afternoon."

Once they'd left, she went back to the table. Tristan's plate was a psychological study: everything had been shifted to the right, picked at, barely touched. He'd signed for the whole bill. The tip was calculated at 15 percent to the penny.

In the corner of the slip, a phone number was written, along with the name *Bridges Spencer*. Beneath it, he'd drawn a smiley face with devil horns.

THREE

AT THE END of her shift, Pearl stepped through the patio doors into evening heat and held her breath, listening. In the distance, a motor hummed. One of the zero-turn mowers, somewhere near the golf course's ninth hole. Dad.

As always, the club seemed to observe her as she crossed the western lawn toward the golf course. Measuring her, taking stock. It was Pearl's habit to keep her tie knotted until she was over the cobblestone bridge spanning the pond, well out of range of the many gleaming windows.

The club was an imposing three-story block of New England architecture, all white clapboards and Victorian-style gingerbread trim. It was due to turn one hundred years old in July, celebrated by a monthlong series of gala events that had the members buzzing. It was a determined sort of buzz, white noise to cover the steady pulse of unease. Six months had passed since tragedy had soiled their summer playground; not nearly time enough for the dead to rest easy. Better to bury the Garrisons in talk of formal balls and silent auctions, of ladies' teas and regattas on the bay.

Usually, you had to be ready to duck and cover on the links, but at this time of day most of the golfers had headed home or to the bar. The groundskeepers' main building was off to the left, silver-shingled and gambrel-roofed. The guys were locking up for the night, but Dad wasn't among them.

Dickie Fournier saw her coming, hooked his thumb toward where the links curved off into invisibility. "He's way the hell out there. Take a Gator."

"Thanks." Grabbing a set of keys, she tossed her bag into the passenger seat of one of the utility vehicles and put the pedal down, loving the shock of breeze through her hair.

Around the bend, the links opened into a panoramic view of Frenchman Bay and Little Nicatou Island, which sat a mile offshore from their corner of Mount Desert Island. Living on an island sounded romantic, but MDI was the second largest on the Eastern Seaboard, and easily accessible by bridge— no storm-tossed ferry rides required. It was starkly beautiful here; academically, Pearl knew this, but she'd also lived the other side, post–Labor Day: shutters on most of the shop windows, the single stoplight blinking yellow, the whole world buried under feet of suffocating snow.

Most of the course had been freshly mowed lengthwise, green to the tee and back again, but here, the lines ended. She spotted the zero-turn abandoned near a sand trap, Dad nowhere in sight. She hit the horn lightly and parked. "You here?"

No answer. Pearl climbed out and walked the ragged edge of the bluff, running her hand along the wire fence. She finally spotted him, out there on the embankment, standing on the ledge, facing seaward.

She gripped the fence posts, afraid to speak and startle him. After a moment, he sensed her and turned, a man torn from a dream. "Hey, Pearlie." He sounded fine, same old Dad, but the late haunted nights had seamed his face, already full of sharp angles, like her own. He was responsible for all of it: her small build, the slight wave in her hair, her habit of biting her lips whenever she was nervous or upset.

"It's five o'clock." She still couldn't move. He seemed to understand, then, how much he was scaring her, and walked over, squeezing through a rolled-back panel in the fencing, where she immediately hugged him hard around the waist. "What were you doing out there?"

"Looking around." He kissed the top of her head. She caught a hearty whiff of him: spearmint gum, fresh sweat, and booze, but not recent—hopefully none since this morning,

Irish in his coffee while she was out of the room. "Hey, I got something for you."

"It's not a golf ball, is it?"

"Hey. You used to love that when you were little." He took something from his pocket and pressed it into her palm.

She opened her fingers and saw a tiger-striped sea scallop shell, perfectly intact. "You found this out there?"

"Thought you'd want it for your collection." The gesture almost made her forget that he hadn't answered her question. "How was work?"

Memories of Tristan flickered by. "Typical. Doing stuff for rich people."

"Sounds like we had the same day. How about I grill tonight? Got some burger half off at Godfrey's."

"Sure. But the grill needs gas." He swore. "I can fry it up on the stovetop instead. Make pasta salad?" She was rewarded with a nod, half a smile. "Race you back."

Dad made for the zero-turn. She ran to the Gator, already rolling before he even had the mower started. She kept him in her side-view mirror the whole way. Better to focus on that than on how her stomach had plummeted at the sight of him on that ledge, how everything she'd become so afraid of seemed encapsulated in that moment. Better than asking him the hard questions, the ones that really needed answering: *When are you going to be okay? Were you thinking about them?*

★ ★ ★

Dad's Beetle Cat sailboat sat on the boat trailer in the front yard with a spray-painted *For Sale* sign leaning against it: *$3,500 OBO.* The original prices of $4,500, then $4,000, were blacked out. Dad stood with his back to it, hosing road dust off his battered pickup, the first Bud Light of the evening in his free hand.

It was the final ass-kicker in the whole ordeal, selling the boat. Dad had owned it since before she was born. When Pearl was a kid, sometimes they'd drop a line in the harbor on a Sunday—never with Mom, that wasn't her thing. Her parents had so little in common it was amazing that she'd ever been conceived. So, it was Pearl and Dad, fishing buddies; poker buddies; throwing the ball around on warm evenings and tinkering with projects in the shed. Mom used to complain about feeling left out of their little club of two, but whenever she and Pearl tried mother-daughter stuff, it always ended in a fight; they just didn't seem to speak the same language. When the divorce finally happened, Pearl was thirteen, and the judge had let her decide for herself who she wanted to live with. She was surprised he'd even had to ask. And Mom never forgave her. Why else would she have taken that job down in Kittery, almost a four-hour drive away?

Now a sedan drove down Abbott Street and slowed, checking out the Cat. Pearl sat up in her lawn chair. After a second, the driver accelerated again. Relaxing, Pearl pulled her feet back up to sit cross-legged and continued reading *Sense and Sensibility* on her tablet.

"Maybe I should knock the price back." Dad popped the tab on Bud Light #2.

"It's too low already."

"Not if we want to unload the damn thing." Dad's profile was stony as he sprayed the mud flaps.

They didn't want to, but they were drowning. The mailbox was crammed with notices from collection agencies; snail mail was the only way they could reach the Haskins household now that Dad had canceled his phone service, both to save money and escape the reporters begging for comment, to find out what he'd seen that night. Dad's caretaking business, which kept them afloat during the off-season at the club, was bust. All because of the Garrisons, and what everyone in town was saying: it was Win Haskins's fault. A few tips of the flask, and he'd let the wolf in the door.

The image brought back the memory of Tristan today, sitting close enough for her to add his brand of aftershave to her cache of Garrison knowledge. Pearl slouched down, closed out of her social media accounts—Mom was always trolling, hoping to catch her online; after their latest fight, it probably seemed the safest way to communicate—pulled up Google, and entered the familiar search criteria *David Garrison family deaths* with the sound of Mom's old wind chimes pinging off each other in the background, miniature anchors.

Pearl had reread those first *Mount Desert Islander* and *Ellsworth American* articles countless times. She knew the photographs they'd run to the smallest detail, starting with the full-color spread of the Garrison house with a scorched hole in the roof, the blackened clapboards, the second-story east window a gaping hole into what had been the master bedroom. Firefighters were roaming around the front yard, their gear smudged with soot. The *American* headline read "Multimillionaire David Garrison, Three Family Members Killed in Tenney's Harbor Blaze."

The fire—cause undetermined at that time—had originated in David and Sloane's bedroom, spreading down the second-floor hallway to where Cassidy and Joseph slept, and up through the ceiling to the attic level, which had been converted into a loft for Tristan when they bought the house three years ago. On the morning of December 24, David's, Sloane's, Cassidy's, and Joseph's bodies had all been transported to the county morgue; Tristan was unaccounted for.

Pearl straightened her spine. She'd woken up to an empty house that morning, and a message on her phone from Dad, received at three a.m. *Something came up, be home as soon as I can.* Turned out he'd been calling from the hospital ER, where he was receiving treatment for second-degree burns on his hands and lacerations from punching through window glass. She could still see the Christmas tree tinsel swaying with the throb of the furnace as she'd eaten breakfast, facing the front window so she could watch the street for him. Then Dad had called back, with the rest of the story.

"Garrison Blaze Ruled Arson, Multiple Homicide." The next article was the first to use that family portrait, the one that would haunt the case to its current state of open, unsolved. Taken maybe two years ago, the photo showed the whole family wearing various ensembles of navy and white. The photographer must've told them not to smile.

Pearl's phone went off and she jumped, answering without taking her eyes off Tristan's face. "What's up?"

"Nothing. It's just that we've got way too much cake over here." Reese chewed as he spoke.

She'd hoped he'd call; he always kept her in suspense until dusk. "Cake sounds good." She watched Dad, now sitting on the front steps. She'd lost count of the Buds. "You could bring it over here."

"Yeah, but then I'd have to move." He waited. "Pe-arl, come on. I'm going to watch *Evil Dead 2*."

Now that was fighting dirty. "Text you in a sec." She hung up, turning the phone over in her hands.

"Reese?" Dad watched the sunset above the roofs of neighboring houses.

"Yeah. But I think I'll stay in. The dishes—"

"I'll do them. If you want to see your boyfriend, go ahead."

"He's not—"

"Whatever you call him. I can hold down the fort."

But chances were, he couldn't. Chances were, Dad would get to thinking, and there'd be nothing on TV, nothing to keep the walls from closing in, so he'd decide to drive down to the Tavern for a few. And she'd lose another little piece of him.

A text popped up from Reese: *chain-saw hand just sayin*

"I won't be late. Promise." Dad waved her off as she jogged up the steps past him. In the bathroom, she combed her hair (no visible change) and spritzed on the tiniest bit of Chantilly from the sample bottle Mom had forgotten in the medicine cabinet. Reese would laugh his ass off if he could see her.

She drove her old Civic over to the Dark Brew bakery and coffee shop, where Reese lived with his technically ex-stepmother. Dark Brew was on the ground level of an old general store built in the 1800s, and as manager, Jovia had been given a break on renting the second-story efficiency.

Pearl found them in the kitchen, Jovia doing her nails at the table, Reese sitting on the counter, eating what was most likely his second or third piece of chocolate cake.

Jovia shook her head at Pearl. "I don't know how you stand him. Having a metabolism like that should be against the law."

"Did you save me any?" There was one slim piece left in the takeout box. "Seriously? That's disgusting."

"Back off. I skipped breakfast this morning."

"Only because you didn't haul your butt out of bed until ten minutes before you had to be at work." Jovia blew on her nails and pointed at him. "I am not your wake-up service, mister. Next time, you're on your own."

"Sounds good to me."

Pearl dug into the cake. "Thanks, Jovia. This is awesome."

"Better be. I made it." Now that tourist season was in full swing, the kitchen would be stocked with day-old muffins and croissants; by the time Jovia got home, she was usually too wiped out to cook. Jovia and Reese were physical opposites: she was short, dark, and plump, fortysomething, favoring tight jeans and trendy tops; Reese was wiry, his eyes gray and lively, his uniform composed of thrift-shop finds, band tees, and the leather cuff bracelets he wore even to work, defying dress code. Their personalities were oil and water, but somehow they made the living situation work, probably because Reese did most of his living on the second floor of the carriage house out back.

Reese drummed his fingers, jumping down to his feet as soon as Pearl took her last bite. "Let's go."

Jovia jerked around. "You two aren't watching that psycho crap now, are you?"

"Yep," Reese said.

"Oh God. People getting heads chopped off, guts ripped out. Give me a nice romantic comedy any day, people being good to each other."

"Rom-coms suck." Reese held the back door for Pearl. "Two idiots meet cute, find insta-love, get in a fight over something stupid, and spend the rest of the movie figuring out what the audience has known since ten minutes in. Roll credits."

"Listen, smart-ass, love *is* stupid. Doesn't mean it's not worth the ride."

"We've got to get you your own line of Hallmark cards."

With a growl, Jovia turned to Pearl. "He tries anything out there, just slap him, okay?"

"Okay." As Pearl stepped through the door, Reese dodged her and ran down the steps. She gave chase, following him along the flagstone path into the shadows of the carriage house, where towers of boxed napkins and coffee stirrers stood as tall as she was. Up the spiral staircase to the unfinished second floor, where Dark Brew stock took up most of the space except for Reese's corner. A mattress on the floor, a set of plastic drawers, a box for a bedside table, and a standing lamp. Jovia had offered him the fold-out couch when he first moved in, which he'd flatly refused because he wanted his own space.

Reese tackled her onto the bed, and she shrieked, laughing. Pearl tickled his sides, and he yelped, rolling off. When he lifted her shirt and blew a raspberry on her stomach, she shrieked for real, scooting back on her heels and yanking down her hem.

Reese dropped back against his pillows, breathless and grinning. "If you really want to be safe, you could staple your shirt to your underwear."

"Shut up."

"Not like I saw anything." A silence. "So, bras come in negative cup sizes. Who knew."

She pummeled him. He covered his head and laughed until she tired herself out, kicking him once for good measure before flopping back and starting the movie on his old laptop. "Jerk."

After about half an hour, he rolled onto his side and hung his arm over her waist. "You can't fall asleep," she said softly. He nearly always dozed off when they watched something together.

"I'm not." It seemed to be growing between them, this closeness, in awkward fits and starts. Dad didn't know how much freedom they had over here, how much privacy, and she wanted to keep it that way.

She and Reese had been friends since the start of junior year, when Reese had moved here from Portland. Why he'd picked her of all people to hang around with, she didn't know; proximity, most likely. Same school, same job. She'd always been a square peg in both places: no good at currying favor with the queen bees, too old now to run with the boys. She and Reese had never kissed except for the night before Christmas Eve, such a humiliating memory that she'd tried to bury it as deeply as possible. Now she reached down and linked her fingers with his, feeling a small charge when he didn't pull free.

His phone began vibrating on the bedside table. Groaning, he reached over, checked the screen, and put it back on the table before she managed to glimpse the screen. Indigo, maybe. He lay down and put his hands behind his head, watching the mayhem on the screen. "You okay?" he said finally.

"Me? Yeah." But she was tense now, and she sat forward, hugging her knees. "Feel like a drive?"

After texting Jovia that they were going out—she wrote back *not too late, be SAFE*—they set off, Pearl driving, Reese riding shotgun with a Coors Light from his stash held below the sight level of any passing police cruisers, which were a common sight since December. The night smelled like ocean, car exhaust, the stifling perfume of peonies.

"She has to know you're taking those." Pearl headed down Ocean Avenue, passing a stretch of sprawling bed-and-breakfasts and inns lit by streetlamps, quaint little shops displaying souvenirs and work by local artisans. For those who found Bar Harbor ostentatious, Tenney's Harbor was the place to summer, to leave behind the hectic pace of New York City, Boston, Chicago. Tenney's Harbor's population more than doubled from late June to mid-August, wealthy families returning to their summer homes and their yacht and country club memberships.

Reese shrugged, popping the top and sipping the foam. "I think Jov's just glad I'm not cooking crystal in somebody's basement. A couple beers missing from the fridge are no big."

"Has she heard from your dad lately?"

Another sip. "Nope." Jovia and Reese's dad, Liam, had divorced almost three years ago. Reese's mom was caught up with the two young children she had with her second husband, and Liam's current wife, his third, hadn't exactly loved the idea of having a teenager around, especially not one with Reese's mouth. It was decided among the adults that Reese would move in with Jovia to finish high school. Liam had ignored his promise of financial help ever since. Last Pearl knew, Reese hadn't spoken to his dad in over a year.

As they cruised down Ocean, Reese shook his head, reading aloud, "Vacationland," from the license plate of the car in front of them. "That has to be crappiest state slogan ever." He raised his beer to a Toyota Tundra from New Hampshire that cut them off at the lights. "Live Free or Die. Damn straight."

A flock of summer kids strayed into the crosswalk, texting, talking, paying no attention to traffic. They were the same ones who sunbathed poolside at the club in chaise lounges, held languid tennis matches on the courts, and set the standard for unstudied cool around the bandstand in the town square. As Pearl hit the brakes, Reese's hand shot over and honked the horn. He stuck his head out the window. "Hey,

Alligator Shirts? Lacoste outlet is that way. You're blocking the road."

One boy flipped him off, and Reese returned the gesture, settling back with a grin.

"Feel better?" Pearl exhaled slowly, accelerating again. "You shouldn't have done that."

"Why not?" His voice dropped to a whisper as he looked skyward. "You think the club's got drones up there?"

"No-o-o, I think if those guys recognize us from the dining room and run to mommy and daddy about it, we're screwed."

"Oh, come on. They loved it." He brushed at some drops of beer he'd spilled on the console. "That's why they come up here to the land of the lost, right? Rich people get off on local color. We fulfill some salt-of-the-earth delusion they have. They seriously think we sit around the woodstove eating whale blubber and singing sea chanteys all winter long." When she finally smiled, he reached over and ruffled her hair. "Relax. Nobody's getting fired."

They continued out of downtown to where the woods deepened, toward Millionaires' Row, the local nickname for Cove Road, which was reserved for the summer getaways of the ultrarich. The Spencer mansion was first and oldest, a Georgian colonial with three smaller guesthouses arranged on the lawn below like a tiny village. The grandfather, Frederick Spencer, now lived in Tenney's Harbor year-round, where he was rarely seen anywhere but the club, although his name was ubiquitous in town: the Spencer Wing on the public library, the Frederick L. Spencer athletic track at the high school.

"Flag's out. Brats must be in town." Reese nodded to the guesthouses below, where a bright nautical flag hung outside one of the cottages, an eccentric Spencer custom that meant family was visiting. Pearl remembered Bridges, considered telling Reese about being hit on by a Spencer. Better not. If she talked about Bridges, then she might talk about Tristan, and she wasn't ready to do that yet. Reese glanced at her. "Did your dad ever work down there?"

"No. Spencers go through some guy from Winter Harbor." Dad was just one of many caretakers on MDI who maintained these grandiose homes, most of which were occupied for only a few weeks or months a year.

Each driveway was marked by a single, understated sign bearing the family name. *Wooten. Montgomery-Hines. Mertz. Langstrom.* She'd been this way many times, first as a kid, accompanying Dad on his duties—clearing snow, checking locks, making sure all the furnaces were maintaining a steady sixty degrees so the water pipes didn't freeze—and now, since December, on solitary drive-bys, defying the empty, winterized homes with her presence. They could shun Dad, but they didn't own Tenney's Harbor.

All the little sounds Reese usually made to fill

silence—finger tapping, humming—grew quiet. He must've figured out their destination by now: 168 Cove Road, the long, winding driveway marked with a carved granite block reading *Garrison*.

They didn't speak as she urged the car up the crushed rock drive. The gatehouse was first to emerge from the darkness, a small brick structure with a window, an intercom system, and the controls to open the sixteen-foot steel gate beside it. The modern fencing contrasted with the home itself, set far back from the gate, another two-and-a-half-story colonial worthy of a *Down East* double-page spread. Instead, it had appeared in *Time*, accompanying the article "Study in Flames: The Slaying of Millionaire David Garrison," which Pearl had pored over until she'd memorized entire paragraphs like a catechism. Dad was mentioned in that article. How he'd been filling in as night watchman for the regular guy, who had an off-season job he couldn't leave at the Garrisons' last-minute notice, yet someone had gotten into the house anyway. Someone who still hadn't been caught.

She and Reese sat there, thinking their own thoughts in the face of the house, a puzzle box waiting for someone to figure out the first move. There was a new caretaker now: the crime scene tape had been removed, the burnt rubble hauled away from the yard, the grass mowed. A tarp had been laid over the hole in the roof, and David and Sloane's ruined window was covered with a sheet of particleboard.

Pearl recalled the diagram from the *Time* article, detailing the killer's route through the sleeping second floor, the path of the accelerant.

"Why do you think he stayed?" Her voice sounded far off. It wasn't necessary to name Tristan.

Reese shifted. "No clue. Seems like he'd get out of here and never look back. I would." He hesitated. "They're not buried in town, right?"

"No. Connecticut." Tenney's Harbor had been stunned when news got out that Tristan had rented one of the new homes in the development over on Narragansett Way, had been seen driving his father's Bentley, playing alone in the club racquetball courts. Why, after everything, wasn't one of the richest young men in the country going back to his life? To Yale, or the family home in Greenwich? Why stay in a Maine tourist town where he had no one, where people either turned their backs on him or gawked as if he were the equivalent of a wreck on the highway?

"Dad thinks it's his fault." Now her voice sounded thinner than ever. "I know it." She took a breath. "He wasn't drinking that night. He swore to me."

Reese was silent nearly ten seconds, a new record. Then she felt his hand close on the nape of her neck, a gentle pressure.

They sat together until a scraping sound made them both turn wide-eyed on the night. It was the tarp, a loose corner shifting in the breeze. Reese swore and sat back. "Let's go.

Too many freakin' ghosts out here."

She took him home, watched until his silhouette moved past the carriage house's second-floor window shade. When she got to her house, Dad was gone. He hadn't washed the dishes.

FOUR

THEY WERE BACK the next day, this time numbering only two: Bridges and Tristan. The maître d' seated them in Indigo's section, beneath the windows on the far wall. Tristan spread his napkin in his lap, and then his hands lingered there, like he'd forgotten his task. Pearl glanced away, keeping her hands busy counting change.

What had been on their itinerary this morning? Sleep until ten, maybe. Linger over coffee and girl-watching in one of the shops on Ocean, then hit the club pool with the rest of the members' kids until it was fashionably late enough for lunch.

When Pearl circled back from the kitchen, Bridges sat

alone at a booth in her section.

"Hi," he said. "You didn't call."

"You should go back to your table."

He really was the smilingest person she'd ever seen. "Let's do this right." He stuck his hand out. "Bridges Spencer. Nice to meet you." She looked at his hand. "Your turn."

She tapped her name tag. "The *a* is silent."

He laughed. "Come on, don't leave me hanging." She gave him a quick, hard handshake. "So. I've seen you around a lot." He sat back, getting comfortable. He had a slender build, blue eyes the color of faded denim, a nose with a slight upward tilt. "What do you do when you're not working?"

From the corner of her eye, Pearl caught a flash of bright color. The Malhotras were crossing the dining room with their friends and business partners, the Fraziers; Akil trailed a few feet behind, earbuds in place. Akil's mother wore a fuchsia sundress with a matching shrug, her husband more subdued in the preppy dad uniform of polo shirt and khaki shorts. When Akil saw Tristan, he split off from the adults without a word and joined him at the table. Akil's father, an elegant, imposing man, didn't so much as look his way, but his mother did, her brow wrinkled, lips compressed.

"You still with me?" Bridges touched her hand.

"I really can't talk right now."

"Okay. I get it, you're busy. But listen. There's a party tonight. Nothing crazy, just some people getting together.

I figured, if we're both going, you know . . . why not go together?"

She stared. "You don't even know me."

"I want to. That's how people get to know each other, right? By hanging out?" He paused. "Isn't it?" He surprised a soft snort of laughter out of her. "No pressure. Think about it. We'll be here awhile."

"Excuse me? Miss?" The Wootens signaled her from table five.

Pearl took a breath, released it in a rush. "I'll let you know."

At the register, Pearl printed the Wootens' check, watching Tristan openly around the monitor. Her mouth was dry, fingers ticking off points on her thumbnail. A summer kids' party. Nobody from town went to those. If she were somebody else, somebody like Indigo, maybe she could do it. Cross that invisible line to the place where people like Tristan existed, see him in his natural habitat. See what he knew. Because that was one thing everyone agreed on, from locals down to conspiracy theorists online: the son knew something.

A few moments later, Indigo came around the partition at the end of the room, Reese close on her heels. Pearl stepped back. The tension between those two was electric today; everyone had picked up on it. Indigo hadn't spoken a word to Reese since the shift began, tossing her head and finding something else to look at whenever he passed by. Pearl kept thinking about the phone call he'd blown off in favor of hanging out with her last night. Triumph blossomed briefly, then died as she watched Reese catch Indigo's elbow, turning her back, whispering something close to her face. Indigo said nothing, but she allowed him to steer her through the ballroom doorway, where they disappeared.

By the time they came back, Pearl had delivered checks to two more tables. From the corridor, she watched their brief exchange as they stood mostly concealed in the doorway, watched Indigo's hand steal up and squeeze Reese's ass before they went in opposite directions.

Pearl felt heat, then chill. She shut her eyes for a moment, then went into the kitchen to place another order.

She waited until the boys were done eating before going over to them, sensing more than seeing Tristan shift his attention her way. Bridges stopped stirring his straw in the ice at the bottom of his glass. "I'll go," she said abruptly. "Tonight." Her heart was galloping.

"Really?" Bridges pushed his sun-bleached hair back, grinning. "Cool. Where can I pick you up?"

"I'll meet you."

"Okay. Whatever. Yacht club, slip D12. I drive a Talon. Can't miss it."

While Akil smirked openly at them, Tristan's look was unfocused, as if she and Bridges were a reality show, one he'd soon turn off if they didn't start doing something interesting. "What time?" Pearl asked.

"Nine-ish?"

She nodded and left, slowly sinking into the truth of what she'd done.

Pearl checked her phone one last time. No texts, no missed calls. Well, one from Mom, but she didn't plan on returning that anytime soon. All Mom would want to do was quiz her about Dad—was he taking care of himself, eating well, staying away from the Tavern—and Pearl was in no mood.

It wasn't like she'd made plans with Reese tonight. They never made plans. Things either fell together or they didn't. The difference was, this time it was because *she* had something else to do. No doubt he was busy, too, or she would've received a summons by now. *I'm bored. Come over. Help me feel safe enough to sleep.* Apparently, that was one service Indigo didn't provide.

She jammed her phone into her pocket so hard it hurt—nothing compared to the splintery heart-stab of being mad at Reese—and stepped out of her car into the night.

The yacht club landing was lit by old-fashioned lampposts that made her think of Narnia; Dad had read those books to her growing up. She walked through pools of light, passing rows of yachts and powerboats, reading the slip numbers, half expecting some official type to come up and demand proof of membership. She'd explored this place plenty in the off-season, but never during the summer. The public landing was for locals like her, where the water rippled with prisms of diesel fuel and the benches were sticky with ice-cream handprints.

"Pearl. Hey."

Down the floating dock, Bridges stood aboard a huge, muscular-looking speedboat. Pearl walked down to meet him. "Holy shit," he said. "You actually showed."

She shifted. "I said I would."

"I know, but . . ." He shrugged. "Climb aboard. Need a hand up?"

"I got it." She didn't, but he let her find her own footing on the ladder, ending up nose to nose with him. His eyelashes were light, sun-washed, like the rest of him.

There was a thump, and Akil came up from belowdecks, dropping into the passenger seat. "So, she's here. Let's go," he said.

Pearl sidestepped Bridges and perched on the bench seat, watching him pull the lines free and coil them. No sign of Tristan, no movement from below. "Where's this party?" Bridges cocked his hand, pistol-style, at the dark, rocky mass crouching in the harbor. "Little Nicatou? That's private property. Nobody goes there."

The boys traded a look, but whatever Bridges said next was lost in the roar of the motor.

Pearl twisted around to watch the dock grow distant, all her tension and mental preparation dissolving like sand underfoot. He wasn't coming. She rested her chin on the back of the seat, squeezing her eyes shut, wondering how she was going to survive this night—then swore as Bridges opened the throttle and almost pitched her to the floor.

They shot across the harbor, both boys standing, facing into the wind. Akil looked back once and laughed at the sight of her sitting stark upright, belted in, gripping the seat as spray buffeted her from all sides.

The headlights of three other boats were visible ahead of them now, cutting their own paths to Little Nicatou. There was a dock on the island—Pearl had seen that much from the harbor—and tonight it was lit with electric lanterns. Firelight was visible on the beach. Bridges muffed the landing twice, finally dropped anchor, and tied off on a piling before he noticed Pearl brushing water from her arms and face. "Sorry. I'm a pretty crazy driver."

She had an answer for that, but when she saw Akil's look, she swallowed it. One bitchy remark and she'd fail the first test, be labeled a typical girl: whiny, temperamental, and weak. "No worries." Wiping her face, she took Bridges's offer of a hand-up onto the dock ladder, passing Akil without a glance.

The beach stretched out to their left, Adirondack chairs strategically placed here and there. Globe string lights illuminated a pathway up into the trees, where windows glowed through the branches and hip-hop pounded from unseen speakers. There must be one hell of a generator up there—and an Exxon tanker to fuel it.

Most of the summer kids sitting around the portable fire pits were at least somewhat familiar to her, faces she'd seen in the dining room, or coming and going from the fitness center or spa. Even money none of them recognized her without her club colors.

Bridges grabbed two beers from an ice-filled cooler in the sand, microbrews Pearl had never heard of. Not a Bud or a Coors Light to be seen, and nobody seemed the least bit concerned about drinking right out in the open. Local kids made campsites in the woods, holed up in abandoned houses just to get some privacy. She didn't drink anyway, but tonight, it seemed safer to carry one as a prop.

He put his free hand in his pocket, taking in her running shorts, gray V-necked T-shirt, and flip-flops. "Wow. You look . . . really . . ."

"Butch?" Akil hooked three beers under his arm and set off across the sand.

"Dude, don't be like that." Bridges looked back at her. "Ignore him. He's pissed at the world, not you."

"What a relief." Pearl watched him choke on his first sip, his shoulders shaking. "What?"

"Just—you're always on defense, that's all." He put his

hands up. "Not a bad thing. Don't maul me."

Smiling despite herself, she gestured to the others. "Sorry. I'm a little out of my tax bracket here."

"Ah, who cares. None of that shit matters."

"Says the guy who owns an island." She nodded at his hesitation. "That's what I thought."

"It's my grandpa's island, okay?"

"Right. You just use it to entertain a few hundred of your closest friends." He tipped his head back and laughed. Pearl laughed with him; it was impossible not to. "How come I've never heard anything about this place belonging to the Spencers?"

"Gramps kept the deal pretty quiet. The family who owned it for, like, sixty years decided to sell, and I guess the old guy figured, why not? He loves Tenney's Harbor. Been coming here ever since he was a kid." He shrugged. "So, we own a big chunk of rock now. Don't hold it against me."

"Okay. I won't. How long are you in town for?"

"Until August fifteenth. It's just me this year. My mom and sisters usually come, but the girls wanted to go to some horseback riding camp in Kentucky this summer, so Mom sent them and stayed home to take a vacation from the family. It's cool. They don't really get this place the way Gramps and I do, anyway, why it's special. Your turn." She glanced over. "I said I wanted to get to know you."

"Why?"

"Because you have the coolest eyes I've ever seen." At her withering look, he planted his feet. "I'm not moving until you tell me something about yourself. Think about it. I'm your ride. You'll be stuck on Little Nicatou forever."

"Foraging for beer and canapés. Rough life." She sighed, ruminating. "I graduated a couple weeks ago. I'm starting at the College of the Atlantic in the fall, keeping my job at the club."

"Nice. I'm going to UMass, rushing Sigma Phi Epsilon."

"I thought all you guys went Ivy League."

"You mean guys with money? Nah. I mean, I've got an uncle who went to Stanford, he could pull strings. But we both know I don't have what it takes."

"Not like Tristan." The words spoke themselves.

He snorted quietly. "You have no idea." He flipped a mussel shell over with the toe of his sandal. "Anyway, it's cool that you're staying in the area. It's beautiful here." He paused. "Used to be like paradise, you know? Feels different this summer." He shrugged. "I guess it should."

She watched him. It was the first remark, indirect or otherwise, that she'd heard any summer person make about the Garrisons since the season began.

A knot of girls moved up the beach toward them, and now they stopped, heads together in conference. A tall, lanky blond girl stepped out and called, "Really, Bridges? Really."

His expression froze. "Hey, ladies."

The blonde marched over, dragging along a petite brunette with long, side-swept hair who looked like she wished she was anywhere else. "So, this is like compulsive behavior with you," the blonde said. "New summer, new girl."

"Not really your business, Quinn." Bridges glanced at the brunette and said, "Hey, Had."

"Hi." Her voice was soft.

"It's absolutely my business. My friend got her heart stomped on. I know how she feels, remember?" Quinn folded her arms. Pearl recognized the brunette: Hadley Kurtzweil. Her parents had let Dad go in an email this spring, claiming they'd "made other arrangements" for the caretaking of their home on Millionaires' Row. "And FYI, watching you slobber all over your trailer-trash date is only like the biggest turnoff ever. So, yeah. I'd lose that."

"Christ, Quinn, do you even hear yourself? Look, if you've got a problem, there's the door." He jerked his thumb at the water and stepped around her. "Nobody made you come tonight."

"I happen to be hanging out with Hadley, if that's okay with you. Unless you want to kick her off, too?"

Akil came up then, finishing his last beer. "Hey, girls. We've got a game of quarters going. Winner gets to sit on my lap. You in?" Quinn held her middle finger in his laughing face and left, pulling Hadley along.

Hadley called "Bye" to Bridges, who nodded before

taking a deep breath and turning to Pearl.

"Uh, about all that."

"No explanation needed."

"I'm not some letch. I swear. I dated Hadley last summer, but it didn't work out. She lives in Colorado during the year—"

"Seriously. I don't want to know."

"You dumped Quinn." Akil sat heavily, tipping his bottle back. "That's the real problem. That's going to come back to haunt your ass forever."

"We were fourteen."

"Doesn't matter. You should've waited until *she* dumped *you*."

Pearl faced Bridges. "Anyway. I need to pee. I'm assuming you've got a bathroom up there?"

"Oh, yeah. Composting toilet and everything. Spared no expense."

When she was halfway up the path, she glanced back. Bridges stood below, watching her. Once she stepped past a spray of spruce branches, he said something sharply to Akil and kicked sand at him.

The little A-frame cottage sat on a rocky outcropping, clam and mussel shells scattered over the walk and pressed whole into the mortar of the stone steps. Inside, tables were spread with food that had barely been touched.

As Pearl crossed the room, a woman solidified at the edge

of her vision: midforties, dressed in a white blouse and apron, standing with her hands folded in front of her. Clearly some member of the Spencer help. For Pearl, it was like seeing herself run through age-progression software. "Hi," Pearl said. The woman gave a slight nod, avoiding eye contact.

Afterward, still rubbing in hand sanitizer, Pearl went back down the path, sidestepping a reeling, giggling couple. She checked her phone. One missed call. Reese. It felt like years since they'd talked, and now she had all this fodder for conversation: the Night Pearl Went to a Posh Party and Survived. She hadn't intended to tell him about it, at least not right away. But he'd called. Maybe he'd never had any plans with Indigo. Maybe she'd had no right to get so angry in the first place. It wasn't like she didn't know what those two were all about.

Her thumb was still poised over the screen when a light went on by the base of the cliff. A flickering, unreliable light, like a bulb not fully screwed into a socket. It was far enough away from the party that she stared. A doorway was visible, seemingly in the middle of nothingness, the glow spilling onto the beach.

Pearl continued down the path, then took a fork in the direction of the light. It was a stone boathouse, big enough to accommodate a large sailboat, the floor stained with rust. Someone stood inside, casting a long shadow as he circled beneath the bulb.

Tristan Garrison. Exploring, reaching up to trace his fingers over an ancient, cracked buoy slung over a hook. He held that position, arm outstretched, then sank into a crouch, fanning his hand through the debris scattered across the floor, crushed shells and sand. Pearl stood motionless, not daring to draw breath. Nothing on the floor was of interest, so he folded his arms across his knees and lowered his chin onto them, rocking back on his heels. She'd never seen him look that way, pulled into himself. Backing away, she slipped off her flip-flops and escaped on bare, silent feet.

When she got back, she found Bridges and Akil sitting around a fire pit. Bridges got to his feet as she came up, brushing sand off his shorts. "Did you get lost?"

"No." Sitting, she hugged her knees, willing her heartbeat to slow down.

Bridges sat beside her, holding her token beer. "Want me to open this for you?" She let him have his moment with the twist-off. As he handed her the bottle, his expression changed. She followed his gaze to Tristan emerging from the boathouse. Bridges said, "I thought he wasn't coming."

For once, Akil didn't have an answer.

By the time Tristan reached them, many of the partyers had faded back, found other places to be, other people to turn to. His separateness was a physical force; even Pearl had to fight down the need to make room. He stood looking at the fire, his hands in the pockets of his shorts. In the charged silence, Akil leaned forward. "S'up, man. Want a beer?"

"How'd you get here?" Bridges said. "Where's your boat?"

"On the other side of the cliff." Same tone as in the dining room, low, distracted.

"You walked through the woods?"

Tristan sank down, removed the screen from the fire pit so he could use the poker to hook out a piece of flaming kindling. Pearl got the feeling he was in the habit of letting people believe he could see in the dark. "Do you have any Grey Goose?"

"I told you, my gramps won't pony up for hard stuff."

A slight lift of his brows as he turned the kindling over, then dropped it, wiping his hands and straightening. "I'm going for a ride."

Bridges and Akil both rose. Pearl stood behind them, feeling as though she'd missed a cue. Tristan didn't seem aware of her; he led the way down the beach, never glancing back to make sure they were keeping up. She watched Bridges, waiting for him to say something, like maybe explain why he was willing to desert his own party at the first word from Tristan.

They followed the path that led past the boathouse up into the trees. The blackness was total here, towering spruce and balsams blotting out the moonlight. A moment later, a glowing square appeared: Tristan's phone, lighting the way.

They emerged on a steep ridge that switchbacked down to the water. The path was precarious, but not nearly as tricky as getting aboard Tristan's boat was going to be. Pearl couldn't see it, could only hear water lapping against the hull. No one spoke.

The ledge provided barely enough room for them to stand as Tristan unknotted a line tied around a tree trunk. He tugged, and finally the shape of the boat was discernible against the night, drifting closer. He made it all look easy, bracing his palms flat on the deck and boosting himself into the aft entry, going up the starboard walkway to the helm, where he started the motor, the running lights bursting on. The gauntlet had been thrown. Follow the leader, if you can.

Akil leaped first, then Bridges. His sandals slipped on the wet stern. Pearl's shoulders jumped involuntarily, but he pulled himself into the walkway, safe.

Now the gap between the ledge and boat stretched out before her. No room for a running start, nothing to hold on to. Bridges held out his hands. "Come on. I'll catch you."

Another second of hesitation and all her credibility would be lost. Instead of looking at the gap, she focused on Bridges's hands and lunged for them.

Her toes barely made the stern. Then he had her, pulling her into an embrace, rubbing her back. "Gotcha. You're okay." Akil was laughing.

Pearl extracted herself, cheeks burning. She wasn't a

hugger, except for Dad and Reese, and she sat down, jaw clenched, her skin tingling from the uninvited touch. Bridges sat beside her, stretching his arm across the top of the seat. She stayed clear of it, watching Tristan's back, the wind tossing his hair around.

He was a better driver than Bridges, cutting across the water at a steady clip, his attention never wavering as he took them out into the blackness. The boat was a beauty, a Stan-Craft 290 Rivelle with a cream leather interior. His father's boat, Pearl was almost certain. Dad had pointed it out in the harbor once, saying that in his next life, he'd own a wooden speedboat. Classiest things on the water.

After a couple of minutes, Bridges called, "Tristan." No response. Bridges moved forward. "Dude." He gestured to Pearl. "We have to take her back now. Right?"

Tristan glanced over his shoulder. "Oh." He made a wide turn and took them into the harbor, returning to the yacht club dock. He leaned back, waiting.

Bridges stepped onto the dock with her. "Sorry about . . . well, everything, I guess. Tonight was pretty much a fail. I'd like to try again, if you want."

Pearl opened her mouth, not entirely sure what was going to come out. From the corner of her eye, she saw Tristan tilt his head, roll his shoulders as if working out a cramp. "Sure. Why not?"

As Bridges entered her number into his phone, Pearl felt

it for the first time. Tristan's full attention, focused squarely on her.

She grew intensely aware of her body, the awkwardness of how she stood, slightly hunched, arms folded. She straightened her spine by degrees and lifted her chin, her skin thrumming.

She wasn't the only one who felt the scrutiny. Bridges shifted, met her eyes, took an uncertain step closer. Of course they wouldn't kiss; it would be ridiculous. It hadn't been a real date. But it was as if the decision had been made for them, an invisible hand moving his knight to take her, the pawn.

Bridges's lips touched hers. Her eyes remained open, her nostrils full of his cologne, spicy and fresh. When he pulled back, he said softly, "I'll call you."

She turned and left without a word, blood roaring in her ears, counting each plank she put between them, counting the seconds until she reached dry land. There, she gripped a lamppost and watched the boat's taillights disappearing across the water, heading toward a destination they hadn't wanted her to know.

FIVE

DAD WAS UP, making his hangover special: scrambled eggs, black coffee. He'd been asleep on the couch when she got home—not late, before the national news started—but this time, she hadn't woken him. Hadn't fixed him toast and asked him to watch the *Tonight Show* with her. Instead, she'd slipped into her room, where the light from her tablet crept beneath the door until the wee hours.

Now she rubbed her lips, trying to erase a memory as Dad moved between fridge and stove. She looked at the scars on his hands. The burns had healed well, but the cuts from where he'd punched out the parlor window to get inside the Garrisons' house had required almost twenty stitches, the pinkish scar tissue twining up his wrist like young roots.

"Missed you coming in last night," he said, as if partially catching the flow of her thoughts. "Good party?"

"Not bad."

"Any puking?"

"Not that I saw."

"Sounds like a success to me." He fixed her a plate, squirting on lots of ketchup, the way she liked it, and she felt such a rush of guilt and affection for him that her eyes burned. Always being a relatively easy, responsible kid had earned her his trust, especially now that she was eighteen and Dad had done away with her already lax curfew for good. If he knew where she'd really gone and who'd she'd been with last night, if he knew about Tristan—she blinked rapidly, stirring her fork in her plate. She'd told him she'd gone over to Katy Scanlon's house for one last party with her graduating class; Katy was a sort-of friend who she hadn't spoken to since the last day of homeroom.

Dad watched her as he swallowed two Excedrin with his coffee. "I'm headed to the club. Wysocki-Tillman wedding needs one hundred and fifty folding chairs set up before eleven."

"You guys already put up the tents?"

"Fought with those things all day yesterday. Meriwether was hanging around bitching about 'divots in the grass.' Dickie told her if she can think of another way to hammer in stakes to let us know."

Pearl laughed. "I'm working the reception, thank God."

It was infinitely better to arrive after the ceremony was over; you didn't want to be within a mile of the tents with the wedding planner, Meriwether, and the mother of the bride all swarming around, sniping at one another about floral arrangements and seating plans. Meriwether was already in a snit over preparations for the upcoming formal ball and charity auction; club members were donating antiques and passes for all-day boat tours of Frenchman Bay faster than anyone could keep up with them. Seeing Dad and a couple of other groundskeepers lugging massive carved armoires or boxes of carnival glass past the dining room windows on their way to the storage building had become a regular occurrence.

Pearl studied Dad over her juice glass. His eyes were red from the six-pack he'd killed last night, but otherwise, he seemed okay, complaining about familiar things that had always been in their lives: the tight-ass club, management breathing down his neck. An outsider would never know he'd been called into a closed-door meeting this spring with General Manager Gene Charbonneau and the board to discuss the Garrison incident, and how exactly they were supposed to continue to put their trust in him. After fifteen years with the club, Dad had been made to beg for his job. Few people would blame them. Even after the state police chief came out to say that the killings had all the earmarks of being an isolated incident, and that the murderer had almost certainly left the area, people were scared. If there was no arrest, you just didn't know. It could happen again.

"How about we hit North Beach after supper one of these nights?" Dad said suddenly, and Pearl glanced up. "We haven't been out there yet this year. Might be some good glass."

"Yeah, absolutely. Anytime." Beachcombing on North was a summer tradition for them. The currents around the cove made for some unique finds. Pearl had done some research online about rare sea glass colors; she'd found both purple and aqua on North, not to mention a scalloped white that looked like it might have come from an antique serving dish.

Down the hall, her ring tone trilled. She went to her room and picked up the phone, reading *Bridges Spencer* on the caller ID. She stared, the scrambled eggs she'd eaten doing a lazy loop-de-loop in her stomach. Two more rings. Her voice mail would pick up in a second. She answered.

"I didn't wake you up, did I?" He sounded casual. "What're you doing this morning?"

"Not much. Breakfast."

"Listen, I have to head back out to the island. Thought you might want to come along." At her hesitation: "It'll be just us. Akil doesn't get out of bed until noon."

It wasn't Akil whose gaze had left her feeling harrowed and raw last night, who she'd proceeded to read online articles about until she could barely keep her eyes open. From the kitchen, Dad called good-bye, and the front door shut. She leaned across the mattress, parting the curtains to watch him go down the steps to his truck. To her right and left spanned her collection, mason jars of shells and sea glass lining her windowsill, beachcombing treasures she and Dad had collected over the years. More jars of glass—mostly common colors, green, brown, and clear—sat on her desk, catching sunlight. "I'll bring coffee," Pearl said. "Twenty minutes?"

After the disconnect, Pearl retrieved her tablet, looking at the article she'd left open last night. Curtain up on act two of the Garrison tragedy.

By Christmas Day, Tristan had been found. It took that long to locate his cell phone number, provided by some member of the Garrisons' household staff back in Greenwich. State police took him into custody at the Sugarloaf Mountain Resort, a three-and-a-half-hour drive from MDI. On the evening of the twenty-third, while his family was dining at the club, he'd driven his BMW through the snowy dark to stay with a friend from Yale whose family owned a condo near Sugarloaf's Burnt Mountain Road. According to Tristan, there'd been a disagreement at his house: he'd wanted to spend the holidays skiing, his parents wanted him to stay home. He'd left at the earliest opportunity.

Pearl exhaled steadily. Here was Tristan's senior photo from the Brunswick School, unsmiling, yet not without a certain sardonic implication. Gold crest on his blazer, school tie of brown, white, and gold. *Accelerant used. Autopsies revealed that Garrison, his wife, and two of their three children were each shot in their beds multiple times with a semiautomatic handgun before the fire was set.* Tristan's hands, folded one over the other on a polished mahogany rail, a photographer's prop. *Oldest son in custody. Person of interest. Under suspicion.*

It was a blindingly sunny day, the brisk wind raising white-caps across the surface of the harbor. A banner advertising the Centennial Celebration Regatta, cosponsored by the country club, flapped against the railing of the yacht club's waterfront deck.

This time, Pearl saw Bridges first, bent shirtless over a tangled line on a small two-seater powerboat. She thought of last night, the taillights of Tristan's boat fading into the darkness, leaving her behind. *Where did you go after that? Where in hell did you three go?*

She came up behind him and cleared her throat, watching him snap around. "Good thing I wasn't a bear." She held up a big Coleman thermos. "As promised."

"Whoa. That's old school." He took it from her, sniffed under the lid. "Something tells me you brew it strong."

"Might put hair on your chest."

"Finally." They both smiled, relieved; the kiss could go unmentioned. "Hop in."

"Where's your other boat?" As she stepped into the

cockpit, his hands briefly found her hips, guiding her down, another unnecessary touch that she let slide.

"Still at the island."

"Tristan didn't bring you back for it last night?" She stared. "Somebody could've stolen it. Stuff like that happens all the time in the summer."

"Tristan doesn't think like that." Looking uncomfortable, Bridges started the motor. "Buckle up."

This morning, Little Nicatou was back in the hands of nature. There were a few stray beer bottles on the beach, but the coolers, chairs, and fire pits were gone, cleared away by somebody other than Bridges, obviously. Pearl thought of the servant in the cottage, then tried to remember how she'd disposed of her own bottle last night; she couldn't.

The Talon was still moored at the dock where they'd left it, bobbing with the pull of the tide. Bridges was on his feet before the engine died, straining to see. "Looks okay."

"Except for the metric ton of gull crap." As they approached, Pearl took the wheel, which Bridges seemed to have forgotten. She brought them about, then made a soft sound. "Looks like your friend Quinn left you a love note."

Manwhore was written in lipstick across the entire length of the starboard side. Cursing, Bridges tied off and clambered into the Talon.

Pearl went up the ladder and down the dock, giving him some privacy while he tried to clean up.

She walked along the beach toward the boathouse. It was more impressive in the daylight, with steps that led up to a sitting area on the battlemented roof. The year 1922 was carved into the cement over the doorway. She walked into the shadowy recesses, discerning shapes that turned out to be fragments of rope, dried seaweed pods. Who knew what Tristan had seen in the dust?

Pearl walked out of the boathouse and onto the sand, blinking as her eyes adjusted to the light. Her gaze landed on a crumpled foil square by her feet.

In the same instant that she realized it was a condom wrapper, she felt Bridges standing behind her. She jerked around.

He was looking at the wrapper, too. He shifted slightly, lifting his gaze to her. "It's not true, you know." When she stared, flushing, he gestured back to the boat, where *man-whore* had become a five-foot-long burgundy smear. "Quinn's crazy."

"Okay." Her toes curled against her flip-flops.

"I brought the coffee. If you still want it."

She nodded, grateful to move. She sat on the lip of the boathouse floor, swinging her feet, willing herself not to be the kind of girl who got flustered, whose whole body blushed.

They drank cups of Dad's Folgers and watched the tide. Gulls had dropped mussels and clams on the rocks, shattering the shells to dig out the meat; iridescent fragments were everywhere. "I'm surprised Akil missed this." She cleared her throat, took a sip. "I thought you guys were grafted."

"I'm a morning person, he's not. He'll have to get his ass up next Saturday, though." At Pearl's look: "For the regatta. Race starts at ten a.m. Are you going?"

"Hadn't planned on it."

"You should come. Tristan's racing his dad's Islander. We're his crew. We'll just hang out, drink, whatever. It's Tristan's show. You know if it was anything like work, Akil wouldn't be there."

She ran her fingers over the step. "Tell me something. How did Akil's family manage to keep their club membership after he stole that golf cart last year?" Bridges laughed, ducking his head. "Seriously. Last summer was the Malhotras' first season here. I've heard about new members getting kicked out for wearing socks with sandals."

"Hey, you know how it works. You abuse the club, they hit you in the wallet. His dad paid for a new cart and made a huge donation for pain and suffering or whatever. Plus, his dad's business partners with Timothy Frazier. That carries a lot of weight. Fraziers have been summering here forever. They recommended the Malhotras for membership, even though some people think their color kind of clashes with the scenery, you know?" He shrugged. "Akil didn't exactly steal it, anyway. He borrowed it. Took a joyride."

"Too bad that telephone pole ran into him."

"So he was wasted. Go easy. He was nursing a broken heart."

"Anybody I know?"

"Cassidy Garrison."

Pearl's mouth fell open. "You're kidding."

"Weird couple, right? It only lasted a few months, but he was crazy about her. Really messed him up when she ended it. After what happened . . . he's having a hard time."

Beautiful, slender Cassidy, fingers on the keys, the deep blue luster of her dress under the lights. Not weird; unimaginable. "Why'd she dump him?"

"She said it was because of the long-distance thing, with summer ending and all. Akil blamed her dad. He thought David made her break it off."

"Did he?"

"Probably. It was the kind of thing he'd do. Power play."

"Was David one of those people who didn't like Akil's color?"

"Maybe." Bridges paused. "But Cassidy . . . she was different. Smart and talented and everything, but kind of fragile, too, you know? I think she hung out with her little brother more than anybody else. Couldn't really blame David for being overprotective when it came to her." He flicked sand from the hem of his cargo shorts. "She needed somebody to look out for her."

"Are you always this fair?" When he shrugged again, she

said, "Sounds like you knew them pretty well. The Garrisons, I mean."

"Some. We used to hang out at their house. Up in Tristan's room." Some of the color had left Bridges's face beneath his tan. He set his cup down, giving himself a shake. "Holy caffeine rush. Okay, now you tell me something. Why are they like that?" He gestured to her eyes.

"Oh. It's called heterochromia. It's a genetic thing. I've got a cousin with one green, one blue."

"But that's not as cool. I mean, yours are totally different." He considered her face so steadily, so frankly, that she was compelled to look back. "Almost like they belong to two different people."

She reached up, touching the skin near her right eye. "Really?"

Bridges leaned in. This time, she closed her eyes, too, feeling his lips part against hers, moving deeper, her body responding without waiting for permission. She finally put her hand against his chest. "Bridges . . ."

"Too soon, right. Damn it." He sat back, giving her a sidelong look. "Did you mind?"

Pearl bit her lip, then shook her head. No way was she getting into Reese with him, or the real reasons she'd said yes to the party last night, or why she was here right now; not with his body heat still on her. "You know, you're not making a very good case for yourself." She nodded toward the boat with its clouded slur. "Maybe Quinn and I should compare notes."

For an instant, she was sure she'd gone too far. Then his face relaxed, and he leaned back on his elbows. "You seem like you can make your own decisions."

"Ha. Nice technique. You're all set for Psych 100 next semester."

"Sweet Jesus. I think I just got frostbite."

"Try wearing a shirt." They held each other's gaze for a long moment. Pearl let a hint of a smile show. Bridges did the same. She stood. "Come on. I have to be at work by one."

They towed the smaller boat behind the Talon, leaving Bridges no choice but to take it slow. Pearl looked back once. The boathouse gazed inscrutably back, standing sentinel over the same view of the harbor it had watched for more than ninety years.

SIX

ONE HUNDRED AND fifty white wooden folding chairs stood empty on the eastern lawn, formed into two groups with an aisle down the middle leading to a rose arbor. The wind had carried red, pink, and yellow petals everywhere, some clinging to the plastic windows of the reception tents like thumbprints.

Wedding pace was about five notches faster than dining room pace, and Pearl had almost collided with another server twice already. There was a schedule to keep, speeches to be made, hokey traditions to be carried out, and nobody wanted to be the server who photobombed the wedding party because they couldn't keep up.

At this point, guests were winding down on entrées and speculating about the cake. Pearl cleared her own tables—busboys were catch-as-catch-can in the tents—and hefted her tray through the open patio doors, almost slamming into Indigo coming out of the kitchen.

Indigo stopped short, blew a stray curl out of her eye, and threaded around her, saying nothing. Fine by Pearl. She dumped her dirty dishes and returned to the dining room, which had the gilded *Closed for Special Event* sign propped in the lobby entrance.

Somebody said, "*Pssst.*" She looked around, saw no one, kept going.

"For chrissake, I said *pssst.*" As she approached the bar, abandoned by Chas for a table under one of the tents, the top of Reese's head appeared, then sank again.

She tucked herself in beside him, glancing back to make sure no one could see them from where they sat. "They're going to cut the cake in a minute."

"Cool. Save me a piece." He flicked her cowlick. "Where were you last night? You didn't pick up." He propped the toes of his vintage wingtips against the back bar. "I called, like, once."

"With a guy." A little surprised at herself, she didn't look away from the mirrored shelves of liquor bottles.

"Oh. Your dad again. Hey, you ever need help with that, you call me, okay? Doesn't matter how late."

She shut her eyes. Right. Not only was he throwing her an undeserved pity party, but he apparently couldn't conceive of Pearl Haskins having Friday night plans with any man who wasn't her father. "You'll jump right on your white horse, huh."

"You know it. I got a cape and some tights, too."

She smiled. "Come on. Our tables probably think we died."

"They wish. *Salud.*" As she watched, Reese reached down, picked up a shot glass, and tossed back the contents, wincing.

"Do you *want* to get fired?"

"Ooh, now there's a question for the Magic Eight Ball." Reese stood, rinsed the glass, then paused, fixing her with a look, one eyebrow raised. "Pearl, relax. Nobody's going to get close enough to smell it."

"I can."

"That's because you've got a nose for it." She didn't flinch; she didn't have to. He was quiet a second. "Sorry. That was shitty." He popped a couple of olives into his mouth as he passed her, gesturing to the room at large. "There. Virtually undetectable."

She followed on his heels into the afternoon sunlight, where Indigo was being death-marched back inside by Meriwether.

The assistant manager was a small woman in her early thirties, her lips thin and colorless, her fine hair twisted into a chignon. As always, her look was one of grim focus, her hushed tone that of someone who'd spent her entire life operating behind the scenes. "You and you. Come." Her gaze flicked between Pearl and Reese, lingering on him, perhaps detecting the junipery smell of whiskey as Reese looked blandly back at her and did what he was told.

Meriwether steered them into the kitchen, where the wedding cake sat on a lace-draped cart, five massive tiers covered in ivory fondant, piping, and sugar flowers. "I need you to take it straight through to the doors to the center of the main tent." She crossed her arms. "Do not jiggle the cart. Do not fraternize. This is a major photo op. Nobody wants to see your mouths moving."

Somehow, it made perfect sense that Pearl ended up steering, gripping the edges of the cart while Indigo and Reese walked point. With painstaking care, they rolled the cart out of the kitchen and through the dining room, Meriwether following. They hit the slope of the lawn, and their trio closed in, close enough to share breath.

"Slow down." Indigo's lips barely moved.

"I *am*." Pearl.

"People." Meriwether.

One of the cart's wheels snagged on a rut—Pearl thought *divots* and had to bite the inside of her cheek—and the cake trembled. Indigo swore. "It's slipping."

"If Pearl says she's got it, she's got it." Reese's voice was flat. "Relax."

Indigo glanced at him, a sharp, private look, then away. A

warm feeling—was it schadenfreude?—spread through Pearl as the shadow of the tent fell over them, oohs and aahs and camera flashes erupting from the crowd.

Once the cart was parked, the three of them broke in opposite directions, Pearl ending up in the far corner of the tent by the member lot. A flash of St. James Red caught her eye, and she watched the Bentley Continental GT pull in and claim one of the last open spots. Tristan got out, slung a sports bag over his shoulder, and went into the fitness center entrance.

The sight of him stayed with her as she served paper-thin slices of cake and poured coffee from silver pots, moving on autopilot until a woman said, "Hello, Pearl."

Beth Zimmitti, resident of Millionaires' Row. Her slightly protuberant eyes were wide, and she fiddled with her bracelets as she looked at Pearl.

"Hi." Pearl's voice was faint.

"I hadn't seen you yet. Around the club, I mean. So I wondered . . ."

What? If the Haskins had been exiled to Siberia? Much less awkward for the Zimmittis, no doubt, who, after seven years employing Dad as their caretaker, had fired him in a one-paragraph letter, simply stating that his services would no longer be required at 112 Cove Road, though they wished him much luck in his future endeavors. And Beth was one of the few who'd always gone out of her way to ask after Pearl, to send a Christmas card with a little bonus in it each year. Pearl heard the click in her throat as she swallowed. "Would you like more coffee?"

"Oh—please." Another pause; then, in a lower tone, "How is Win doing?"

Pearl thought Beth might actually reach out and squeeze her hand, at which point she'd be forced to dump the coffee into her lap. "Fine." What was she supposed to say? *You know, he really had the drinking in hand until you people got through with him. Thanks for that.*

Beth nodded in the increasingly painful silence; the cup seemed bottomless, like some nightclub magic trick.

"Young lady?" The Texas accent was unmistakable. Mimi Montgomery-Hines hallooed from five tables away, flapping her napkin in Pearl's direction. "SOS, honey."

Pearl felt her body unlock, and she left Beth Zimmitti with a brief "Thank you." Even that tasted bitter.

"Oh, hell's bells, I'm a mess, aren't I?" Mimi, smelling powerfully of Chanel Misia, dabbed at a spill on the tablecloth. Mineral water, by the look. "You'd think a lady my age would be able to drink from a glass, but you'd be wrong."

"Told you we should've kept her away from the bar," one of her friends said.

"Hush." Mimi gave Pearl a nudge in the ribs as she helped Pearl dry the spot. "How they treatin' you around here, dumpling?"

Pearl flushed slightly. "Not bad."

"Not so good, either, I bet. Any time you need somebody to throw their weight around for you, let me know. Weight I got, and plenty of it." She dropped Pearl a wink. "Tell your daddy I said hello. My roses are gonna be prizewinners again this year, I just know it, and it's thanks to him."

Emotion sealed Pearl's throat; she smiled, nodded, and took her leave.

Not long after, the guests migrated to the ballroom for music and dancing. Servers started tearing things down: linens were balled and carted to laundry, furniture was carried inside, the PA system was dismantled.

After Pearl dropped the last stray table number into the trash, she slipped through the dining room into the lobby. If the rumors were true about how Tristan worked out, he might still be in the fitness center. She passed the front desk, the stone fireplace, the overstuffed chairs. Photos taken at the club over the decades hung in the corridor: men in antiquated golfing garb, couples in costume dress. There was a recent group shot from a fund-raiser; Sloane Garrison smiled down from the upper-left corner, blond and sleek in a white linen shift and wide-brimmed hat.

The fitness center was in the renovated ell, decked out with floor-to-ceiling mirrors and TVs flashing muted CNN.

Tristan was using the treadmill in the far-right corner, facing the mirrors. The center, otherwise deserted on a Saturday evening, was consumed by the pounding of his steps.

He had an erect running stance, but at just shy of the two-and-a-half-hour mark, he was losing form, a dark V streaming down the back of his T-shirt to the band of his shorts. His breath sobbed out of him.

Pearl edged to the doorway, watching until he finally fell, landing heavily on one knee. The safety key clipped to his shirt popped free of the machine, cutting the power. He knelt there, gasping, head hanging down. Finally, like an act of prayer, he touched his brow to the track and sat back, tossing his drenched hair out of his face.

She let Tristan find her there, deep down in the mirror. Their reflections watched each other. It wasn't clear if he recognized her at first—puke or pass out was still in question—but then his gaze sharpened. With effort, he gripped the railing and pulled himself up, turning to face her. His legs were trembling.

Pearl went to him. No thought, all instinct. She held out her hand.

The tableau held for a moment, Tristan looking down at her hand as if it were something foreign and unreliable, as if he'd never seen the gesture before.

"Do you need help?" It was the wrong question; his expression was remote, unyielding. She tried again: "Where do you want to go?"

He hesitated, looked like he might throw up. "The locker room."

She held his arm as he stepped down from the treadmill.

They crossed the room together. Once they entered the men's locker room, their balance was dependent on each other.

Inside, everything was ecru tile and stainless steel. Tristan led her straight to the open shower area and twisted a knob, bracing one hand against the wall as the spray came down on him. Pearl moved back, watching as he slid to the floor and sat with his head hanging, letting the water soak through his workout clothes. She felt like a voyeur staying, yet she didn't dare leave, instead standing back by the sinks until he finally lifted his head.

She brought him a towel from the shelf. "Are you going to be sick? I can get the trash can."

Eventually: "No."

"You need water."

"I have some." He swallowed, nodded over his shoulder to the lockers, closed his eyes. "Seventy-eight."

Pearl went to his locker, unsurprised to find it was one of the only ones without a padlock. She reached into his gym bag, touched folded clothes, travel-size toiletries, a bottle of water. When she gave it to him, he drank half without stopping, downed the rest a moment later. He was still pale, with faint, shocked shadows beneath his eyes, but when he looked at her, the keen focus was back, the sensation of being under a 400x microscope lens.

"You should eat something." She suddenly felt very wrong being here, where the air smelled like men's soaps and acrid cleanser, where anyone could walk in and find them together.

He stood, now with only the slightest sign of weakness, and went around the corner. Pearl took a step forward, stopping abruptly when she saw, over the chest-high partition, that he was getting undressed.

His voice caught her at the door. "Nobody ever said your name. Last night, on the boat."

She didn't turn. "It's Pearl."

Tristan remained silent so long she had to look back. He now stood at the partition, watching her. His shoulders and pectoral muscles were chiseled, not an ounce of extra flesh on his frame. His skin gleamed damply under the fluorescents. "Thank you."

He said it without inflection. She barely nodded, lifting her gaze from his body a moment too late, knowing he'd seen. She left the fitness center quickly, not slowing her step as the desk attendant came out of the women's locker room pushing a cleaning cart and stopped to stare after her.

SEVEN

THAT NIGHT, PEARL jerked awake in the bluish darkness of her living room. The digital clock read 12:18 a.m. Her phone was ringing. She put it to her ear, staring unseeingly at the TV, which she'd fallen asleep in front of two hours ago. "Hello?"

"Pearlie?" Dad sounded distant, muffled.

She swung her legs to the floor. "Are you okay?"

"Oh, yeah, yeah, but . . ." Voices in the background, a bellow of laughter. He was borrowing the Tavern phone. "Don't think I can make it home."

"It's okay." Her words were quick. "It's fine. Hold on. I'll be there."

No good-bye, just a soft fuzz of distant music and bar noise, then the disconnect.

Sleep addled, she crept around, looking for her flip-flops and car keys. She stepped out into the night.

The Mermaid Tavern was the bar's original name, and you could still read the letters on the sign, if you squinted right. What had first opened as a whimsical watering hole for tourists had, over the years, been claimed by local hard-core drinkers. It was as if their hopelessness had drained the place, weathering the periwinkle-and-lavender-trimmed paint job to gray, starving the window boxes to dirt.

Pearl hesitated outside the door, clutching the strap of her shoulder bag as she stared at the figurehead of a bare-breasted mermaid mounted by the door. The siren, collecting lost souls. Like the rest of the building, she was chipped and peeling, her right hand carved to grip the pole of the "open" flag like a pike. Pearl steeled herself, pushing through the door into the smell of booze and fried bar food.

Inside, there was recessed lighting over the bar, and green-shaded lamps above the pool table, where dark shapes hunched and leaned and drew from glass steins. They knew Pearl here; she was allowed as far as the stools, where Dad always sat.

She put her hand on his shoulder; his head hung down, nearly resting on the bar. "I'm here. Let's go."

"You need any help getting him into the car, dear?" The rusty voice of Yancey Sanford spoke into her left ear, and every nerve in her body revolted. The big man spilled over the stool beside her, grizzled gray curls covering the tops of his ears, eyes shiny with drink and mocking good humor. "I tried to cut him off, but you know how it is. He goes on a tear sometimes."

Saying nothing, Pearl drew her shoulder up automatically, making a barrier between them. "Dad, time to go, okay?"

He finally turned to her. For a moment, she expected a different face, somehow unfamiliar. Maybe monstrous. Too many horror movies with Reese; he was the same old Dad, only bleary-eyed, and somehow gone from her. Belonging more to these people, the same ones you stood in line with at Godfrey's Market and the Citgo station, their faces seamed with cold weather and monotony and drink. "Yup. Okay."

"Sure you gonna make it, bub?" Yancey's voice rose for the benefit of the other drinkers, who chuckled, craning their necks as Dad navigated the stool, holding on to Pearl's arm. "Now, don't give that girl of yours any grief. She's awful good to cart you around." More laughter.

Bull*shit*. They were the ones: buying Dad shots after he tried to cut himself off, encouraging him to give in, to drown it all so they could have a night's entertainment and some gossip to spread around town tomorrow. Pearl tugged too hard, making Dad stumble, then slid her arm around his middle, propping him up.

"Yep, my boy would do that for me. Wouldn't you, Ev?" Yancey's twentysomething son Evan sat to his left, peeling the label on his Sam Adams, not bothering to look up. "'Course, I always manage to get myself home, one way or another. . . ." Yancey's words caught her ear on her way out the door. Never mind that nobody ever offered Dad a ride home when he was like this, never thought to call a cab.

When Dad was in the passenger seat, he pinched the top of his nose, squeezed his eyes shut. "Christ. I'm sorry." He sounded hoarse.

"Don't apologize. Those guys are assholes." She pulled the seat belt across him, buckled him in.

"I'm sorry." Wheezing now, his eyes still closed, as if he wasn't talking to her at all. "Sorry."

They drove down the night streets in silence, Pearl so focused on getting home that she started a little when he said, "I walked all around that goddamn yard. Snow was ass-deep. Didn't see anybody, didn't hear anything. Swear to God." He turned his face to the window.

Cold filtered in slowly, from the crown of her head to her fingertips. This was the only time he talked about it, when he was drunk and numb. "He was in the woods, they said." Her voice was soft. A stranger, hiding, biding his time, watching the sleeping Garrison household through the trees and the storm. "You couldn't have known."

"Nobody came over that fence. Would've been footprints."

"It was snowing too hard." All the prints, even Dad's, had been lost under the ashy, frozen mess left by the fire hoses, destroying the only proof that Dad had made his rounds at the one-hour intervals marked on the clipboard with his initials. The proof that he'd seen nothing, could've done nothing to stop the stranger who'd later walked the quiet hallways of the second floor, pushed David and Sloane's bedroom door open to watch them breathe. Put a bullet in the base of David's spine, another in his head. The discharge from the silencer might not have even woken Sloane before he did the same to her.

"I don't care what they say. Had to be somebody who knew the house. Knew the schedule." Dad scrubbed his face and sat back, closing his eyes. "I just looked back . . . and the place was on fire. Alarm was screaming. How'd he get in without setting off the goddamn alarm?"

They didn't speak again until they were home, Pearl watching him tug ponderously at his laces until she finally knelt and pulled the boots off his feet. She guided him to his bed, laid the chenille blanket over him. Dad curled onto his side, his breathing slow, labored. He licked his dry lips before he spoke. "I didn't have the flask with me. Swear."

"I know." She was positive it was Yancey who'd started

that rumor after the news broke about the Garrisons. That Win Haskins had a flask he carried around with him everywhere, that he was probably drunk as a lord while murder was being done in the big house.

The flask was real enough. It sat on the bureau, engraved with Dad's initials. He used to bring it with him on fishing trips, weekend outings, never on the job. "You shouldn't go to the Tavern anymore." She felt empty, hollowed out by the smallness of her own voice in the room. "Please don't go there anymore."

Dad promised nothing. He was snoring, mouth open, one fist clenched beside his head. She stuffed the extra pillow against his back so he'd sleep on his side—that had been a persistent fear these past months, that he'd vomit and choke, she'd read about that happening—switched off the lamp, and continued to sit on the edge of the bed in darkness, her own fists balled.

She didn't know who this helpless anger was for, if she could pick just one target, but it left her knotted with tension that could be eased only by going over the facts, digging up the bodies again and again and hoping for something new to emerge.

In her room, her tablet glowed with cold comfort, glinting off the sea glass and shells in their neat rows. There were more true-crime nuts out there than she'd ever imagined, entire sites dedicated to unsolved cases. The Garrisons were hot right now, that familiar navy-and-white family portrait reused again and again, the same links reposted to Cassidy's website, which showcased her musical career and a video journal she'd kept while touring. The videos were usually shot in some greenroom right before Cassidy went onstage, featuring the girl in full makeup and formal gown, saying how very excited she was to perform. Despite the difference in their coloring, there were similarities between her and Tristan: the shape of their jaws, the arch of their brows. Cassidy was animated, high energy, with none of the aloof detachment Pearl associated with her older brother.

Pearl read all the message boards she could find. Tristan's name leaped out repeatedly. As much as everyone liked him for the crime—the only survivor, the sole heir to all that money—it was impossible. He couldn't have committed the murders.

A security camera in the Sugarloaf condo complex had caught Tristan driving in around nine thirty p.m., nearly three and a half hours after he'd left Tenney's Harbor, exactly the time it would take to drive straight there with one pit stop for gas. Five witnesses—two of them Tristan's vacationing Yale friends and three "guests" (girls, Pearl assumed)—corroborated that he'd arrived at that time, free of blood or wounds. One of the girls must've been intended for Tristan, put on reserve until the crown prince made his appearance.

A notification popped up on one of Pearl's social media

accounts; this late, there was no worry of Mom being online. A friend request from Bridges Spencer. Pearl accepted.

A few seconds later, an instant message box appeared with a thumbnail selfie of Bridges: *U always up this late?*

The cursor blinked. A muscle moved in Pearl's jaw. Her fingers flew over the pad. *When I'm bored. I thought you were an early riser.*

And a night owl.

Bridges, you amaze me. As she awaited his response, she accessed his page, scrolled through photos, read old posts, hunting for signs of Tristan. Searching, endlessly searching, for what was written between the lines.

EIGHT

THE DAY OF the regatta seemed tailor-made for sailing, the sky cerulean and clear, the wind pulling steadily northeast. The crowd swarmed all the way from the public landing to the yacht club, tourists and locals mixing, snapping pictures of the yachts, eating ice cream and fried seafood sold at the takeout on the waterfront walkway.

Pearl put her hand up to block the sun, spotting Bridges sitting on one of the granite posts by the yacht club marina entrance. He wore a navy-striped hoodie, chino shorts, and boat shoes without socks. "Very nautical," she said as he slid down to his feet. "Did a big kid take your captain's hat?"

"Hey, I'm just the first mate. We don't get hats." They fell into step, the silence self-conscious but not uncomfortable.

More experimental, trying out the new intimacy between them. They'd been chatting online almost every night this week. Silly verbal sparring on the surface; beneath, reaching out to each other while the rest of the world was asleep. She often wondered if he'd just come back from another clandestine boat ride with Tristan, going God knew where on the bay at an hour when almost no one was on the water. "I only got here a couple minutes ago." He checked his phone, snorted. "Akil's bitching at me to hurry. This way."

She followed him through the crowd. A steel drum band was playing somewhere, hammering out a deafening rhythm as they passed other sailboats lined up for the race.

Tristan's Islander 36 was at the end, brilliant white with a blue cabin housing. The name stenciled across the stern was the *Cassidy Claire*.

Akil sat in a deck chair above, mirrored aviator shades on, one foot propped up. "Dude. We thought you'd bailed."

"When have I ever."

Pearl stepped onto the deck and saw Tristan kneeling by the mast, pulling the lines off their cleats and winches. He stopped what he was doing at the sight of her, one arm resting on his knee, the wind stirring his hair around his collar. She'd taken more care with her appearance today, khaki shorts and a white gathered top she'd bought last summer and only worn once because she didn't think it was really her style.

There was movement on the opposite side of the deck,

and Hadley Kurtzweil walked into view. She stopped at the sight of Bridges, flushing slightly. "Hi." She held up a bottle, giving it a shake. "Water?"

Akil waved at the cabin door. "Go ahead." Hadley went below, and a moment later, Quinn followed. She wore a black crocheted bikini that showed off every sinewy inch of her; she caught the cabin door and held it, facing Bridges and Pearl. "Akil sent us an invite. Hope you don't mind. Oh, wait." She tilted her head. "Is this awkward for you, Bridge?"

Bridges didn't speak right away. When he did, his voice was flat. "It's Tristan's boat."

Quinn turned to Tristan, hand on her hip. He was silent for a beat, then looked back to his work. "You should stay," he told her.

She smirked and disappeared down the steps. Bridges slowly turned to Akil, his eyes wide, jaw set. "What . . . the hell."

Akil tipped back in his chair. "Hey. You bring around whoever you want, why can't I?" The look he leveled at Pearl blew away any pretense: she was a joke that had worn very thin. She held his stare.

Tristan straightened. "Akil, let the topping lift out."

Akil got up and let down one of the lines that held the boom until it hung loosely, then recleated it. Bridges turned to Pearl. "I'm so sorry, I didn't know. We can leave—"

"It doesn't matter." She heard the girls' laughter below,

tinkling and faint. "I can take it if they can."

"Are you sure?" She nodded briskly, and after a second, he breathed out. "Cool. Okay."

She found an out-of-the-way place to perch and watch the boys finish prepping. Tristan started the motor and steered them into the direction of the wind while Akil and Bridges hoisted the sails, which luffed briefly against the mast before Bridges cleated them off.

There were eight yachts already at the designated starting area near the end of the breakwater, one by the name of *Freedom,* another *Starchaser*; from here, the crowd on the docks was little more than distant color and sound. The girls came back up and resumed their positions on the far side of the deck, stretching out on towels with tanning lotion and magazines, seemingly oblivious to the competitive tension in the air.

At ten, the starting shot sounded. Tristan came forward from the cockpit. "Starboard tack." He switched places with Bridges, trimming the jib while Akil did the same to the mainsail. The *Cassidy Claire* tilted to the right, sails puffing with wind, sliding with surprising nimbleness toward the rocky breakwater.

They glided past the *Freedom,* the *Penobscot Princess,* the *Stand Fast.* Rocks loomed large.

No one spoke as the hull passed within twelve feet of the breakwater. Pearl gripped her knees, straining for the grinding sound of rock against wood. Bridges was rigid at the helm; Akil crouched on the deck, waiting.

They slipped along soundlessly, close enough to see a Styrofoam cup wedged in a crevice. Tristan called, "Port." The boys trimmed the sails again, Bridges turning the wheel to the left. They cut off the front-runner, *Starchaser*, so narrowly that Pearl heard Bridges curse under his breath.

The wind pushed them out into the open, and as the other eight yachts struggled to keep up in their wake, a distant cheer went up from the docks. Tristan stood against the mast for a moment, looking back, then went to Bridges, pulling a flyer out of his pocket as Akil moved up beside them. "This is the course." He unfolded the sheet to show the line diagram. "Windward toward the Nicatou buoy, then southeast to the Whale's Tooth buoy, southwest around the entrance of Somes Sound, then home."

"Three, four hours?" Bridges glanced back.

"Less. If we do our jobs." He tucked the map away, in full possession of himself and the day. It was as if the white, shaking boy in the gym had never existed, and she wondered if his wingmen had ever seen that side of him. "We bought ourselves some time. Set the sails." He turned away, adding vaguely, "The bar's stocked."

Bridges and Akil exchanged a look, grinning.

Bridges and Pearl went below first. The cabin was polished teak, a galley to the right, a chart table nearby with two white leather settees and a stained-glass lamp mounted above. Gilt-framed photos hung on the walls: a candid of Cassidy and Joseph standing on the Islander's deck, holding a just-caught fish with tropical-looking water in the background. Another professional family photo, everyone dressed in denim shirts and khakis, barefooted, sitting on a beach somewhere. Tristan was much younger, maybe twelve, his hair cut short, sitting chin-up, his fingers spread on his thighs. The more Pearl studied the photo, the more the pose took on a rigid show quality, like a Labrador waiting for the Westminster judges.

Bridges went straight for the galley, locating the liquor cabinet, where expensive-looking bottles sat in a rack coated with a fine layer of dust. "You want anything?"

Pearl dragged her eyes from the photo. "Do you guys sail a lot?"

"Tristan and Akil and I usually just knock around in the motorboats, cruise the islands and stuff. Competitions like this were something he did with his dad. David entered regattas all over the world, had a whole case of trophies."

"Sounds like he and Tristan were pretty close."

One of the ice cubes Bridges held dropped into a snifter. He cleared his throat, let the rest fall into the glass, and broke the seal on a bottle of brandy. "Not really."

She sank onto the settee, watching him.

"Truth?" Bridges glanced over at her. "David was a real

hard-ass. Nothing was ever good enough, you know? He was one of those self-made men, had to remind everybody about his amazing work ethic all the time. Especially his kids."

"New money."

He glanced up, gave a laugh. "Yeah. And he was a dick to Tristan. Like, bad. Cassidy was his princess, and Joe was his favorite." He paused, fingering the foil seal. "I shouldn't have said that."

"I won't tell anybody."

Bridges was silent as he poured his drink. "My gramps would say that's bad luck. Speaking ill of the dead." He gave a humorless smile. "Bet you don't think I'm so fair now."

"I think you're being honest. Sometimes that's better."

He was still frowning. "Are you hungry? There's supposed to be cold cuts and stuff in the fridge."

"Sure." She went to find the head, fastening the catch on the door. There was a toilet, sink, and shower, thick towels with Gs embroidered on them. Pearl ran the faucet and carefully opened the medicine cabinet. A small first-aid kit, a hairbrush, a box of tampons. In the sink drawer, there were some prescription bottles with Cassidy's name on them, dated a year and a half ago, nearly empty. Pearl slipped her phone out of her pocket and Googled the medications. Sertraline: antidepressant. Trazodone: antidepressant and sedative.

She hunkered down and opened the cabinet below the sink, painfully aware of the passing seconds, of how long she could stay in here without drawing attention. There were more first-aid supplies underneath: Ace bandages, gauze pads, more boxes in the shadows behind. She pushed through, heard the rattle of a small object being dislodged. After a quick inventory, she heard it again when she shook the box of gauze.

Inside was a memory card no bigger than her thumbnail, the kind used for file storage in digital cameras. Pearl turned it over in her fingers, mind racing, then jumped at the sound of Bridges's footsteps passing by outside. She pocketed the card, turned off the faucet, and went to meet him.

Carrying two plates loaded with sandwiches and chips, they went back on deck, sitting together where Bridges could keep tabs on the sails while Akil went below. She could feel the memory card against her thigh, as if it generated its own heat. Tristan stood at the helm, seemingly oblivious to all of them, his gaze on the green navigational buoy about a quarter mile offshore from Little Nicatou.

Akil brought up a drink for himself and white wine for Quinn and Hadley, leaving the bottle between the girls. The wind shifted, and the boys went back to tacking, only Tristan speaking now and then to issue orders. The boat heeled around the buoy, avoiding bad waters, bearing southeast toward Whale's Tooth. Pearl sat by herself, glancing over once or twice to catch Hadley and Quinn looking in her direction. They didn't seem to be whispering about her, just looking, sizing her up. Feeling increasingly foolish sitting alone with a plate of half-eaten sandwiches, Pearl stood and made her way over, leaning on the cabin housing for support when the boat pitched.

Quinn and Hadley said nothing as she sat on the deck beside them, her stomach knotted, already regretting this. Approaching two girls bonded in their hatred for you was like sticking your head into a wolverine den and hoping for the best. They were painting their toenails ruby red, trading off the brush. None of them spoke for so long that Pearl almost stood and left, though the shame of retreat made her hold out for an extra minute. Quinn said, "Bridges won't like you being over here with us."

"It's not his call." She shrugged at their long looks. "We're friends."

Quinn's mouth quirked. "How original."

"It doesn't have to be original. It's true." Quinn gave her a moment's appraisal before facing back to the ocean. Silence settled in again.

"So . . ." Quinn leaned back, crossing her long legs at the ankle. "Does anybody else find it weird that we're basically sitting on a floating mausoleum right now?" Hadley shushed her, glancing back to see if Tristan had heard. "Seriously. He hasn't gotten rid of anything. I saw some of Cassidy's hair elastics and lip gloss down there. That's like one step away from saving fingernail clippings."

"It's only been six months." Hadley spoke in a hush. "He's probably not ready yet. I mean . . . can you imagine? The last time you see your parents alive, you get into a fight over something stupid?" She shook her head. "How do you get over that?"

"He could hire somebody to put their stuff in storage. He'd never even have to look at it. My mom did that when my aunt died. I mean, you have to deal with these things." Quinn adjusted her sunglasses. From this angle, it was obvious that she was no more a natural blonde than Pearl, but her highlights were exquisite, ranging from honey to platinum. "Do you think their house is like that? Everybody's stuff still lying out, like, creepy as hell?"

Hadley coated her pinkie nail. "I heard the fire was really bad. There probably isn't much left."

"He should bulldoze it." Hadley burst into exasperated laughter. "What? Look, I'm not being a bitch here, I'm serious. It cannot be healthy to live across town from a monument to your murdered fam while you try to work through your PTSD issues. He never should've spent the winter here." Quinn glanced back at Tristan. "He doesn't look good."

"He's beautiful." Hadley's voice was faint.

"Well, yeah. But he doesn't look good." She gave a barely detectable nod in Pearl's direction. "Too bad you weren't around the last couple summers. Tristan, in his prime? Basically ruled the whole Tenney's Harbor party scene. Some *craaazy* shit went down."

Pearl raised her brows. "Wow. He seems like such an introvert."

Hadley looked thoughtful, finishing her wine and refilling her glass. "He's changed a lot. After everything being in the news and the reporters . . . I guess he just wants to be left alone. But when his family first summered here? Oh my God."

"What happened?" Pearl watched them exchange a look, familiar helpless frustration rising at their telepathy, the higher plane of girl friendship that she had never reached herself. "What?"

Quinn settled back, smugness playing across her lips. "Debauchery. That's all I'm saying."

Hadley giggled. "You oughta know."

"Shut up. I've *heard* things, I didn't say I was a joiner. Becoming a YouTube porn star doesn't exactly make my bucket list. Besides"—she let the pause drag out, resting her head back against the chair—"it's mostly townies who get into that stuff. Give them, like, one wine cooler, and they'll do anything the guys want."

Pearl turned to the water, measuring her breathing, waiting for the red to fade from her vision. Looking embarrassed, Hadley bit her lip, finally saying, "For real, Quinn? I mean . . . the guys really made a video . . . ?"

"I'm not saying who did what. You must know. You were with Bridges last summer."

"He'd never do something like that."

"Look, all I know is some freaky Skinemax action got posted for a week or two before somebody took it down. Maybe it wasn't Bridges or Tristan who made it, but it happened at one of their parties. It got like a zillion shares."

"Who was the girl?" Pearl said.

"As if I watched it. I already said, some random townie." Quinn glanced up as a second bottle lowered down between them, Akil holding it by the neck. "And now the Wine Fairy's here."

"Drink up. This is the good stuff. Ol' Dave left the place loaded." He took Hadley's glass and topped it off, clinking it with his own. "May all our ups and downs be between the sheets."

Hadley laughed, coloring slightly, while Quinn looked coolly back. When he'd gone, she said, "He's trying to get you drunk."

"It's working."

"Do you think he's cute?"

"Yeah. I mean—yeah." Hadley flicked distractedly at her hair.

"But he's not Bridges." Quinn shook her head. "Remember what today's about. Proving you don't need him to have a good time."

When Pearl glanced back, Akil was conferring with Tristan, who made some small comment without taking his eyes off the Whale's Tooth buoy in the distance.

Akil crept up behind Hadley, tickling the exposed skin between her tank top and shorts, making her shriek. Pearl took the opportunity to remove herself, going back to pick at the food and watch Bridges, who was watching Akil, his brows drawn. The memory card held a new weight in her pocket, and she squirmed a little, thinking of what Quinn had said about freaky videos.

Time spun out in the sunbaked quiet. The water was jewel green, endless. Akil led Hadley down below, his hand on the small of her back. Bridges stood stiffly, then walked away from the sails, taking up a solitary position on the pulpit.

The boat lost some speed, no longer angled properly into the wind, but Tristan didn't seem to notice, sitting in the captain's chair with one knee drawn up, his right forearm draped across, lost in thought. Bear Island lay ahead, the lighthouse crowning the rocky heights. Maybe this was the direction the boys had gone after they left the party on Little Nicatou; there were any number of small islands out here, not to mention harbor access to all the little towns dotting the coast of MDI. Not much else to do after ten p.m. on the open water.

Some sound or intuition made Pearl glance back. The *Starchaser* was closing in off the port bow, crew members in bright Windbreakers scrambling around on deck, adjusting sails. Pearl raised her voice: "Should they be passing us like that?" No one answered. She went to Tristan, stopping a couple of feet away from him. "They're passing us."

He turned, saw the *Starchaser*, and got to his feet, his expression freezing when he saw both Akil and Bridges gone.

She hesitated, thinking how long it had been since she'd sailed, how little she knew about handling a boat this size. "I've got it." Pearl ran for the sails, loosening the line with a few tugs. She looked back to find Tristan staring. "Trust me. Grab the wheel."

NINE

PEARL CHECKED THE telltales and pulled the mainsail about fifty degrees from aft; the jib sheets were next, and she tried not to show her relief when she felt the boat heeling beneath her. Maybe sailing was one of those riding-a-bike things, all the afternoons with Dad on the Cat indelibly imprinted—either that or they'd end up in irons out here, and none of these people would ever speak to her again.

Once she'd finished trimming the mainsail, they were moving swiftly, neck and neck with the *Starchaser*. The other yacht was running with the wind now, maneuvering in front of them, mirroring what Tristan had done back at the starting area. He called "Bear off" over the steady rush of waves against the hull. After Pearl trimmed the sails again, he relaxed slightly, watching the *Starchaser* move past them.

She looked back at him, blocking the sunshine with her hand. "What're we doing?"

"Letting them get ahead of us."

Pearl waited for him to expand upon that. His silence was complete, as if, for him, she'd dropped out of existence again. She released a breath and sat back on her heels, chewing a nail she'd barely been aware of ripping on one of the lines.

They continued around Bear Island, watching the *Starchaser* pull ahead, leading the way past the opening to Somes Sound, around Sutton Island.

Tristan glanced at her. "Do you know how to jibe?"

"Uh, I've seen it done before, but—"

"Then tighten the mainsail and the jib sheets." She did it, loosening the preventer line, biting back her doubts and questions, her memories of what Dad had told her about jibing, especially at speeds like this. Tristan pointed off starboard, where another navigational buoy could be seen. "There's some bad water over there. They'll do the smart thing and avoid it."

He turned the wheel, aiming them into the rough current on the far side of the buoy. The boat pitched and rocked; there was a faint thump from below, like something or someone being thrown to the floor. "I'll tell you what to do from here," he called.

He turned the boat across the wind, the mast shaking with resistance. The jib blew backward, and he shouted, "Watch the boom," not even giving her enough time to gasp.

The boom and the mainsail hurtled at her. Pearl threw herself to her knees, air whooshing over her head and back as the thick pole passed close enough to part her hair.

She pressed herself to the deck, sick with reaction, afraid to sit up and see the boom flying back at her. She heard Dad clearly now, telling her how risky jibing could be, how sailors had been struck in the head and knocked overboard, unconscious, to drown.

Tristan called something, but the blood was roaring in her ears, her pulse pounding with adrenaline. She finally understood: "Haul in the jib sheet and trim it." She looked up and saw the sails flapping wild.

Scrambling, she ran for the jib, unaware of Bridges by her side until he grabbed the line and helped her pull in the sheet.

"I've got the mainsail," Bridges said, waving her back, and she stepped away, hands on hips, breathless. She glanced at Tristan, but he was steering, totally focused, banishing her to wherever it was he sent people when they stopped being of use.

Bridges finished trimming and turned to her. "Jesus, that was close. You okay?"

"Fine."

He let out a breath and laughed, shaking his head. "Why didn't you tell me you knew how to sail?"

"Why didn't you ask?" She ran an unsteady hand over

the top of her head, ensuring it was still there, then set her shoulders.

Tristan's gamble had worked: they cut in front of the *Starchaser* with plenty of breathing room, and from there, Pearl and Bridges handled the sails together.

Little Nicatou was visible in the distance when Akil and Hadley came back on deck. Hadley went straight to Quinn, looking at no one, while Akil took a moment to stretch lazily, stopping when he saw Pearl trimming the sails in his place. The other boys didn't acknowledge him at all.

A moment later, Akil went below again, leaving the cabin door open and banging.

When it was all over—the applause Pearl dodged, the photographs she managed to stay out of (the last thing she needed was Dad opening the *Islander* to see a picture of her with half the club's young elite), the awarding of the trophy, the fuss over them being the youngest crew in the race—they moved through the crowd as a group, Bridges and Akil singing a drinking song, Pearl following a half step behind Tristan, close enough to watch his shoulder blades move against the fabric of his shirt. It was the same loose black polo she'd seen him wear several times, and she imagined him picking out shirts online in the silence of his rented home, the lost boy again, the one who'd always had a fashion-conscious mother to make sure he left the house looking right. But now he carried a trophy held loosely in one hand; the posture of the winner fit him like a second skin.

"I'm starving. Let's eat somewhere." Bridges was wind-burned, exhilarated, eyes only slightly bloodshot from drink. His hand found Pearl's back. "Honorary first mate makes the call."

She didn't think she'd ever wanted to go home so badly, the memory card seeming to grow heavier in her pocket with each step. "Anywhere but the club." Truth was, even if she wanted to go there as a guest, she couldn't afford the club; her car insurance payment had pretty much wiped her out until next week's paycheck.

Quinn tapped Akil's arm, taking a few steps back. "We're going now." Hadley stood behind her, fiddling with the strap on her leather tote bag, looking off.

"You're bailing already?" Akil tried to catch Hadley's eye. "Come on. Eat with us."

"Got stuff to do." Quinn took Hadley's arm. "'Bye-bye." They took off through the parking lot without a backward glance.

Akil scrubbed his hand in his hair, watching the girls leave.

The four of them went downtown in Tristan's Bentley—spotlessly clean, smelling of conditioned leather, the trophy deposited in the trunk—and claimed one of the last free parking spots on Ocean. When Pearl realized where they were headed, she balked, one foot on the sidewalk, one hand on the car door. Bridges hesitated, looking back. "What's the matter?"

Dark Brew's sign hung above, whimsical lettering paired with a silhouette of three witches stirring a cauldron. Weekend afternoons were Reese's time; he wasn't always seated at the corner booth with a coffee and a leftover chocolate croissant from that morning, but the odds were not in her favor. "Nothing. I just don't . . ."

He tilted his head, smiling. "I know. It's kind of a dive, but the coffee's awesome. Trust me. Once you get it here, you won't go anywhere else."

She tried not to show how it grated, being told about her own hometown, having Jovia's baby called a dive. There was no way to bow out now—she couldn't even make a quick getaway without her car—so she followed him inside, barely able to hear the entrance chimes sound over the hum of summer madness.

The line snaked to the door, and almost all the pub tables were taken; the air was dense with the smells of coffee, baking, the sounds of conversation and clinking dishes. No sign of Reese. Lots of people seemed to have come straight from the landing, and the four of them got plenty of looks as they queued up in front of the counter, where Jovia was working at high speed along with two college-age girls in aprons and

Dark Brew T-shirts. The boys ordered before Pearl, and she braced herself as Jovia glanced up. "Oh! Hey, hon, didn't see you there."

"I was hiding." All too aware of who stood beside her, Pearl ordered a black coffee, grateful to be able to fix her gaze on the hunt for her wallet somewhere in her bag.

Bridges was faster, sliding his from his back pocket. "All on one?" Jovia's hand hesitated over the cash register keypad.

"No—" Pearl broke off as Tristan reached past them both and ran his credit card through. Jovia watched, making brief, questioning eye contact with Pearl before handing over the receipt and coffees, saying, "We'll bring you your meals in a minute."

As they moved away from the counter, Pearl whispered to Bridges, "Does he always pay for everything?"

"Not always." A hesitation. "Most of the time."

"That's handy."

"That's just Tristan."

Summer kids sat at a table nearby, and they called out to Bridges; only two chairs were free, but Tristan claimed one, joined by Akil, and like that, the table began to empty. Not all at once—there was some chitchat about the regatta, some congrats handed around—but one boy moved to the counter, and two girls took their iced mochaccinos and left the shop for a bench on the sidewalk. Soon, it was just the four of them, together.

Pearl took the chair Bridges pulled out for her and found

herself facing Tristan. He was watching people pass by, some of whom stared at him, then whispered to a friend.

"So, where'd you learn to sail?" Bridges asked her, folding his arms on the table.

She took her time in answering. "My dad taught me. You?"

"Yacht club, here and in Southport, where I'm from. My parents and Gramps had me tying anchor hitches before I could walk." He gave her an approving look. "You were pretty badass out there today. Saved our butts."

Akil rolled his eyes. "You guys could've called down to me or something. Not like I was unreachable."

"You wanted to have sex more than you wanted to win." Tristan's tone was even, declarative, and he didn't spare Akil a glance as he wiped a ring from beneath his mug, laid down a fresh napkin as a coaster. "You made your choice. Own it. If Pearl hadn't stepped up, we'd still be making our way back from Somes Sound right now." One of the counter girls appeared with their order and began handing out sandwiches; Tristan stirred his coffee, continuing to speak as if she weren't there. "Hadley wouldn't have sex with you, would she?"

Akil's jaw tightened as he glanced at the girl, whose eyes widened before she quickly moved on to the next table. "I got enough."

"No, you didn't. If you did, you wouldn't be taking it out on Pearl." Still such a calm tone. "Admit that's what you're pissed off about, not that she helped us win. You never cared about that."

It was the fastest, most complete dressing-down Pearl had ever seen. Akil didn't argue; in fact, he shrugged and began eating his fries, a little sullen but somehow mollified, like it was a relief to be called on his own bullshit. Pearl glanced at Tristan—had he just defended her?—but he was preparing for a meal he wouldn't eat, adding pepper and salt. She barely registered the sound of the rear entrance jingling open until she heard Reese's laugh as he traded friendly insults with one of the counter girls.

Pearl was on her feet immediately, crossing the room to head him off. Reese wore baggy board shorts and a David Bowie T-shirt, and he smiled, surprised. "Hey. You missed a classic this morning. Mrs. Rosenthal lost an earring in her brunch strata and had me dig around for it so she wouldn't ruin her manicure. It was awesome. Ten bucks it went down her shirt, but I wasn't ready to go, like, spelunking. You eating by yourself? Grab your stuff and come out back. I downloaded *The House on Sorority Row*."

"I can't." She couldn't pretend to be normal, couldn't relax the tension written all over her face. "I want to, but . . . I can't right now."

"Um, okay. Why?" His gaze traveled to the table she'd come from, the empty chair with her bag hanging over it. Bridges was watching them with interest. "You're sitting with them?"

She opened her mouth, closed it. Time hung suspended, tension deepening with each second.

"They asked you to sit with them?" Flatly disbelieving.

Unexpectedly, some part of her bristled at that. "I came with them."

Reese stared at her for a long moment, then forced a laugh. "What is this, Be Kind to Second-Class Citizens Day? Why'd they ask you?" Another laugh, harsher, before she could speak. "Let me guess. Tristan Garrison's gone all Howard Hughes and hired you to be his handler. No, wait—this is some social experiment and you're their Eliza Doolittle. Who gets to stick the marbles in your mouth?"

"Will you stop? Can I say one thing before you talk over me?"

"Nope. I'm good." Reese stepped away as if to leave, and she reached for him.

"It's not—"

He turned, holding his finger in her face. "You've got no idea about those kind of guys, Pearl. You've got no idea what they really want." His intensity silenced her. "You think you're the first townie they let hang out with them? You going to party with them? Get wasted?" He made a disgusted sound. "Wake the hell up."

Heat rose in her face. "Don't tell me what I know about. And don't talk to me like I'm stupid—"

"Whatever." He put his hands up, turning away. "Enjoy your rich pricks." He pushed past a tourist family and went out the rear door, letting it bang shut behind him.

Pearl took a step to follow, but she was mad, too—furious—so she lifted her chin and turned away. Jovia had been watching with a pained expression, but now she looked back to the cappuccino machine, saying nothing.

The chaos of the shop had a dreamlike quality as Pearl returned to the table, everything seeming distant and muted compared to the hammering of her heart. "Everything okay?" Bridges glanced back at where Reese had made his exit.

"What's this?" There was a sandwich waiting on a plate for her, grilled cheese with tomato on rye, one of her favorites.

"I figured you must be hungry." He slid some napkins her way. "Come on. Everybody's eating." And then he was back in the conversation, laughing at some story from Akil's private school days that had even Tristan wearing a slight smile, his gaze sliding once to Pearl, then onward. She wondered who had first mentioned that she wasn't eating, whose idea it really was to order for her.

As the conversation flowed around her, her pulse slowed, her breathing evened out. The sandwich smelled good. Tasted even better.

TEN

PEARL TOOK THE front steps two at a time and then threw the chain lock home, something she and Dad never did. This moment called for extra security, extra privacy—she felt like she'd been caught in a whirl of people all day, when all she wanted was her bedroom, her tablet, and two minutes of peace to see what was on the memory card.

It was a little past five p.m. She'd told Bridges that her dad was expecting her, maybe holding supper. In truth, Dad wasn't even here. Maybe at the Tavern, maybe at Yancey's house shooting the shit, who knew. She slid a pair of his boots out of her path, then heard the telltale click of the oven, which meant that he'd heated up leftovers for his meal and forgotten to shut the oven off again.

By the time Pearl reached her room, her fingers were clumsy with nerves. She dug the memory card out of her pocket and slid it into the slot in her tablet, Quinn's words about last summer's viral video fresh in her mind, about random townies not even worth remembering.

There were seven video files on the card. It wasn't necessary to expand the thumbnail stills to recognize Cassidy Garrison's smiling face held close to the screen. Pearl even recognized a few of the dresses she was wearing. These were some of the entries for Cassidy's video journal, the ones she'd uploaded to her website. The two most recent files were unfamiliar, the thumbnails of nothing Pearl could identify; she clicked on the first one, dated almost exactly a year ago today.

A glimpse of what must be Cassidy's stockinged feet as she walked soundlessly through a doorway into a spacious room with a cream-colored settee. Joseph sat with his back to her, propped up on a throw pillow, engrossed in some handheld game. The camera shook as Cassidy pounced, seizing his shoulder, making him yelp and whirl.

"Hey!" Joseph made a grab for the camera. In some ways, he was a younger version of Tristan, except for the ease of expression, the playful light in his eyes.

Cassidy backed away, laughing. "Mom says you can't use it unless I say so—" End of video.

The final video on the card was dated August 16 of last year. It began with a rushing sound, like fabric or a hand rubbing across the mic. When the camera steadied, Pearl recognized the teak paneling of the Islander's head, the gleam of the towel rack; this was the angle from the far corner of the room by the shower stall.

The camera held shakily on the closed door. The mic was full of breathing—presumably Cassidy's—hard and raspy, like she'd been sprinting.

Wham. Something slammed against the other side of the door.

Wham. Cassidy made a keening noise in her throat and backed up—a rattle of shower curtain rings across the rod as she brushed by them.

Another *wham.* Then whoever was on the other side of the door went into a frenzy, hammering, slamming their full weight against it, the force threatening to explode the flimsy catch.

Cassidy cried out, fumbling the camera down. A kaleidoscopic whirl of paneling and floor tiles—then the video cut off.

Pearl stared. She clicked play again and again, pressing one fist to her lips as she watched.

Cassidy might've been moving to hide the memory card at the end—too scared to keep filming, to risk whoever was after her bursting through the door and finding her with the camera in her hand. Maybe separating the card and camera was the only way she could think of to save the video, to ensure that somebody, at some point, might find out that she'd been attacked. It was the act of a girl who wasn't sure if she was going to survive.

But Cassidy had survived—another four months. And she'd never gone back for the memory card. The Garrisons probably flew home to Connecticut a matter of days after this video was shot—summer families left Tenney's Harbor by mid-August at the latest to get home in time for the start of the school semester—and they hadn't returned to Maine until that unexpected visit during the week of Christmas. It was possible that Cassidy simply hadn't had a chance to get back onto the Islander before then; by December, the yacht would've been winterized and stored in a boatyard some-where. But what the hell had happened after she stopped filming that day?

Pearl played the video again, her skin tingling. Palpable rage was on the other side of that door; she could taste Cassi-dy's terror in the back of her own throat, bitter, acidic. Pearl's fingers flew, opening a browser window, Googling the Ten-ney's Harbor police department phone number. Then she sat, motionless.

Not yet. This wasn't enough. She didn't have a face, didn't have a name. And she didn't have a fix on Tristan Garrison, not even close.

She sat, hugging her bent knee, listening to the wind chimes outside the window. She played the video again. She didn't want to leave that terrified girl on the screen alone, trapped in that moment, recording whatever was about to come through that door. Cassidy Garrison had reached across four long seasons, and found her, Pearl, waiting on the other side.

Pearl had become invisible.

This was what it was like to be off Reese's radar. She might as well have been one of the pool attendants, or a spa stylist, peripheral characters who had nothing to do with the social whirl of the dining room. When it came to close friends, Reese was it; without him, she was on the outside again, maybe more so than ever. It was Sunday; she was only three hours into her shift, but his anger, his refusal to look at her, was like a wall she kept slamming into.

Reese was serving Mimi and company, laughter rising and falling as always, mock flirtations on both sides as he dialed up his charm to eleven. Pearl watched him hard for a moment, willing him to notice, hating herself for caring so much. He was the one who was being an ass, treating her like some clueless tween with a crush, like she didn't know the first thing about the way summer people operated. She couldn't imagine herself telling anybody but Reese about the video of Cassidy Garrison—and she also couldn't imagine being the first one to break the silent treatment, either.

"Pearl." The maître d' signaled to her. "You've got a phone call."

"Here?"

"Out on the lobby line. Go ahead, I'll keep an eye on your tables."

She'd never gotten a call at the club before. Meriwether was waiting for her at the front desk, having relieved the receptionist of the phone, and she watched with pursed lips as Pearl approached. "You know"—she didn't hand the phone over—"staff aren't to receive nonemergency calls on this line."

"I didn't give the number out. I don't know who it is."

"Mmm." After a long, considering pause, Meriwether held out the extension, making her reach for it.

"Pearl?" The voice on the other end was strained, all too familiar. Mom. "Finally. The switchboard bounced me all over the place."

"What's going on?" She turned her back on Meriwether. "Why didn't you just call my phone?"

"Why do you think? I knew the club was the one place where you'd have to pick up."

It was too late for lies about missed voice mail; Pearl had ignored three calls from Mom this month. As she gazed ahead, trapped, staff members carried cardboard boxes and an extension ladder through the lobby into the ballroom;

preparations for the formal ball and auction on Friday were well underway. "Well, I'm working right now. I'll call you back on my break."

"I want you to promise me."

"Promise, promise." She was increasingly aware of Meriwether's eyes boring into the back of her head. "Give me an hour."

There was a picnic table tucked around the corner of the club, mostly hidden from view by the low branches of an oak tree, where staff could eat their lunches without ruining the ambience. Pearl sat cross-legged on the bench, listening as the line rang twice before Mom picked up.

"So. How are things?" Now that Mom had her where she wanted her, her tone was careful, hesitant.

"Good."

"I never see you online anymore."

"I don't go on much."

A sigh. "Am I allowed to ask how Dad's doing?"

Pearl hated it when she put it like that—"Dad"—like they were still a unit, like Mom didn't have her own life way down in Kittery, and her own live-in boyfriend, Scott What's-His-Name, who seemed completely inoffensive, and who Pearl had absolutely no interest in getting to know. "He's fine. Everything's fine."

"Oh, Pearl." A long silence, waiting for Pearl to fill it with reassurances. "Does he ask you not to tell me things?"

"No. Why would he?" Dad didn't need to; it went without saying. A holdover, perhaps, from when Pearl was younger, when both she and Dad knew that a slipup could end with them back in family court, debating custody. The one solid understanding between Dad and her since the Garrisons happened was *don't tell your mother*. Don't tell her there's nothing but spaghetti in the cupboard and half a six-pack in the fridge. Don't tell her we're behind on the mortgage. Don't tell her the wolf is at the door. Don't tell her.

"How's his drinking?" This time, Pearl didn't speak at all. "Honey . . . I know he's been through a lot. I just want to know what's going on. I'm getting nothing from either of you. Your father doesn't even have a phone anymore, for God's sake." In the silence, tension grew. "You two always do this. Stonewall me. Just you against the world, nobody gets in, right? How do you think that makes me feel?"

Pearl wanted to shout, *Well, whose fault is it*, to drive Mom back from the receiver with the sound and force of her words. *Whose fault is it you left? Who made you move to the other side of the state? Who made you?* But the resentment was old, and it exhausted itself quickly, leaving her feeling how she always did after a chat with Mom: like she wanted to curl up with a pillow over her head and block out the world. "I don't know what to tell you. We're doing okay."

"What's okay?" Mom's tone was delicate again. "Listen

to me, please, for one second. Your father has a problem. We were together fifteen years, Pearl, I know better than anybody. I know how it is to hang in there for somebody, hoping they'll change—"

"I have to go now."

"No, you don't."

"They need me inside. I really have to go. I'll get back to you, okay? I will." And Pearl disconnected, holding the phone cupped in her hand, squeezing her eyes shut when it vibrated a few seconds later. Mom, wanting the last word. She turned the phone off, imagined dropping it in the trash can on her way inside. In the end, she pocketed it and went back to work.

Reese's section was liveliest, as usual. Always leave 'em laughing. How the hell could he act so normal when she felt like she was walking around with a blade stuck between her shoulders? She thought about confronting him in the kitchen, cornering him the way he'd done with Indigo the other day, forcing him to listen to her.

Across the room, their gazes met, the briefest of magnetic pulls. But Reese didn't linger; he went back to chatting up members, pointing out items on the menu, refilling glasses, making time to get a slow smile out of Indigo whenever she passed.

Stiffly, Pearl went to her section, pushed a chair into a table harder than necessary, and tried to match his pace.

Maybe she didn't make it look as good, but she could freeze him out just as easily. The two of them moved like figurines on an ornamental skating pond: gliding, spinning, repelling whenever they grew too near.

Pearl and Dad left for North Beach after supper. It wasn't necessary to talk much. She knew how he was feeling after the night at the Tavern. They'd survived enough lost weekends that he didn't embarrass her with apologies. He had cut himself back to two beers a night for the last week, and she'd pretended not to notice his restlessness, his short temper as the evening wore on. It would be something of a relief when he gave in and went back for that third, fourth drink.

But tonight, they were going beachcombing, and there was peace and timelessness in the ritual. Pearl might've been ten years old again, riding shotgun, hoping for a stop at the ice cream takeout on the way home. And when they got to the house, Mom would be sitting on the couch, flipping through a magazine, waiting to see what they'd found. Funny; sometimes Pearl would go months without thinking about the way things had been, and then a nothing-special memory like that would pop into her head, bringing with it an unexpected sense of loss.

North Beach had a paved parking area with a hot dog stand in the far corner, its striped awning faded and tattered around the edges. Dad parked nearby, said, "Want a dog?"

which earned him the usual dirty look. He knew Pearl hadn't touched a hot dog since she ate a bad one at the Blue Hill Fair in sixth grade and threw up on the Sea Dragon.

They walked together, each of them with their hands in their pockets, speaking only when one of them spotted something of interest: a shard of beach pottery veined with cracks, a particularly big crab shell. Now and then, Pearl stooped to examine pieces of sea glass winking up from the sand, leaving most of it for somebody else to discover. She had more than enough common colors in her collection already.

Dad said, "So you talked to your mom today, huh."

"She *called* you?"

"At the club, after you hung up on her, yeah. She was pretty upset."

"It wasn't like that. I mean, I didn't yell at her or anything, I just . . . didn't have anything else to say." She glanced at him. "Did she freak out on you?"

"Well, she had some questions about what's going on, how you were. I said you were okay." He rubbed the sides of his mouth, watching a dog splash into the water after a stick. "Are you?"

It was no small thing, Dad asking that. He was the opposite of Mom, tending to give Pearl more space than she wanted. She thought of thundering fists on a door, the trapped-animal sounds Cassidy had made on the video, tried to push them away. "I'm fine. She's the one who's always having a meltdown over nothing. If she wants to know what's happening with us, why doesn't she ever come up here and see for herself?"

"Because her life's down there now. She's asked you to stay at her place for the weekend plenty of times. You never want to go."

"So I can sleep on the inflatable mattress and make super-awkward small talk with what's-his-name? No, thanks." Pearl bit her lip as they walked. "That was mean."

Dad shrugged. "You're her kid. She worries about you."

"You mean she worries about you. I'm just the go-between."

"Bullshit. She loves you and you know it." Dad picked up a stone and skipped it across the water's surface. "You need to call her more, or email, something. Stay in touch."

"Okay. I'll try." In that moment, she meant it.

A few minutes later, her phone chimed—new text. Pearl glanced, saw Bridges's name, kept the screen angled slightly away from Dad as she texted back, *not much* in response to his *wuz up?* Not that it was Dad's style to sneak a peek, anyway.

Bridges: *missed u last night.*

She hesitated, typed, *did you guys go out later?* On the water, maybe, in Tristan's Rivelle?

A pause. Then, an emoticon, a smiley face with devil horns.

where?

No response for so long that she almost put her phone back in her pocket. Then: *u into tennis?*

Okay, random. *never played.*

tomorrow @ 2ish?

Pearl exhaled slowly through her nose, sent back a thumbs-up. As she tucked her phone away, she noticed a shard of cobalt-blue glass near her foot. Probably from an old medicine bottle, smashed who knew how many decades ago on another coast, tumbled smooth by time and tide. She wiped it off with the hem of her T-shirt, held it up to the dusky light.

"A keeper?" Dad said.

"Definitely."

ELEVEN

THEY HADN'T CHECKED the mail in days. From the
kitchen, where Pearl threw together a bag lunch to bring
to work, she could see the mailbox door hanging open, letters and drugstore flyers sticking out. Neither she nor Dad
wanted to be the jerk who brought the bills into the house.

Sighing, she went outside into the bright morning, yanking on the mail until it came free. The Clarence Agency: bill
collector; Central Maine Power: past due; a heavy cream-
colored envelope with her name and address printed in
calligraphy across the front. The return address was the club.
For a crazy moment, she wondered if it might be a pink slip,
but not even Meriwether would be that pretentious. Brow

furrowed, Pearl tore open the seal and pulled out the square of card stock inside.

You are cordially invited to
the Tenney's Harbor Country Club
Formal Ball and Benefit Auction

She stared for a long moment, running down the details. Eight to eleven p.m., open bar and heavy hors d'oeuvres, auction to benefit the local nonprofit tutoring program. She checked again to make sure it really said her name on the envelope. This made no sense, unless she'd ended up on the list by mistake, somebody mixing up their spreadsheets at the club.

She heard the screen door open behind her and quickly shuffled the envelope in with the other mail, keeping her head down. "You want toast?" Dad said from the front steps.

"Coming." She slid past him into the house.

She tried not to glance at the stack of mail until Dad was in the bathroom, at which point she grabbed the invitation and took it down to her room, hiding it between the mattress and box spring, along with Cassidy's memory card.

Reese moved past her, no acknowledgment. Breakfast/ brunch shift was tough on everybody, even on an average day: the prep cooks and busboys were still blinking sleep from their eyes, and the servers were sneaking coffee every chance they got. It was ten minutes before the dining room doors opened for the day, and as Pearl watched Reese taking chairs down from tabletops and setting places, she suddenly felt like hitting him—or at the very least, throwing some eggs Benedict at him.

"Really?" She stopped in the middle of righting a chair, looking at him across their sections. "You're just not going to talk to me now?"

He dropped a chair heavily onto its legs, grabbed another.

"Fine. But you're being stupid." She glanced at him. He still had his back to her. "You don't even know what's going on. You didn't even ask."

Thump. Another captain's chair landed on the hardwood.

"Reese—"

"Pearl, I don't give a shit. Okay?" The next chair dropped so far that the bang echoed to the rafters. "Save it." As she stared, speechless, he turned and went into the kitchen.

The morning continued as it always did, sunlight slanting across the room in the usual patterns, Lou Pulaski and some golf cronies meeting for artery-clogging breakfasts, talking too loudly and laughing too much for Pearl to keep her thoughts on anything but Reese's words. How had they gone from holding hands in the dark to *I don't give a shit*? She'd seen him annoyed before, irritable occasionally, but never like this—never to the point of completely shutting her out.

Feeling slightly stunned, she went through the motions until she noticed a palpable shift in atmosphere, a redirection of focus to the patio entrance.

Frederick Spencer Sr., the patriarch, came in, removing his cap and smoothing the pure white feathers of his hair. He wore a pale-yellow sport shirt, khakis, and Italian loafers. Beside him, Bridges was a young, trendy version, Ralph Lauren to the old man's Gucci. When the maître d' abandoned his podium—seldom done—to hurry over to seat them, Bridges said something quietly to his grandfather and pointed Pearl out.

The maître d' led them to Pearl's section, Mr. Spencer meeting and greeting the whole way, patting shoulders and exchanging good mornings. Pearl felt a blush growing; she'd waited on him a few times before, but always as a nameless server, someone who would fade from memory before Mr. Spencer's crepes had fully digested.

She walked over, provided menus, said, "Good morning, gentlemen," in a tone that she hoped made clear to Bridges that she wasn't out to endear herself, wouldn't be leaping into his lap like a giddy cocker spaniel in front of the great man.

"Hey. I wasn't sure if you'd be working this morning." Bridges smiled. "Gramps, this is Pearl. Pearl, this is my grandfather, Fred."

She hesitated, caught between roles. "Nice to meet you, sir."

Mr. Spencer put his hand out. It was tanned, deeply lined, and she was surprised to feel calluses on the palms. "Likewise, young lady." His eyes must be the wellspring of the Spencer blue, vivid and lively. "My grandson's quite impressed by you. I hear you sail?"

"A little." Everyone must be looking at them now, wondering what possible reason Frederick Spencer would have to shake his server's hand. "I'm a novice. Not like Bridges."

"Don't listen to her. She knows her way around a boat better than a lot of the guys in sailing club ever did," Bridges said.

"Sounds like we have a mutual admiration society here." Mr. Spencer smiled. Something in the expression hinted that lady-killing might be a family tradition. "Will you do us the honor of joining us for breakfast?"

"Oh. Um—"

But Bridges spoke up. "Come on, she can't do that. You'll get her in trouble."

"Well. Another time, then. When you're off duty." He continued to study her, then broke into another smile. "Do you happen to have any of those currant scones this morning?"

Pearl leaped on the segue, taking their orders and walking swiftly away. Everyone might not have been watching, but Reese was; she locked eyes with him for a moment. His expression lingered somewhere between disbelief and disgust before he turned back to the table he was serving.

Imagine his face if she'd pulled up a chair across from Old Man Spencer and his golden grandson, right here in the same room where she and Reese had scrubbed hardened lobster bisque off tabletops and returned meals two, three times for members who didn't feel that their swordfish was "blackened" enough. Pearl got it; at the same time, she resented the hell out of it, gripped by that same *why not me* feeling she'd had in Dark Brew Saturday afternoon. Was it so unbelievable that these people would want anything from her other than bowing and scraping, that she couldn't possibly have anything else to offer?

When she delivered their breakfasts, Bridges said, "So. Tennis?"

She was aware of Mr. Spencer's bright gaze. "I'll be a terrible partner."

"No worries. It's not like any of us will be making the US Open anytime soon. I just want to hang out with you."

She thought of the invitation to the ball, swallowed her questions for the time being. "See you at the courts."

She didn't expect to find him there, reclining in one of the patio chairs, a tennis racket dangling from his fingers as he waited for her.

Pearl hesitated in the doorway, looking back at Tristan, then stepped the rest of the way out of the dining room and shut the door behind her. "You're not Bridges."

He balanced the racket on the floor on its handle, picked it up again. "I was told you don't know how to play tennis."

"Guilty." She hoped she sounded as blasé as he did. She'd changed into street clothes in the staff restroom right after she'd punched out, her tan shorts again, the nicest T-shirt she'd been able to find.

"You'll learn." He straightened up. The decision had been made to move, and they were moving, Pearl pulled along as if by inertia, down the steps and around the building, past the pool where summer kids lounged in swimsuits and played with their phones, soaking up the midafternoon rays. Some of them stared at her, then cast speculative looks at her company; she could hardly believe it herself. Tristan Garrison, not only walking beside her, but seeking her out. "If you can control how hard you hit a ball," he said, "you can play tennis. You might not be great at it, but you can participate. Watching is for the Hadley Kurtzweils of the world."

Pearl kept her expression deadpan. "Being Hadley Kurtzweil. A fate worse than death." As soon as she said it, she wished she'd chosen any other turn of phrase.

"That depends. Here." He put the racket in her hand. "It should be the right grip size for you."

She looked at it. It wasn't club-issue, rented from the sporting equipment counter. She didn't want to ask where he'd gotten a girl's racket. She casually swung it back and forth, acting like it meant nothing. Her mind was full of the video in the Islander's head, of Cassidy's hard breathing. *I saw your sister scared to death. I saw her running for her life.* And what did he know about it? Watching his still profile, it was possible to believe everything or nothing.

There were three tennis courts, and Bridges had reserved the one on the far left. He stood, smacking the ball lazily back and forth with Akil while other summer kids hung around, mostly girls, leaning against the fence to watch the matches in play. Pearl was surprised to feel Tristan's hand graze her arm as he held the gate for her, then saw what he was indicating: Hadley and Quinn, sitting with their backs against the fence, watching the action.

Bridges's face went blank at the sight of Pearl and Tristan together.

"Look who I found," Tristan said mildly.

"She was going to meet us here."

"And she has." Tristan went to the fence, retrieved his own racket from his bag.

He stretched his left triceps, gripping his elbow. "Pearl and I against the two of you." Bridges's gaze went to him. "We need to even the odds. I'm the strongest player, she's learning."

Akil looked at her. He wore sweats with one pant leg pushed up to his knee, a Puma tank with his aviator shades hooked over his collar. "You've never played? You work, like, ten feet away from the courts."

"Yes. She works here." Tristan approached the net. "When exactly would she be playing tennis?"

Akil shrugged. "Well, you can't suck any worse than Bridges."

"Shut up, man." Bridges pegged the ball at him, and Akil let it bounce off his shoulder. "You're as bad as I am."

"Yeah, but you don't have an excuse. You should have tennis in your genes. Your grandfather was practicing his backhand when mine would've had to carry somebody's golf bag to get into a place like this."

"Come on," Tristan said. "Flip a coin. We call heads."

Bridges and Akil won the first serve, but Bridges was subdued, watching as Tristan showed Pearl how to hold the racket properly for a beginner—grip at the bottom of the handle, fingers spaced apart—and helped her with her swing. His touch on her forearm was sparing, his body close enough that she could sense his proximity, but not feel him; if she made a misstep, he was there, correcting her again with his touch, not words. From the corner of her eye, she could see Hadley and Quinn watching.

Preparing to serve, Akil said, "Thirty, bitches. Hey—look who's coming."

Bridges glanced toward the parking lot, and when Pearl swatted the ball back, it bounced out of his service box, forgotten.

Indigo crossed the side parking lot, her designer-imposter bag over her shoulder, her mass of sandy curls hanging loose down her back. The boys took in her rolling hips, the way her slacks clung to her. "No handicaps for boners." Akil grinned at Bridges and Tristan. "Don't even ask." He went to the fence, calling, "Hey. Hi."

Indigo turned to him, squinting against the afternoon sunlight. Once recognition set in, her body language changed, all the lazy panther looseness that Pearl associated with her tightening, tensing. "Hey." She didn't come over.

"So . . . are you going to hang out this summer?" Akil worked his fingers into the chain link, rocking back on his heels. "Because the invitation's open. Anytime, anywhere."

Indigo moved her gaze to Tristan, who'd retrieved the ball and now tossed it, caught it, tossed it again. She finally seemed to notice Pearl standing off to his left. The girls stared at each other, Indigo frowning slightly, revealing nothing. "Yeah. Maybe." She turned away and continued toward the club, tossing her hair over her shoulder. If the word wasn't out that Pearl Haskins had been seen with the summer boys, it would be now—how long before Indigo made this kitchen gossip, before she made sure Reese found out all the details?

"Don't be a stranger." Akil gave an exaggerated wave, speaking too loudly. "'Bye!"

Bridges shook his head, smiling ruefully. "That was evil."

"Hey, somebody's got to let the girl know she's wanted."

Quinn sighed, calling, "You guys are pathetic."

"How do you know her?" Pearl watched Bridges and Akil exchange a look, hide smiles. Tristan started bouncing the ball off the clay, catching it. "Am I missing something?"

"Nothing. It's just . . . everybody knows her. She's"—Bridges carefully avoided her eyes—"one of the townies who comes to the parties. You know."

Pearl flexed her fingers. "Townies. Right."

"I don't mean—not like you."

"Tell her the nickname." Akil took a few practice swings. "Go on, Bridge, don't be such a goddamn southern gentleman just because your girlfriend's here. Say it."

"I'm not saying it."

"Okay, eww. I'm done." Quinn stood, brushing off her white denim skirt, nudging Hadley with her foot. "Tell your little conquest stories after we're gone."

"Whatever." Akil smiled. "You just wish you were in one."

"With a walking hard-on like you? I don't think so."

A murmur of laughter from the kids nearby. Akil glanced over, laughed along sharply. "I meant Bridges. Pretty sure you guys never even made it to second base—or wasn't anybody supposed to know that?"

A quick, naked flash across Quinn's face, a glance at Bridges, who turned away, running his hand back through his hair. "Wait," Quinn said to Akil, "just so we're clear—you're trashing me for *not* putting out when I was fourteen?"

Akil snorted, shrugging her off, but she followed him. "Seriously, what does a girl have to do to earn a vote of approval from you guys? Or is that even possible?"

Akil dug into his bag. "Just forget it, Quinn."

Hadley touched Quinn's back. "Let's go."

"No. I want to hear what he has to say." Quinn folded her arms as he gave her a sidelong look. "I mean, it's obvious you think you can do whatever you want because you're a guy. It's okay to act like a heartless horndog slut, because later, all your buddies will buy you beer and tell you what a stud you are, right?" She raised her voice for the benefit of their audience. "I think you should have to explain why it's not a karmic issue for you to have a random hookup on a boat named after your dead ex, who—let's face it—only ever got with you as part of her Get Back at Daddy campaign. Any thoughts on that?"

Half a second of shocked silence. Hadley's face was white. Akil swore, threw his racket to the side, and went for Quinn.

Bridges slammed into Akil's chest, catching handfuls of his shirt, moving with him. "Dude, no—"

Akil shoved at him, tried to twist around him, still locked on Quinn, who gave a *bring it on* gesture, stepping lightly back.

"Stop it!" Hadley's voice broke. "Quinn, let's go! Please!"

"I'm shaking. Really, Akil. You're such a badass. You have to beat up a girl to make her be quiet?" Quinn allowed

Hadley to tug her toward the gate, calling back at them, "Nobody's impressed. Just so you know."

Bridges held on to Akil, kept talking him down until Akil finally ripped free, turning off balance to face Tristan.

Who was leaving. He was already through the gate and onto the walkway, bag over his shoulder, moving at a steady pace toward the parking lot without looking back.

Akil swore a final time, grabbed his things, and left too, shoving by Pearl and heading in the direction of the club.

Bridges watched him go for a moment, then sank onto the ground into a sitting position, hanging his head. Pearl walked over and sat beside him. "That was fun." She glanced toward the parking lot. "Will Tristan be . . . okay?"

"Tristan doesn't really need people." He was quiet a moment. "Akil's the one who's freaking."

"Quinn had a point. About the boat."

He rubbed his face. "I know. Akil knows it, too. That's the whole reason he did that with Hadley. To prove something about him and Cassidy."

"And he had to prove it with your ex-girlfriend?" Bridges didn't answer. "Was it true, what Quinn said about Cassidy using Akil to get back at her dad?"

"Cassidy wasn't like that." He released a pent-up breath. "I dunno, maybe it was a little bit true. But it wasn't like she planned it. I mean, Akil came on to her hard, right from the beginning. Said stuff most guys wouldn't say to somebody's sister. Not that Tristan seemed to care." He looked at her, his expression pained. "It wasn't like she had a lot of experience, you know? Last summer was the first year she started hanging out with us. She just kind of showed up at the parties, had a few drinks, whatever. We were always Tristan's friends before that . . . she stayed away. I don't know if David made her or what. I don't think she'd ever had a real boyfriend before Akil."

Pearl pushed her hair behind her ears, watching a nearby match without really seeing it. "Tristan didn't mind that his little sister was tagging along with his friends?"

"I guess not. They didn't talk much. She always found her own rides places, things like that." Bridges paused. "She said she was on a break." He shook his head. "I don't think I heard her playing at all last summer. Weird. Usually her music was all over their house."

A silent piano. A suddenly full social calendar. And a video of someone breaking a door down. Pearl wanted to keep pushing, to reach into Bridges's mind and rake through what he'd seen, what he knew—he'd been there, in the Garrisons' house, at the Little Nicatou parties—but she was on the verge of prying too hard as it was. She picked up a pebble, tossed it away through the fence. "Think Akil really would've hit Quinn?"

"Everybody wants to hit Quinn. But, nah. You've got to know by now that Akil's ninety percent talk."

Interesting, considering how fast Bridges had gotten between them. Pearl looked off at the club, picturing Akil's face on the other side of that door on the Islander, his shoulder slamming the wood. "Would he have hit Cassidy?"

"Are you kidding? He treated her like a princess—for him, anyway. Akil's not stupid. He knew he was getting crazy-lucky. I mean, Cassidy Garrison? That's like . . ." Bridges hesitated, got to his feet. "Well, lots of guys would've traded places."

Pearl plucked at her racket netting, feeling the slight twist of—not exactly jealousy, but a resurgence of what'd she felt the night before Christmas Eve when she'd watched Cassidy's poise and grace and known with a hollow certainty that she'd never, ever have that. Not even close. What did it take to inspire awe in people, to be the kind of girl that guys treated like royalty?

"So . . . do you ever check your mail?"

Pearl looked up sharply. "What?"

"I've been waiting for you to say something, but you should've gotten it a couple days ago, so . . ."

She stood. "How'd you manage that, anyway? Those invitations were mailed by the club."

He grinned. "Are you saying you'll come? You don't have to work it, do you?"

"No. I'm working lunch that day." Going as Bridges's date would mean total exposure, see-and-be-seen by both members and staff. Word would almost certainly get back to Dad.

It was a risk. "I don't know. Hoity-toity people in diamond tiaras . . . ?"

"I'll leave mine at home, promise. Come on, my gramps is making a big deal out of it. The whole club's going to be there. He really wants me to go. And he likes you. I can tell."

"All I did was bring him some scones."

"It's because you were cool. You didn't try to kiss his ass. He respects that." Bridges stood up. "So . . . do you have time to get a dress before Friday?"

She gave him a look. "I'll get my designer right on it."

He loped over and picked up the tennis ball, reminding her a bit of a golden retriever puppy, shaggy-haired and guileless. "Still feel like learning to play?"

They spent an hour batting the ball around, laughing at their mistakes; when Pearl stopped, winded, she realized she was having fun, genuinely enjoying herself with Bridges, and not for the first time, either. Then she heard one of the mowers approaching.

Dad rode by, following the nearest edge of the golf course. Bridges's conversation faded behind the sound of her own heartbeat, the blood rushing in her veins as she stood still, sure Dad must've seen her through the chain link, that he'd cut the engine now and come over to ask her what the hell was going on.

But his gaze passed over her and moved on without hesitation. As if, without her uniform, with a racket in her hand, she was unrecognizable. A completely different person.

TWELVE

SUMMER DUSK, A long, shimmering stretch of afternoon bleeding into twilight.

Pearl was home with supper ready—mac and cheese, Veg-All—when Dad got out of work. They ate in companionable silence; then she cleaned up, turning from the sink when she heard him putting his shoes on by the door. "You're leaving?"

Dad didn't look at her, taking his time checking his pockets for his truck keys. Was it her imagination, or was there more gray in his dark hair than the last time she'd noticed, more salt in his two days' growth of stubble? His scarred left hand found the key chain, jingled it into his palm. She wondered if she'd ever be able to look at his hands without picturing him trying to get into the Garrisons' burning parlor, being held back by the flames, finally having no choice but to retreat to the fence and watch the place go up until the first responders arrived, the whole time thinking the family was alive, unreachable. "Heading over to Yancey's to help him with the tractor."

Ah. The project without end. "Has that thing ever run?"

"Once in a blue moon." He hesitated briefly, something in his posture making him seem no older than Pearl herself. "You mind?"

"No. Go for it." But she sounded stiff, and she saw a flash of Mom standing at this same sink, up to her wrists in soapy water, turning her back on Dad for going out. "Be safe."

Dad didn't say anything as he left. They both knew the tractor was an excuse to start up the drinking again, to sit around Yancey's garage getting numb with the same guys he saw at the Tavern every week. How many hours had Dad spent out there this spring, even when he had to know how much crap his so-called buddy had been talking about him since what happened to the Garrisons? She dropped the pot she was scrubbing back into the water roughly, splashing herself. There was no rule that said she had to stay here and wait to see how long it took him to walk back through the door.

Instead, Pearl drove. Through downtown, past tourists leaving restaurants or toting shopping bags of souvenirs:

balsam pillows, mugs reading *Maine: The Way Life Should Be.* Out into the woods, to Millionaires' Row, past the Spencer compound on its ledge. Daylight seemed to hover, the low sun casting everything in flat, unreal brightness, like an old Technicolor movie. It felt different being here without Reese this time. Desperate, compulsive. In the backseat, her tennis racket lay covered with a sweatshirt. She hadn't known what else to do with it.

She drove up the Garrisons' driveway, reaching the clearing that opened on the gatehouse before she spotted the car parked inside the gate. Tristan's Bentley.

Swearing under her breath, she dropped into reverse and backed down the drive, praying he hadn't seen her. She reached Cove Road, whipped onto the shoulder, and sat parked, rigid, tapping her fingers on the wheel. What was he *doing* in there? It had never occurred to her that he'd set foot inside the house since what happened, actually walked those halls. Just the thought made her stomach take a lazy, nauseating plunge.

Pearl drove down the road to the dirt turnaround and left the car parked under the cover of low branches, walking back to the Garrisons' property at a brisk pace, praying her luck would hold and nobody would drive by and see her.

She followed the driveway as far as she dared, then entered the woods, circling off to the left, always keeping the security fence in sight through the trees.

The house sat on a rise, flashes of white clapboard visible as she walked. She crouched for a time, watching, wondering how far away she was from where the killer had sat that night in the snow. She tried to picture it, flakes swirling around the gate, the way Dad's hunched figure might've looked from this distance, wading through the snowbanks around the perimeter in the dark, a flashlight in his hand. Had the killer drawn his gun, sighted for a time on the back of Dad's head?

The thought made her weak, but it was logical. Get the watchman out of the way. Cove Road was mostly deserted in winter; there would've been no one else around to call 911, no one to smell smoke until it was too late. The house probably would've burned flat, taking with it much of the evidence that the Garrisons hadn't simply fallen victim to an accidental house fire. So why let Dad live?

There was a click as the back door of the three-car garage opened. As she watched, Tristan crossed the yard, following the winding stone path past a brick outdoor oven, a garden with a stone sundial in the center. There was a rear gate in the fence, which he unlocked and left ajar behind him, continuing down the path toward the beach.

Pearl followed at what she hoped was a safe distance, cringing at every snapped branch or crushed leaf. Tristan made his way down the rocky path until he reached sand, where he disappeared from view.

She went to a gnarled birch tree at the edge of the

embankment and knelt, watching him go, hands in his pockets, eyes on the ground, following the line of the tide on his private beach. She recognized the posture well: beach-combing.

He completed the circuit, walking back close to the tree line. Pearl shrank down, her pulse throbbing steadily, her abdomen clenched, wondering what he'd do if he spotted her through the leaves.

Tristan headed toward a structure on the beach some twenty feet away from where she hid, a sort of two-story playhouse made from weathered planks and driftwood. A sign had been affixed to the peaked roof, painted in a kid's handwriting: *The Roost.*

There were other treasures visible on the second-story platform: a peeling lobster buoy, a couple of plastic crates holding pails, shovels, beach toys. Tristan went up the ladder to the platform, looking through the crates for a bit before settling back to watch the tide, letting his legs hang over the edge. He wore a Henley shirt, the sleeves tugged over his hands, and from this distance he looked much like his little brother, Joseph, might've looked the last summer he swam here, played in his fort.

There was nothing but the sound of the wind. Gradually Pearl lowered her head, shut her eyes to rid them of the grainy feeling. She didn't sleep—impossible—but when she looked up, dusk had crossed the seamless threshold to twilight. The sky was two shades darker, and peach sunset filtered through the horizon. The Roost was empty.

Her nerves leaped as a footstep crunched a few feet away. She held motionless, wide-eyed, cheek pressed against the smooth bark. More footsteps followed, heading down the path. Tristan, returning to the house.

She was breathless by the time she reached tree cover outside the fence. She crouched, watching him leave the garage again, this time by the front door, carrying a duffel bag and a couple of big cardboard boxes. He popped the trunk and leaned inside.

Pearl made for the slope along the driveway, running when she thought she was far enough away to crash through the underbrush without being heard.

Once she was back in her car, she accelerated down Cove Road, but the Bentley was already gone. She finally caught up with him on Ocean, relaxing slightly, letting a car pull out in front of her at the intersection with Pine so she didn't feel so obvious. She doubted Tristan had any idea what she drove, but better not to risk it.

Ten minutes later, the Bentley pulled onto Narragansett Way. Pearl drove past the road, continued for a few minutes, then turned around and went back.

Narragansett was a new road on land recently clear-cut to make way for the housing development. The homes were identical: two stories high, a cobbled-together architectural style resulting in odd angles and many windows. The streetlamps winked on as she drove past number 23, where the Bentley sat in the driveway. There were no lights on inside the house yet, and no curtains, only featureless blinds in the windows. What would it be like having an entire house to yourself, all those empty rooms surrounding you at night as the clock ticked down the minutes until dawn? Given the choice, she'd rather be waiting up for Dad.

She turned around at the end of the cul-de-sac and left, taking one last look back at the blank facade of Tristan's house, where he had yet to turn on a light.

The week passed, though Pearl never would've thought it possible. Every shift, she'd think she couldn't stand another day of being ignored by Reese, of spending her breaks alone at the picnic table beneath the patterned shade of the maple tree, but then Tuesday faded into Wednesday, into Thursday, and still nothing changed. She did receive a voice mail from Mom, though: *What I really wanted to tell you the other day was that it's not your job. Fixing Dad, I mean. He's a grown-up, he's responsible for himself. Please call me when you have a chance. Love you, honey.* Pearl almost called back, but she couldn't face that conversation right now, dissecting Dad piece by piece. Not with how the rest of her life was going.

She caught Indigo watching her a few times; Pearl gazed back, trying to feel some measure of triumph over what the summer boys had said—*everybody knows her, comes to all the parties*—but what really separated the two of them at this point? A nickname, maybe some rumors. They were both townies, blue-collar in a white-collar paradise, allowed entrance to the summer world because the boys were tired of hooking up with the same girls they'd seen every school break since third grade. How much did Reese know about Indigo's rep? Pearl guessed not much, which gave her some leverage, if she was interested in using it. She hadn't made up her mind yet. Stupid, really; like Indigo had wasted any time telling Reese all about seeing her at the tennis courts on Monday.

Preparations for the ball continued: the floor buffer hummed steadily through the lunch hour on Thursday, and the voices of the staff charged with decorating the ballroom echoed back and forth. Pearl peeked through the doors at one point and glimpsed dozens of circular tables, shimmering white tulle drapery streaming out from the chandelier.

Then it was Friday.

Pearl had one dress. Bright-pink raw silk, spaghetti straps, a hem that ended just above the knee. Mom had mailed it to her for graduation, said she'd gotten some great deal at one of the outlet stores in Kittery. Pearl had worn it under her graduation gown because Dad made her, even though it was so not her, not even close, and Mom should've realized it the second she saw it on the hanger.

After work, Pearl showered with care, rinsing away the cooking smells and sweat, taking more time with the razor than usual. After a couple of swipes at her lashes with a mascara wand she'd forgotten she had, she studied the results in the mirror, decided she could live with it. Put in her birthstone earrings, citrine chips, another present from Mom. Better memories connected with that one: a tenth birthday party, just the three of them, a lopsided cake decorated with strawberries, Mom and Dad laughing over something. Outside the window, the anchor wind chimes clanged, tangled in their lines.

She left the empty house, carrying a backpack with street clothes to change into before she came home, in case Dad was back before then. Bridges had offered, but she'd insisted on driving herself. Next stop: the Spencer compound.

A long, paved driveway sloped down to lawns burnished in fading sunlight, the bay glittering beyond. The main house was set slightly off to the left. It had a wraparound front porch dotted with hanging flowerpots and deck furniture, cozy, more like a typical summer home of the less-endowed except for the little touches of extreme wealth: a massive stained-glass window with an *S* set above the entrance, professionally manicured flower gardens, and of course the little village of guest cottages below.

Feeling like a trespasser, Pearl drove down to the cottages.

Bridges had told her it was okay to come right in, but part of her still expected alarms to go off, a row of spikes to rise from the pavement and shred her tires.

Bridges was staying in the last cottage, the one with Delta-Echo-Foxtrot nautical flags flying from the pole out front. Pearl parked and went up the steps, catching a wavy, distorted reflection of herself in the glass pane in the door, all peony pink. She was forced to choose her steps carefully, thanks to the matching stack-heeled sandals Mom had sent along.

Bridges opened the door before she could knock, his tie hanging in two ribbons down the lapels of his gray tattersall suit. The contrast with his untamed hair and deep tan was striking, and whatever she'd been planning to say died on her lips, and she simply looked at him.

"Whoa. Pearl." He stepped back to take her in. "Amazing. Seriously. That dress is you."

She almost laughed. "Thanks. You look pretty okay, too."

"Come on in. Want something to drink?"

She shook her head, following him into the spacious main room of the cottage. The interior was "weathered beach house," everything painted white or dove gray, a huge impressionistic watercolor of a dory with lobster buoys hanging above the fireplace, bleached shells that didn't look like they'd come off any Maine beach arranged artfully on the mantel and filling a bowl on the coffee table.

Bridges leaned in front of the mirror, knotting his tie, making a frustrated sound. "I suck at this."

"I can do it." She stood in front of him, crossing the wide end of the tie over the narrow end, tucking it through the neck hole. He smelled good, fresh out of the shower, like expensive shaving lotion and sporty deodorant. It didn't feel strange being so near to him now.

Somehow, she wasn't surprised when his hands found the small of her back, but she didn't expect the intensity of his touch, almost desperate. His fingers slid south, and he gripped her there, lifting her slightly to him as he leaned against the back of the couch. Her breath caught—she should say something, put on the brakes—then held as he kissed her. She didn't remember putting her arms around his neck, but when they finally came up for air, she was eye to eye with him.

He didn't let go, so she finished the Windsor knot with their noses touching, snugging it up to his collar and patting his lapel. "There."

"You know"—he kissed her again, softer, just beneath the jawline—"we could blow this whole thing off. Stay here."

She breathed out, gaining a little equilibrium, as his lips slid to her throat. "You said your grandfather really wants you to go." She moved back a little, but he was still holding her; she was almost straddling his leg.

"I'll tell him you got sick or something."

She laughed a little—she didn't know what else to do—and pushed away from him, walking over to the windows, which looked out on the cliff and water, a wooden stairwell allowing passage to the beach below. "Nice view." She kept talking, words shoring up her defenses. "I can totally see it. Handsome young socialite Bridges Spencer swirling a snifter of brandy as he looks down on his private world." She turned back. "Tell me you've got a velvet smoking jacket around here somewhere."

He stared at her. "Where do you get this shit?"

She shrugged, flicking a carved sandpiper figurine on the windowsill. "Too many books."

Bridges straightened, checked out his tie in the mirror. "Sweet. How'd you do that so fast?"

"The things you learn in food service."

"What's it like?" She glanced at him. "I mean, working at the club." He took a few steps, hands in his pockets, checking out his shoes. "I've never done anything like that. Do you guys, like, totally hate us?" He laughed quickly, but there was vulnerability there, something very un-Bridges in his look.

"Hate you?" She moved to the coffee table, picking up an urchin shell from the bowl, pressing the spines gently into her fingertips. Kitchen talk came back to her, a thousand snarky remarks, plenty she'd made herself, an attitude she'd settled into. She pictured Dad hunched in the Garrisons' gatehouse that night, hands numb with cold even with the space heater going, just trying to get through until morning and earn his under-the-table two hundred bucks to take the edge off the usual Christmas cash drain. "It's just . . . you know, there's a line. Staff on one side, members on the other."

"Is there a line between us?" He came up behind her, slid a finger under one of her straps, smoothed it out. "I don't want there to be."

She couldn't find any answer that he'd want to hear. "Don't get deep on me, Bridges."

His smile was slow in coming, but then he chuckled, shaking his head. "One of these days, you're not going to have a smart-ass remark. It'll happen. I'm going to get you."

"Never." She led the way outside.

It was strange to have Bridges in her car, his legs filling the space where only Reese and Dad had ever stretched out. "Can you pull in for a sec?" Bridges pointed to the circular drive in front of the main house. "Gramps wants to see us off."

Pearl's nervousness returned in full force. She parked and followed Bridges through the gleaming foyer into a parlor, where Mr. Spencer stood by a liquor table, pouring himself a glass. He was already dressed for the evening in pale summer-weight flannel, a brightly colored handkerchief peeking out of the breast pocket. He turned in mid-sip and smiled, gaze keen and interested. "Don't you two look dapper. Pearl,

I hardly recognized you. You look like a vision in that pink."

A vision of what, she wasn't sure. "Thanks. Nice hankie."

Mr. Spencer insisted on pictures despite Bridges's groan. The old man withdrew a smartphone from his inner pocket and snapped a few times, hardly giving Pearl a chance to smile before he vanished it into his coat again.

"Are you leaving soon?" Bridges picked up a snow globe from a nearby end table, rolled it from hand to hand, sending glitter into cascades.

"Once I'm properly lubricated. It isn't safe to attend these things sober. You run the risk of realizing what crashing bores they really are—" He cleared his throat, took another sip, made a sound of exclamation. "You should take the Mustang. Absolutely. I'll have Gus bring it around."

Bridges glanced at Pearl. "Is that cool with you?"

"Uh, sure."

Mr. Spencer raised his glass in cheers, downed the contents, and came over to squeeze Bridges's shoulder. "I only get to see you a couple times a year. God knows I wish it was more. Thanks for stopping by and giving an old man a thrill." Then he took Pearl's hand and kissed it, something she'd never experienced before; somehow, coming from Mr. Spencer, the gesture didn't seem contrived. "Pearl. A pleasure." He made his way back to the table. "Enjoy the Mustang." He nodded, gaze traveling to the ceiling. "I always had good luck with that car."

Pearl and Bridges waited outside until the gleaming black 1966 Mustang appeared, driven by a tall man who said, "Good evening," and nothing else as he climbed out, handed Bridges the keys, and held the passenger door for Pearl. He continued to stand there after she was seated. She shifted uncomfortably, wondering if she was supposed to tip him, if she had any cash on her at all.

"Give him your keys and he'll park your car in the garage," Bridges said softly.

"Oh." She dug into her clutch bag. "Sorry." As Gus folded himself into the Civic, she saw her hard-won car as it must look to the Spencers: ancient, dented, sagging on nearly bald tires. She cleared her throat. "Wow. An actual manservant."

"Gus has been around forever. He kind of runs the place." They headed downtown, following the tree-lined Harbor Road to the club. "This was Gramps's car, back when he was a little older than me. He almost never takes it out of the garage." Bridges smiled a little. "I'm guessing he made some pretty good memories in the backseat."

So that was what he meant by luck. Pearl looked out the window at the deepening night, unconsciously smoothing the hem of her dress. When Bridges's hand found her knee, she let it stay there.

THIRTEEN

WHITE JAPANESE LANTERNS hung in a luminous solar system above the front walkway and gardens of the club. Nets of twinkle lights glimmered on the hedges, and every window was lit. A banner reading *Tenney's Harbor Club: One Hundred Years* hung across the porch, and Pearl could already hear big band music drifting across the front lawn as they parked.

She and Bridges joined the couples walking arm in arm toward the entrance. She hadn't expected this sudden grip of anxiety, entering the club for the first time without the anonymity of her uniform and station. She and Bridges were on display together, and the doorman's gaze rested on her, knowing her face if not her name as he said, "Good evening, Mr. Spencer. Miss," and let them pass.

The lobby was swarming, people having their photos taken in front of a centennial backdrop, stopping to greet friends before going through the ballroom door, the air charged with energy. When they entered the ballroom, Pearl's eyes were dazzled by light. Gradually, dozens of white Japanese lanterns solidified in her vision like ghost orbs, drifting among the tulle canopy strung across the ceiling.

Everything was black, white, and silver, the room itself resembling one of the old ballroom photographs from the corridor, allowing the ladies' dresses to provide the color: scarlet, turquoise, peach. Servers were dressed in black tie, both men and women; Pearl noticed Indigo moving through the crowd with her serving tray held high, dressed in a fitted tuxedo shirt, bow tie at her throat.

Bridges took Pearl's hand as they cut through the crowd, people hobnobbing with drinks, shrilling laughter, some watching them pass with momentary interest before spotting somebody else they recognized.

Bridges put his lips close to her ear. "Insane, huh?" She nodded, releasing a breath, and he laughed, leading the way through the tables. He rapped his knuckles on one as they passed, where a group of summer kids had congregated, eating hors d'oeuvres and looking supremely bored. Quinn and Hadley sat there, Quinn in a body-hugging strapless dress, cozied up to a big guy Pearl vaguely recognized from around the club, a linebacker type with short-buzzed hair. Hadley wore teal, a pink rose tucked behind her ear, her chin resting on her fist as she watched the crowd. "Hey, ladies," Bridges said.

Quinn slid her hand to cover the linebacker's and said flatly, "If you're looking for the idiot, he's over there." She indicated a nearby table occupied mostly by adults, where Akil lounged with his chair pushed out from the table, people casting him annoyed looks as they were forced to squeeze by.

"Oh my God, dude, where have you *been*?" Akil wore a sport coat over a T-shirt, baggy tuxedo pants, and white athletic sneakers right out of the box.

Bridges raised his eyebrows. "They let you in like that?"

"Amazing, isn't it?" Akil's father spoke, his voice smooth and faintly accented. He slowly turned a flute of champagne on the tabletop. "I see that your friends managed to dress themselves properly for the evening."

"I don't wear ties."

"So you've said."

"No more arguing." Akil's mother wore a purple gown accented with gold, and her gaze landed on Pearl, studying her as she and Bridges sat. "Hello. My name's Aditi. We haven't met."

"Pearl." Ignoring Akil's eye roll, Pearl put her hand out and shook with Mrs. Malhotra. "Your dress is beautiful."

Akil made an impatient sound, said to his parents, "I thought you guys were going to dance or something."

His father held Akil's gaze coolly for a moment, then took his wife's hand. "What a wonderful suggestion." They left the table together.

Akil stood immediately, tugging Bridges to his feet. "Seriously. Three more hours of this."

Bridges laughed, making sure that Pearl was following. "You'll survive. Eat some hors d'oeuvres or something."

"Have you seen that stuff? It's like baby eels and quail eggs or some shit."

"You should've hit Mickey D's on the way over."

"I know, right?" Akil headed for the empty seats at the summer kids' table, where there conveniently weren't enough chairs for Pearl to join them; Bridges carried one over, and she wedged in, uncomfortably close to a couple she didn't know.

As Akil and Bridges exchanged fist bumps and small talk with their friends, Akil and Quinn tacitly ignoring each other, Pearl scanned the dance floor and stage, where Steve Mills was again performing at the piano, this time with a brass quartet. A slide show played on a projector screen behind them, photos taken at various club events in recent years. To the right, three rows of tables had been set up to display the auction items, antiques, and gift baskets donated by local businesses.

Pearl pulled a hydrangea from the table centerpiece and plucked a few petals, starting when a voice from behind her said, "Having fun?"

Reese, holding a tray of hors d'oeuvres. His eyes were half-lidded, gaze on a distant point, mouth set in a line.

She hesitated, torn between relief at the sound of his voice and uneasiness at the expression on his face, the fact that he was suddenly willing to speak to her, period. "I didn't know you were on tonight."

He said nothing to that, looking over the crowd at the table. "Can I get you something, miss? Grilled scallop wrapped in prosciutto? A stuffed pepper with goat cheese?" He was giving her the member treatment, club-ing her; she set her jaw. "Excuse me. What was I thinking? For the refined palate, we have caviar on toast points available at the buffet table—"

"Bourbon, straight up," Akil said without bothering to turn around. The other guys laughed, oblivious to the way Pearl's and Reese's eyes remained locked.

One corner of Reese's mouth went up. "Sorry. Not at the kids' table. But if you ask your parents, maybe they'll let you have a soda with one of those neat umbrellas in it."

Akil looked back, eyes narrowed. "What?"

"And quick on the uptake, too." Reese studied Akil. "Gotta give you props, Haskins. When you go gold-digging, you really know how to pick a mark. Somewhere between fashion victim and dumb as a bag of hammers."

Quinn burst out laughing. Bridges turned around. "What the hell is your problem?"

"Reese," Pearl said sharply, but he ignored her, watching as Akil got to his feet, not even taking a step back. She knew Reese: he'd take a punch to the jaw and never even raise his hand. Let the other guy make himself look like a Neanderthal; he'd already gotten his licks in.

Akil, Bridges, and two other guys moved in; Quinn's linebacker started to stand, but Quinn caught a handful of his jacket and pulled him back down.

Reese smiled, taking a stuffed pepper from his tray and turning it over in his hand. "This is like a joke, right? How many douche bags does it take to win a fight? You guys might need a little more help. Your moms must be around here somewhere—" Akil grabbed Reese's shirtfront; Reese let him, laughing harder, gesturing to Akil's jacket and T-shirt. "You know, this is quite the ensemble. But it needs something. I can't quite seem to . . ." Reaching out, he smeared the pepper down Akil's lapel, leaving a white streak of goat cheese. "That's it."

The summer boys moved in a wave, Akil nearly taking Reese down to the floor before Reese caught his balance and pushed back, the two of them locked together.

"Stop it!" Pearl tried to shove between them, hearing her own voice mix with another's, both saying Reese's name at once.

Indigo wedged in, pushing against Akil's chest. "Let go. Come on"—neither of them released—"let *go*. You stupid. Idiots." She threw her elbow into Akil, and the boys finally broke apart, breathless, eyeing each other.

People were staring, and across the room, Meriwether craned her neck, then started toward them. Pearl dropped to her knees and scooped spilled hors d'oeuvres onto Reese's tray, trying to save them from being ground into the carpet.

Reese backed up a few steps, still smirking. He straightened his shirt with a single tug and walked away, making Meriwether double her strides in pursuit. "What happened?" she snapped as she passed Indigo, but Indigo only shrugged, taking the tray from Pearl's hands in a smooth turn and heading back into the crowd.

Akil swore, brushing at the stain. "I'm going to kill him."

Hadley came around the table. "I bet I can get that out for you."

"I don't care about the stupid jacket."

"Just let me try, okay? They've got seltzer water at the bar. It'll take, like, two seconds." She reached out, tugging his hand. "Come on."

Akil went, letting her close her fingers around his. Pearl sank into her chair, twisting around to look for any sign of Reese or Meriwether. Chances were, they were in her office right now, having a little chat about whether Reese still had a job at the club.

When she turned back, Tristan sat in the chair across from her. His suit was dark, his shirt off-white, open-throated. They looked at each other, the moment broken as Bridges sat beside her, saying, "What's up with that guy? That's the second time I've seen him freak out on you." He noticed Tristan. "Hey." His arm slid over the top of Pearl's chair. "I wasn't sure if you were going to show."

Tristan said nothing, clearly waiting for Pearl to answer Bridges's question. "He's a friend," she said shortly, pinching the bridge of her nose; a headache was now in full bloom behind her eyes. "He's mad at me."

"You think? What's his issue with Akil?"

"He doesn't even know Akil. It's not about him." As she said it, she realized that she didn't understand what it was about, not really. Surely not just seeing her sit with the boys in Dark Brew one time; not just members on one side, staff on the other. "Be right back."

She grabbed her bag and went to the ladies' room, hoping she wouldn't run into Akil and Hadley, but there was no sign of them; they must've gone to the lobby restroom. Pearl sat on the bench in the small restroom entryway, digging through her bag for the tin of ibuprofen she carried with her. She swallowed two dry and leaned back against the wall, trying to relax her shoulders.

What would it be like, if Meriwether really fired Reese? How would she work the dining room without him? She'd done it before he moved here, but that seemed like forever ago, a colorless memory compared to the past year and a half, when she'd looked forward to every shift they shared, every random text she got from him. If Reese was fired now, they might never have the chance to make up.

Around the corner, where the sinks and stalls were, women's voices rose and fell. Pearl was aware of stockinged legs whispering by, the door opening and closing. She leaned her head back, enjoying near invisibility here, tucked away at the extreme edge of the door.

Running water, the occasional click of a high heel. One conversation eventually rose above: "—nice touch. The board's been planning it for a year. There was some talk of making it a masquerade. Thank God they changed their minds."

"Sweating your makeup off under a half mask all night? No, thank you." The second woman paused, maybe reapplying lipstick or powder. "I love the black-and-white thing. So sixties-Capote-New York, don't you think?"

"You know whose idea the color scheme was." A pause. "Sloane's."

Pearl sat up slowly, opening her eyes.

"No."

"Mm-hmm. She was on the planning committee." A faucet went on and off. "You have to admit, she had a talent for decor."

"No, I don't." A shared, hushed laugh. "I'm sorry, that's awful, but . . . Susan and Bill went through with the divorce, did you hear? Their Harbor house is sitting empty this summer. It's such a waste."

"And they're not the only ones." A deliberate pause, voice dropping to a whisper. "Tanya walked in on Sloane and Coralee's husband at some soiree two years ago."

"Stop. How did I not hear about this?"

"She said they were right up against the guest bathroom wall. Tanya was so humiliated she couldn't bring herself to say anything to Coralee, but I gather she found out somehow, because last I heard, she and Seth were taking separate vacations, if you know what I mean."

A soft exclamation. "That woman had serious issues."

"With a husband like that, you almost couldn't blame her. Can you imagine? I've heard he scheduled their day. This is including Sloane. All summer he had those kids putting in something like three or four hours of work on their music, sports, whatever. Some vacation. The whole family was scared to death of him. Total control freak."

"You don't mean he ever—" A group of women came through the door, and the conversation froze for a moment. Pearl had to strain to hear what was said next over locking stall doors and rustling undergarments. "I mean, not with his fists?"

A hesitation. "Honestly? Nothing would surprise me with

David." A final zip of a handbag, and Pearl flattened herself back, studying the floor tiles as the two women, both of whom she recognized well as part of the Garrisons' inner circle, returned to the party.

When Pearl followed a couple of minutes later, the painkillers had started to kick in. Steve Mills was singing "Smoke Gets in Your Eyes" to a nearly full dance floor. She started making her way back over to the table, but stopped when someone came up beside her, touching her elbow.

"There you are." Bridges's expression was uncertain. "I was afraid maybe you'd crawled out a window or something."

"Thought about it."

"We were being assholes, huh?" He studied her face. "Yeah. We were. Sorry. I guess I thought that guy was dumping on you."

Her head was so full of what she'd just overheard that she didn't have it in her to debate. "It's over. Don't worry about it."

"Want to dance? I'll make you look good. Two left feet."

For once, she didn't try to beg off, even though she'd never danced to a slow song outside of a middle school gym before.

Nothing to it, as it turned out. Let the boy lead. Let him hold you so close that he moves for you both, threads his fingers through yours and guides you through the slow spins. Pearl's gaze roamed the ballroom, the indistinct faces of the people sitting at the tables, ordering drinks from servers. "So, after." Bridges spoke softly. "You could come back to the cottage. Hang out for a while."

Pearl brushed close to the couple dancing behind them, pulling her body in, conscious of her chest pressed against his. "Doesn't your grandfather care if you have girls down there?"

"Gramps doesn't spend a lot of time worrying about what I do. He's cool like that." He brushed a strand of hair off her brow. "It's pretty nice in the cottage at night. Turn off the AC, open the windows, and the waves put you to sleep."

She realized what he was asking and looked away, clearing her throat. "Next you'll tell me that it's lonely in that big bed all by yourself."

"Could you stay over?" He touched her chin, turning her head to meet his gaze. "Would your parents get mad?"

Her whole body was growing warm. "Definitely." She had no idea what Dad would do if she didn't come rolling in until tomorrow morning. Probably tell her to leave a note next time, and ask her how she wanted her eggs.

"You're eighteen. Not a lot they could do about it, right?"

She saw Tristan before Bridges did. He moved through the dancers, coming up behind Bridges and tapping him on the shoulder as the song ended and applause scattered the room. "I'm cutting in."

Bridges frowned. "Now?" He glanced at Pearl, who could

offer him nothing, observing in her own state of shock. Finally, he shrugged, stepping back. "Whatever . . . I guess." He turned and left the dance floor, glancing back a couple of times.

The band launched into "Misty." Tristan took her hand and waist firmly, looking over her head at the other dancers as if every action came automatically, without thought. Pearl moved with him, studying his face. The crown prince, member of a family everyone believed to be among the best and brightest. Who knew how much truth there was to ladies' room gossip, but she couldn't shake the memory of it—*you don't mean—not with his fists?*—and now she had a new face to put to the monster on the other side of the door, hammering his way in after Cassidy.

"Do you mind that I took Bridges's place?" Tristan asked abruptly. She got the feeling that he'd been aware of her eyes on him, and had let her look.

"No."

He nodded slowly, still gazing beyond her. "Was he talking you into sleeping with him tonight?" Pearl was quiet. "Maybe you didn't need any talking into. But this would be when he'd ask."

She wouldn't show anything; she'd be as cool as he was, colder, even, while inside, she boiled with embarrassment. "It sounds like you know his routine pretty well."

"By Bridges's standards, waiting three weeks into a

relationship is like waiting until marriage. He must really see something in you."

"Imagine that."

"You're getting offended."

"Well, how is this your business?"

"I'm interested. Specifically, in why you're spending so much time with him if sex isn't on the agenda."

Her hand was starting to sweat inside his. "Is that the only reason you spend time with a girl?"

Tristan actually smiled. It was brief and flickering, yet a stark reminder that he was the kind of boy girls called beautiful, that he was Tristan Garrison, and in what alternate universe would the two of them dance together in the club ballroom? He adjusted his grip on her. "I've been deciding what's going to happen between you two. Maybe it'll be tonight, in his grandfather's cottage. Plenty of privacy there. He knows it's too soon, so he'll try to convince you with promises that nobody will find out, that it'll be your secret. But of course people will find out. He'll tell Akil, and Akil will tell everyone."

It was a battle not to get defensive, but there was a slight opening here, and she stabbed at it. "Sounds like you've put a lot of thought into this. Probably because you're alone so much." She paused, gauging his expression. "This winter and spring must've been hard on you. I don't think I'd like living in a house all by myself."

"Have you been to my house, Pearl?"

It was possible to read anything into that mild tone, and she trained her gaze forward, kept her posture relaxed. "It's a small town. Everyone knows where Tristan Garrison lives."

He made a soft noise that might've been a laugh. "You make it sound so significant. 'Garrison.'"

"Isn't it?"

"It's just another name."

She went for it: "You must miss them very much."

The silence that followed was absolute, like a vault door had closed between them. Her hand was slick inside his. She fought the impulse to apologize, letting the silence stretch out, seeing who would break first.

Finally, he said, "Have you ever been stuck inside a time?"

"What do you mean?"

"I mean, have you ever had a certain time of day or night that you carry around inside you? That defines you." His gaze still went beyond her, but now it was far beyond, past the ballroom and the people and the confines of the club. "Midnight. Give or take fifteen minutes. I wake up at midnight and"—he shook his head slightly—"sleep is just gone. I lie there and I watch the shadows on the ceiling. Then I run."

"Where?"

"On the sidewalks. Sometimes on the beach." His eyes were glassy, and now she read more into the faint redness at the corners, telltale signs of sleeplessness. He didn't say which beach he meant, and it chilled her to think of him driving to his family's ruined house, walking down the wooded path in the dark to reach their private strip of sand. "By two o'clock, I'm home, and I can sleep again. But for those two hours"—he swallowed, trailing off—"I burn."

A little after midnight. The click of a door latch, a studying silence, two muzzle flares each—and then the fire, devouring trails of gasoline to the bedrooms, engulfing beds where bodies already lay still and ruined. Pearl had gone from hot to prickling with gooseflesh.

"It's like—inside me—it's always midnight." His speech came faster, forcing it all out before some internal circuit breaker cut him off. "At least it ended for them, eventually. For me, it just goes on. The fire's always there." He was quiet. When he spoke next, he sounded almost uncertain, as if completely unaccustomed to asking for affirmation. "Does that make sense to you?"

She thought of Dad, trying to drown the fire in alcohol, not seeming to realize he was feeding the flames, revisiting that night every time he'd had one too many. "Yes." She swallowed hard, seized by an overwhelming need to comfort, to fix things. "What happened isn't your fault."

"Then why am I being punished?"

"Because you miss them." There was honest confusion in his eyes. She moved on impulse, squeezing his arm with her free hand. "They were your family."

Her touch seemed to rouse him from his state, and he looked down at her hand, then out at the floor again, where it seemed they'd danced through at least two more songs, and people were applauding again. "I wish it were that simple."

She spent the next two hours at Bridges's side. He was stiff at first, seeming to expect Tristan to join them, but he never came back to the table; nobody commented. Gradually, Bridges relaxed, and he took Pearl out onto the dance floor at least four more times, got her something to eat, tried to coax her out of the pensive state she'd been in since her dance with Tristan.

Reese didn't return to the ballroom. Pearl kept looking, and she kept meeting eyes with Indigo instead as the girl circulated hors d'oeuvres and champagne; it was impossible to tell whether she was keeping watch over Pearl or the boys.

At ten, the band took a break so the club general manager Gene Charbonneau could claim the mic. He wore a tux, his heavy-jowled face flushed, thinning hair combed over from a side part. "Ladies and gentlemen, if you would please turn your attention to the auction tables, it's time to begin the bidding. . . ."

Akil kicked back, stuck his left foot on the empty chair next to him, draping one arm over the back of Hadley's chair as he played a game on his phone.

Two assistants brought items up one by one to a table by the podium. Gene gave a brief description of each piece, took bids as people raised their paddles. There were oil paintings, a sunset cruise for two around the bay, curio cabinets, a Bakelite penny bank featuring a clown and a mechanized seal that flipped a coin into the slot. People were bidding well up into the thousands, more than Pearl would've thought possible.

A set of four blown-glass vases with a distinctive swirl pattern came on the block; there was a faint stirring in the crowd. Gene hesitated, continued, "Bidding starts at fifteen hundred."

The vases ended up going for nearly twice that. A few more items came and went. It wasn't until a Swiss clock appeared that the same table broke into whispers again, one woman sounding most adamant: "Yes, it *is*, I know it is—"

The bidding went quickly. Pearl shifted, crossed her legs from one side to the other; there was an odd feeling in the room now, a rising tension. From the corner of her eye, she noticed someone leaning against the wall near the lobby doors, arms folded. Tristan. As she watched, he straightened slowly and left the ballroom.

Gene was sweating visibly under the lights, looking like there was nothing he'd rather do than take his jacket off. "Next, we have an unusual conversation piece. Really fine work here, and a subject I know we can all appreciate." A large peaked box covered with a dust cloth was brought to the table. Gene pulled the cloth away, and there was an audible intake of breath.

It was a dollhouse, but more than that: it was the club. Two and a half stories high, covered in white clapboards and dark green shingles, complete with a front porch with filigreed gingerbread, flagstones set into the molded grass at the base. "This is by an unknown artist." Gene circled the miniature. "Donated anonymously, and I can tell you that we here at the club were tempted to keep it for ourselves. It opens like so"—he pulled at an invisible seam, and the house split in two on brass hinges, revealing a cross section of the club's interior—"and you can see that each room has been decorated true to life, right down to the wallpaper." He flicked a hidden switch, and there was laughter and applause as electric light fixtures burst to life in all the rooms.

Akil was sitting stark upright, his phone forgotten, staring at the house. "What the hell."

"Bidding starts at seventeen hundred. Remember, folks, this is for a good cause." In the crowd, a paddle shot up.

Akil pushed back from the table and made for the door, followed by Hadley, hurrying to keep up.

Bridges glanced at Pearl, and they went out into the lobby together, which was deserted, and finally onto the porch, where they found Akil and Hadley leaning against the railing. Hadley's hand rested gingerly on his back. "What?" Bridges said.

"That was Cassidy's." Akil rubbed his face. "Joseph's, too."

"The house?"

An engine turned over, and there was a flash of halogen headlights as a car pulled out of the lot and approached, stopping at the curb. It was the Bentley.

No one moved. The window powered down and a slice of Tristan's face was visible in the dash glow. "I'm going out on the water," he said. "Are you coming?" There was an edge to his voice Pearl had never heard before.

Bridges shared a look with Akil. "What about the girls? We can't—"

"Bring them."

FOURTEEN

"DID YOU DO it, man?" Akil faced Tristan as they drove. "Did you give their stuff away?"

"Some of it."

"Why?"

Tristan reached down, raised a bottle from the floor. Vodka, with a pattern of migrating geese on the glass. He took a drink, handed it to Akil. "You know how it is. You've got to deal with these things."

In the backseat, Pearl felt Hadley stiffen beside her; they were Quinn's words, from the day of the regatta. Had he overheard the whole conversation? Pearl remembered all that had been said, the insensitivity of it, the flippancy she'd ignored while busy trying to pump the girls for information.

Akil drank, swore softly, looked out the window. "I saw them working on that house. Out in the garage. Cassidy was trying to get Joe into all that little stuff she liked." He was quiet. "I gave her shit about it. Said dollhouses were for kids."

"Miniatures," Tristan said, "are for people who need the illusion of control. A world where they get to decide everything."

On Pearl's right, Bridges sat silently, tie loosened, hand open on the seat. He took the bottle as Akil passed it back.

"She had OCD," Tristan said. "And an anxiety disorder. Did you even know that?"

Akil paused, said stubbornly, "She didn't act like she did."

"Because she was medicated. She had panic attacks that should've kept her off the stage, but it turns out they have pills for that, too." He fell silent, downshifting as they reached the curve that led toward the waterfront, then spoke again, more quietly. "What better therapy than building a scale model of your life that you can smother under a sheet every night."

Bridges spoke up. "But . . . she didn't do any shows last summer. She actually got to hang out."

"Do you know why last summer happened?" Impatience in Tristan's voice. "Cassidy's psychiatrist told our parents they had a choice. Let Cassidy take some time off now, or accept the possibility that she might not have a musical career beyond the age of seventeen. Burnout. Last summer was a test. Cassidy got a little length on her leash, that's all." He glanced at Akil. "You were a part of that. You think my father tried to get between you two? He tolerated your presence as a part of Cassidy's treatment." When he spoke next, his tone was soft, dismissive. "You were a tool."

The silence was heavy. Something bumped Pearl's knee, and she looked over to see Bridges holding the bottle out to her. She took it by the neck, her nostrils tingling with fumes.

Tristan pulled into the yacht club parking lot and cut the engine. Akil stared straight out his window.

"It wasn't just the dollhouse," Pearl said. "The vases and the Swiss clock, those came from your house, too. Stuff that survived the fire. You tricked people into buying their dead friends' things."

"They weren't our friends. They were followers."

She remembered the women in the bathroom, the casual, gossipy way they tore the Garrisons to shreds while freshening up. These were the friends who Sloane had lunched and shopped with, served on boards and committees with, whose husbands golfed and shot skeet with David.

"It's good stuff." Bridges's voice was low, and she remembered the bottle in her hand. "It won't make you cough or anything."

She knew the attention of the front seat was on her, too, though in the rearview mirror she could see that Tristan's eyes were on the dark water. She put the bottle to her lips and sipped, already anticipating the burn as she swallowed, the vapors flooding her sinuses. No big mystery there; she'd smelled enough of the stuff on Dad's breath to know what it was like. She stuck the bottle back through the seats, and Akil grabbed it as he got out of the car, slamming the door behind him.

Hadley climbed out and lingered by the Bentley, letting the rest of them walk ahead toward the docks. "For real, where are we going?" She reached down and tugged at the sandal strap around the back of her ankle, laughing uncomfortably. "I mean—we're going out on a boat now?"

"Yes." Tristan didn't turn.

"Yeah, you'll never believe it, Had." Akil tucked the bottle inside his jacket. "Boats come with these things called lights." Backing up Tristan, as usual, as if Tristan hadn't just cut him to the bone. Akil gave an impatient gesture for her to come on; when she caught up with him, he slung his arm over her shoulders.

They were taking Tristan's speedboat. Pearl grabbed Bridges's hand as he helped her aboard. "You guys?" Pearl said. "You didn't answer her question. Where are we going? Or are we not supposed to ask?" No immediate response. "You really like your secrets, don't you?"

"We do?" Bridges said, facing away from her as he untied the lines.

"The way you took off after we left the party on Little

Nicatou? Into the darkness, under a shroud of mystery." She sat down on the bench seat, studying the three of them.

Tristan turned the key in the ignition, where he'd apparently left it dangling since the last time he'd gone out. "She's curious, Bridges."

Bridges didn't smile. The bottle had come back to him, and he sat beside Pearl, taking a long swallow. "You'll see," was all he said.

They cut through the bay, the only boat on the water, as far as Pearl could tell. It had been a warm night back onshore, but out here, the wind had bite, and she wished she were wearing anything but this dress.

They passed black, silent Little Nicatou, the boat headlights providing a ghostly flash of tree trunks and rocky cliff side. Akil still had his arm around Hadley, brushing his face close to hers, trying to initiate something that Hadley seemed reluctantly interested in. Before long, they were kissing.

Pearl glanced away, half expecting Bridges to follow Akil's lead, but he was distracted, looking down at the curds of foam rising along their hull, taking occasional sips from the bottle. He passed it back to her. She drank once, handed it off.

Tristan drove for nearly half an hour. When he finally killed the ignition and steered the boat up alongside a sheer cliff, Pearl had no idea where they were. Tristan dropped anchor, tied off on a rocky outcropping, bent to open a storage box beneath one of the seats. The only sound was the sloshing of water against the hull.

Hadley pushed Akil back, slightly breathless as she looked around. "Where's this?"

"A special place." Tristan brought out three Maglites, tossing one to Akil, another to Bridges.

Pearl looked up at the cliff. "If I'd known we were going rock climbing, I would've worn my stilettos." Beneath the words, her own unease mixed with the furred sensation the vodka had left on her tongue, and she felt vaguely sick.

When the flashlight beams hit the rocks, it was obvious that the wall wasn't sheer after all. There was a cave opening, at least twenty-five feet across, the blackness inside swallowing what scant moonlight filtered down to the base. Akil swung one leg over the side of the boat, feeling for the rocks, lunging off as Hadley caught her breath.

He made it, though the force of his leap sent the boat drifting sideways, away from the outcropping, and Tristan had to haul on the line to pull them back. There was a scraping sound as the hull rubbed rock, but he didn't seem to notice or care. "Bridges, help Hadley."

"That's okay." Hadley sat up straighter, pressing her back against the seat. "I'll wait for you guys here."

"Nope. Doesn't work like that." Akil laid his flashlight down, put out his hands. "You come with us, you've got to take the challenge. That's the deal."

"The challenge?" She looked at his hands for a moment, then took them and stood, weaving slightly with the motion of the boat. Bridges boosted her over the side onto the rocks, where she stood hugging herself, shifting from foot to foot.

Bridges was next. Pearl glanced at Tristan, surprised to find him holding a waterproof jacket out to her. "You look cold," he said.

"Thanks." She put it on, tugging the zipper to her chin. Bridges's gaze was on her, she could feel it, but she focused on getting herself across the divide, Tristan close behind.

Tristan moved around her so that he was first through the arch, his Maglite beam cutting through the blackness. Akil finally seemed to notice that Hadley was shivering and held out his jacket. She put it on, folding her arms tightly and dropping back to bring up the rear.

Pearl spoke to Bridges as they walked side by side. "So. This is where you guys go at night." She glanced up, listening as her words echoed up to a vaulted ceiling she couldn't see.

"One of the places." Bridges's voice was quiet, colorless.

The walls of the cave were bumpy and rough-hewn, the floor glistening with moisture and algae left by the tide. Seawater trickled in through small cracks and runnels at their feet.

"Does this place fill up at high tide?" Pearl barely saw him nod. "Kind of like Thunder Hole." Everybody on MDI had been to the tourist attraction in Acadia National Park at least once, an inlet with a small cavern beneath a ledge, where, when the tide came in, water and air were forced out through a blowhole in an explosion of spray.

"This cave is way more badass than that," Akil said, taking a run at the wall, dashing up a few feet before rebounding to the floor. "Like, you have no idea."

Tristan said, "Be quiet," pausing, listening; the air was full of dripping water, small echoes. "It's starting."

"What is?" Hadley stopped, her voice rising slightly. "Bridges?"

"*Shhh*," Bridges said. "It's okay, Had."

"Look, this is cool and everything, but I think I want to go back now—"

"There's no going back," Tristan said. He had led them to a fork. It was more than a cave: it was a system, two broad fissures appearing before them in the rock like gaping mouths. "There's only right or left. You choose."

"Me? I don't—"

"I want to hear you make a decision. By yourself." His voice had that edge again. "And then you have to live with the consequences of your choice. Do you think you can do that?"

The faint outline of her profile was perfectly still. "Yes." Her voice was soft.

"Which way, Hadley?"

"Left."

"Then you lead." He stood back to let her pass, training

the Maglite on the left tunnel. Hadley went, stepping gingerly, slipping and catching herself more than once as she led them through the passageway eroded by wave action and time. There was a sound; Pearl could hear it now, somewhere up ahead, a rushing that cycled on and on.

There was a slight vertical pitch to the tunnel, and Pearl put her hands out, touching the cool, moist walls. "How did you guys find this place?"

Bridges: "Tristan read about it online. Some site on sea caves."

Hadley stopped, glancing back. "I don't"—she lifted a shoulder helplessly—"which way?" Again, two more fissures opened to their left and right.

Enough; Hadley reminded Pearl of a little kid, waiting for permission to move. "Okay, what's this big challenge, if we choose to accept it?"

Tristan turned to look at her. "Finding your way out."

He switched off his Maglite. In nearly the same instant, the other boys followed suit.

Absolute blackness. Hadley cried out—"You *guys!*"—but the only sounds were footsteps over stone, the rush of bodies brushing by. Pearl nearly fell, her shoulder landing heavily against the wall. She clung there blindly, counting the seconds until a light switched back on, until someone called off the joke.

Hadley shouted, "You guys! Come back!"

"Hadley, wait!" Pearl took a step, slipped again, cursed.

"Wait for me, okay?" She walked with her hands out until she collided with Hadley, groping for her arm. "Do you have your phone? We can use the light—"

"No, it's in my bag!" Back on the boat. Which was exactly where Pearl had left hers. Hadley sniffed, shouted, "Bridges!" to a cacophony of echoes.

"*Shhh!* They're not coming back." Pearl's own panic came out as frustration, her airways choked with the smell of subterranean dankness, bringing with it claustrophobia, a feeling of being buried miles, not yards, from fresh air. "Look, we didn't walk that far from the opening—let's just turn around and—"

"How? We can't *see* anything! *Bridges!*"

"Stop yelling!" Hadley yanked her arm free, and this time Pearl did fall, catching herself on her hands and knees with a whoosh of breath. The other girl's footsteps moved away, shuffling and uneven. "Hadley, *no*—you don't know where you're going."

The sound of Hadley's hysterical breathing disappeared behind a wall of rock. She'd gone through one of the fissures ahead, and now Pearl was the one yelling, begging Hadley to stop, to stand still and she'd come find her. Somehow.

Nothing. Pearl sat up in the blackness, her heart trying to escape her chest. What if the boys were hiding up ahead, waiting for the moment to switch on their lights and laugh at her, sitting here, helpless, fighting tears? She folded her arms across her knees, the waterproof material rustling. Tristan's jacket.

She dug into every pocket, and found something. Hard plastic, cylindrical. After some fumbling, hardly daring to hope, she hit the strike. A small jet of flame shot into existence.

A lighter. Now the clue seemed so obvious—what could be less Tristan-like than noticing when another person seemed cold? He'd planted the lighter in the jacket so she'd have it when the time came.

Almost giddy with her ability to see, Pearl went to the fissure on her right, peering in. The passageway stretched off to the right and left. She called Hadley's name.

If there was an answer, it was so distant that it was covered by her own echoes. She didn't want to go in there. She wanted to turn around and the follow the tunnel back to the cave arch, breathe clean air, wait for the boys to get bored with their game. But Hadley. She was down there somewhere, hysterical, totally blind.

Pearl chose left, still calling for the girl. Something crunched beneath her sandal, and she jerked the lighter down—a sea urchin, left behind by the tide.

The rushing sound was still there, growing louder. Whatever it was, she was heading right for it. At this point, anything seemed better than following an endless, curving rock wall, stumble-stepping over an unpredictable floor.

At first, she thought she was imagining the change in the darkness before her, the quality of pitch-black fading into deepest twilight. She let the lighter flame recede.

Another arch lay ahead. Pearl went through the opening. The chamber held a pool beneath the ledge where she stood, filling with tidewater from what sounded like a hundred unseen passages. As she watched, bluish light spread across the surface of the water, amorphous, fluctuating.

She sank into a sitting position, exhausted, for a time full of nothing but the light. She became aware of his presence gradually, a tightening of the skin at the back of her neck, an instinctive knowledge that she wasn't alone.

The silhouette stood and made his way around the ledge to her, switching on his flashlight so that the beam swung at his feet. Tristan sank into a crouch beside her, and they both stared at the light below.

"What is it?" Her voice was hoarse.

"Bioluminescence. I think they're ctenophores, comb jellies. They've been down there almost every time I've come."

The light stretched and separated, living tissue pulling itself through the water by tiny cilia. She felt too exhausted to stand, too damp and chilled and sick of being underground. "We've got to find Hadley. She ran off before I could stop her."

"It wasn't your responsibility to stop her. She had a chance to prove herself and she failed. She panicked, exactly like I knew she would."

"Why'd you give me the lighter?"

"Because I knew you'd have the presence of mind to look for it."

Pearl turned to him, choked with all the things she wanted to say. Speech seemed impossible, pointless. Even if she slapped him, he'd just look back at her, impervious, filing her actions away for further consideration. All she could manage was, "Hadley's terrified. She could be anywhere by now."

Tristan exhaled through his nose, straightening up. "The cave system isn't that big. Six interlocking passages. Between all of us, it won't take long to find her."

He walked back through the arch, and Pearl followed, gripping the lighter in her fist in case he tried to lose her again. Tristan blinked the flashlight three times in the tunnel, then again when they reached the opening Pearl had come through earlier: a signal for the other boys to come back from wherever they were hiding.

Pearl reached out and grabbed the flashlight. "How about I carry this." He didn't argue.

It wasn't long before footsteps came up behind them. As the boys' flashlight beams fell on Tristan and Pearl, Bridges said, "They didn't stay together?"

"Obviously not," Tristan said.

"She just ran off? By herself?" Bridges swore. "I *knew* she'd freak. Crap. We better find her."

Pearl didn't turn or slow down, ignoring all three of them as she pressed forward, running her free hand along the wall to keep from slipping. The floor was noticeably wet now; the tide was coming faster, little streams running along the rocks, soaking her already numb bare toes.

Pearl tried not to think about the water rising higher and higher, about what it might be like, trying to get out of here with it up to their waists, their chins, over their heads. The passageway sloped upward, curved left. They walked on. Pearl sloshed through water now ankle deep, and when she glanced up, it was into a white face, all sightless eyes and keening mouth.

It fell on her, clinging, fingers digging into Pearl's arms. Pearl gasped, her mind registering a moment too late that it was Hadley, of course it was, and she dropped back against the wall to keep from collapsing under the girl's weight.

"Had, it's okay—it's *okay*, we've got you." Bridges tried to pry her free. Hadley was shuddering uncontrollably, her fingertips ten icy pinpoints, her breath gusting against Pearl's neck.

Tristan said nothing, watching as the rest of them, even Akil, tried to talk Hadley down. Finally, her hyperventilating became sobs, and she let Bridges put his arm around her.

Once they reached the cave entrance, rising water was sloshing over the outcropping beyond the arch. It was a struggle to get back into the boat, and Hadley had to be carried. She sat hunched beside Bridges, refusing to speak as he rubbed her back and asked repeatedly if she was okay, to please say something. There was blood trickling down her shin from a gash on her right knee, and her palms were scraped. Akil sat across from her, watching the scene uneasily.

Pearl, meanwhile, still gripped the flashlight. She didn't let go until Tristan moored at the yacht club landing, at which point it dropped from her stiff fingers and rolled across the deck.

Bridges looked up at Tristan. "I think maybe she needs a hospital."

Tristan turned, folding his arms over his chest, studying Hadley. Then he went to the storage box, brought out a first-aid kit, and knelt to apply alcohol to the cut on her knee. She winced, her eyelids fluttering. "It's shock." He opened an adhesive bandage and applied it, then reached into his pocket and handed Bridges his car keys. "Take her home. She'll be fine."

Bridges looked at him for a long moment, finally saying quietly, "Don't you even care?"

Tristan gazed back. "Any sensible person would've followed the sound of running water to the chamber. She could've been out of the tunnels in minutes." He tilted his head slightly, regarding Bridges. "You managed to figure it out. Didn't you?"

Hadley watched as Tristan walked back to the bow, her eyes wide and wounded.

Pearl got off the boat, leading the way down the dock, too furious and half-numb to look at anyone. She only glanced back when she heard the Rivelle's engine roar to life. Tristan, going out again by himself, onto the bay.

FIFTEEN

THE FOUR OF them drove through the streets in the Bentley, Hadley and Pearl in the backseat, both staring out their respective windows. Hadley still wasn't speaking.

They went back to the club to pick up the Mustang. Akil took the Bentley keys from Bridges, glancing at the girls. "Listen, dude, do you—I mean, you got this?"

"Yeah. See ya."

When Bridges and the girls reached the Spencer compound, the big house was dark, but the porch lit up with motion-sensor lights as they drove in. Bridges parked, came around to open Pearl's door, but she let herself out, her gaze following the line of lampposts leading down the driveway to the cottages. She'd been in that living room with Bridges just hours ago, touching him, talking around the subject of going upstairs together.

Now she said, "I need my car," in a tone that made him glance up from Hadley's wan face.

"Pearl—"

"I want to go home. Now."

He made a quick call on his cell phone, presumably to the same manservant who'd taken her keys. His call was answered right away, despite the late hour. Apparently, a middle-of-the-night summons wasn't unusual in Spencerville.

She could feel Bridges's gaze on her, waiting for her to turn to him, but she wouldn't. The headlights of the Civic appeared around the bend in the drive. Bridges said, "Come down to the cottage. Just for a couple minutes."

The Civic stopped beside her, and the manservant stepped out; same neatly pressed clothes, as if he'd slept propped up in a closet. "No." Pearl glanced at Hadley. "She needs you." Then she got into her car and left.

Dad's truck was in the driveway when she got there; he'd left a couple of lights on for her. His snores were audible even from the living room. There was evidence of how he'd spent his evening after coming back from Yancey's—a half-empty bag of corn chips on the coffee table, Bud Light empties, remote wedged between the couch cushions—and she felt more than guilt. It was a genuine longing for how things had been before she'd decided to make herself absent this summer. Not perfect, maybe, but predictable, a routine. She switched off lamps as she went and shut her bedroom door behind her.

Someone in black stood by her closet. Her heart slammed into her throat before she recognized herself in the full-length mirror, still wearing Tristan's oversize jacket, creating a distorted, elongated reflection. She yanked off the jacket, then the rest of her clothes, and kicked the damp heap away.

Pearl curled under the blanket in her underwear, still feeling chilled. She thought of her phone, tucked in her purse, and the one person she wished she could call right now. When she closed her eyes, the strange half-light of the chamber pool was there, waiting for her, and the rhythmic, hypnotizing motion of the ctenophores.

It was relatively quiet for a Saturday morning at Dark Brew. The weather was gray and drizzly, raindrops dewing Pearl's face and eyelashes after the dash from her car to the air-conditioned confines of the coffee shop. As she pushed her hood back, she scanned the seating area for Reese. No sign.

Jovia was behind the counter, putting cinnamon buns into the case from a parchment-lined baking sheet. She noticed Pearl and said, "Oh. Hey, hon."

Well, much better than what she'd expected. On the drive, Pearl had imagined Jovia treating her coldly, asking what had happened at the ball last night to get Reese fired, or maybe ignoring her completely. Pretty ridiculous. Reese was so cagey about his personal life that he probably hadn't told Jovia a thing.

Jovia stopped what she was doing, scrutinizing her. "Are you okay?"

"Are you? You look . . ." Pearl examined Jovia's red-rimmed eyes. "Did you call Reese's dad or something?"

Jovia made a rueful face. "That obvious, huh. You want the usual?"

"Two coffees this time." Pearl hesitated. "And two chocolate croissants."

Jovia didn't remark, filling the order with deft movements. "Yeah, the conversation was typical. Things are a little tight for him right now, but he'll be sure to catch up on what he owes us just as soon as he can." Jovia snorted softly. "Must be behind on his Porsche payments. Don't ask me what the hell I was thinking, not making him sign something legal in the first place. Anyway." She shrugged, fitted lids on the to-go cups, and put everything into a cardboard carryout tray before making Pearl's change.

"Has Reese been down yet?" She failed miserably at sounding casual.

"Nah. He's off today, probably won't stick his head out of his man cave until eleven or so." Jovia pressed her lips together for a moment. "If you see him . . . well." She gave a lopsided smile. "He'll talk to you. He won't talk to me. Good luck." She slid the tray over.

Weighed down by the words, Pearl went out the back

door, across the yard, and into the shadows of the carriage house. She could hear Reese's music playing upstairs, and she steeled herself as she knocked on the door at the top of the stairs.

"Yeah?"

Pearl let herself in. He was stuffing dirty clothes into a bag, getting ready for a Laundromat run. When he glanced back and saw that she wasn't Jovia, he remained silent, looking her over as he balled a uniform shirt in one hand. Then he turned his back again. "What, the Young Republicans won't let you into their clubhouse without the secret knock?"

She looked at him, barefoot, dressed in threadbare jeans and a T-shirt; she'd expected to see evidence of last night's fight with Akil—bruises, something—but he just looked like Reese on a day off. "Do you still have a job?" She kept her voice remote.

He snorted softly, nodded once.

"What'd the Nazi say?" Somehow, it felt forced to use the club nickname for Meriwether now, like she'd given up the right.

"All kinds of things. I wasn't listening."

Pearl exhaled, set the tray down on his makeshift bedside table. She caught a glimpse of what was pulled up on his laptop screen. Apartment listings. "You're moving out?" No response. "Why?"

"Because I can. School's over. I don't need a guardian

making sure I get to study hall on time." He stuffed more clothes into the bag. "Jovia can't put me up forever."

"But . . . what're you going to do? Are you leaving the club?"

"Why, Pearl? Do you care?"

"I'm not the one who said I didn't give a shit."

"Yeah, well, you know what they say about actions."

"Don't you even want to know what's really going on? I've been trying to tell you since the beginning. You're supposed to be—" She stopped, took a breath. "I thought we were friends. But you won't even *talk* to me. So, those are the rules? You can do whatever you want, hang out with whoever you want, but if you even see me with another guy, I'm dead to you? How is that fair?"

Reese turned on her. "It's not just some other guy, Pearl, it's Tristan-effing-Garrison and his trust-fund gestapo. You really need me to explain why it's a bad idea to hang out with people like that? Those guys have no fear. Money and Daddy's attorney can make anything go away. After what happened to your dad, how can you—"

"I don't need you to tell me about that." Her voice belonged to a stranger: harsh, flinty, years older than her. "I know what they did to us. What the hell do you think this is all about?"

For the first time, Reese hesitated, watching her. "You tell me."

"Gee, can I?" When he stayed quiet, she took a seat on the bed, one leg folded beneath her. She lifted her coffee cup from the tray, plucking the plastic seal with her fingernail. "It's more something that I need to show you." She took the memory card out of her pocket. "This belonged to Cassidy Garrison." He watched as she slid the card into his laptop and played Cassidy's video.

When it was done, Reese sank slowly onto the edge of the mattress. The stiff resentment was gone from his expression. "You're sure it's real?" A nod. "Where'd you get it?"

"Found it hidden under the bathroom sink of the Garrison yacht. That's where it was shot, too."

"You've been on their yacht?"

"I've been lots of places. If you want to hear about it."

He scooted back against the wall, opened his coffee, took a sip. "Shoot."

She began with Bridges first approaching her; the party on Little Nicatou; the regatta, and so on, until she finally reached last night. When she finished, Pearl sat with her fingers linked loosely around her bent knee, staring at the pattern of Reese's quilt. It was patchwork, looked like he'd probably had it since he was a kid.

"Sounds like Hadley really lost her shit." Reese tore into his croissant.

"They knew she would, or at least Tristan did. It was all another test, a game. Hadley lost, and now she's out. I don't think Akil will ever look at her again."

"Why'd Tristan set you up to win?"

"I don't know." Pearl bit her lip, shook her head. "It's unbelievable. Those guys go along with whatever Tristan says. He's got total control."

"The alpha dog."

"It's more than that. It's like they're in awe of him, or scared of him, or both. Akil's so mad all the time, all Tristan needs to do is wind him up. And Bridges . . . I don't know what he is. Along for the ride, I guess."

"Tristan sounds intense."

"No. He's actually not that bad." Reese's brows went up. "I'm saying he usually isn't mean or nasty, that's all. And he does stuff sometimes—random nice things, and doesn't take credit for them. I don't know, it's weird. It's like he's always studying people. Playing games like last night in the cave is his way of . . . figuring us out, maybe?"

Reese cleared his throat. "So, as evil eccentric millionaire geniuses go, he rates about a six on a scale of ten. Gotcha." He gestured to the paused video on the screen. "You think he knows about this?"

"If he knew, he would've taken the card before now. Either Cassidy didn't have a chance to get back on the boat to grab it, or for some reason, she decided the danger was gone." Pearl was silent a moment, the consequences of that sinking in. "Tristan said she had OCD, that she had panic attacks. Nobody outside the family knew. And somebody was after her, obviously."

"Somebody pissed off enough to kill the whole family? What about that Akil guy? Maybe he snapped after she dumped him."

"But Bridges said that he treated Cassidy like a princess."

"Oh, Bridges said." Reese leaned his head back against the wall, studying her. "What's the deal with you and Golden Boy? Are you going to keep leading him on after he ditched you in the Caverns of Mystery, or what?"

Pearl opened her mouth to answer, but the words died. She didn't want to bullshit Reese. She thought of Bridges's lips on hers, his hands sliding places where no one had ever touched before, and felt a weakness that made her wonder where the power really lay. "I need more. I have to find out what happened to the Garrisons, to Cassidy. Maybe when I do—"

"People will stop blaming your dad." Reese met her eyes. "I understand why you're doing it. I don't like that you're risking so much."

She forced a smile. "What risk? They're just a bunch of Alligator Shirts, remember?"

"What happens when this guy expects you to follow through on what you've been promising? You think a Spencer who nails two, three girls a summer is going to be happy to hold hands until August?"

"Tristan says Bridges sees something in me."

"And that's all you need to hear."

"Nothing's going to happen that I don't want to, okay?" She'd never seen Reese serious for so long, and she stood, pacing over to the boxes, pushing the shade aside to peer out at the day, where the rain had nearly stopped. "I'm not worried about Bridges. It's like . . . I've got all these pieces, and I just need to figure out how they fit. David was a bully, a control freak, maybe worse. And Sloane was cheating on him, had been for a long time. Everything else is locked up inside Tristan's head. If I can find a way to get in there, maybe . . ."

When he didn't say anything, she turned back. He was starting to eat her croissant, looking thoughtful. "You know who you should talk to? Marilyn Whitley. She cleans for a bunch of the families on the Row. I'm pretty sure she worked for the Garrisons."

"I've met a Marilyn." Pearl remembered the woman from when she used to ride with Dad to check on his houses: small, bird-boned, carrying bags of trash or washing windows with newspaper and ammonia water. "My dad's friends with her. Or they used to say hi and stuff, anyway. Do you think she'd talk to me?"

"I don't know. I only met her once. She lives over in Winter Harbor." Reese spoke around a bite: "She's Indigo's grandmother."

SIXTEEN

WHEN PEARL GOT home, Dad was on the Beetle Cat, checking out the rigging and generally puttering around. She raised her hand to him as she started toward the house.

She was kicking off her flop-flops when she heard an engine. She looked out the screen door to see a silver Jaguar pull into the driveway. As she stared, Bridges got out, glancing over at Dad.

She was through the door and down the steps in an instant. "What're you doing here?"

"I needed to talk to you. Your phone was off—"

"Did you follow me?" When he hesitated, her voice sharpened. "How did you find out where I live?"

Bridges put up his hands. "I asked around the club. Sorry. Was it supposed to be a secret?"

Dad was on his way over. Pearl's entire body felt charged, intensely aware of how their one-story house must look, with scum from the elements clinging to the vinyl siding because Dad hadn't pressure sprayed in a couple of years, the patches of dead grass in the yard, the rusty Fisher plow blade beside the shed.

"Everything okay?" Dad stopped at the edge of the driveway, his worn-out sneakers inches away from Bridges's OluKai sandals.

"It's fine." Pearl couldn't look at him.

"Hi." Bridges put his hand out to shake with Dad. Pearl waited for some flash of recognition in his face, some sign of *hey, aren't you——?*, but of course there was none. To him, Dad was just another faceless servant, trimming hedges and mulching gardens at the club. "Bridges Spencer. I'm a friend of Pearl's. Good to meet you, sir."

Dad shook with him. "Win." His wariness was obvious, maybe waiting for this to somehow relate back to the club, to be told more trouble was coming down on the Haskins family, courtesy of the summer elite.

"He just stopped by," she said lamely. Why hadn't she stayed at Reese's house longer? Bridges probably would've dropped this whole thing when he saw that her car wasn't parked in the driveway.

"Okay. Well. Don't let me hold you up." With another quick scan of Bridges's face, Dad made his way back toward the Cat, watching them go up the steps as he squatted down with his tools.

It had been a long time since a new person came into their house. Everywhere Pearl looked, humiliating things jumped into the foreground: dirty dishes in the sink, windows desperate for washing, faded hand towels, the general clutter on every surface. She went to the kitchen table immediately, stacking mail, sweeping crumbs into her palm, not looking at Bridges.

"Uh . . . sorry if this wasn't"—he stood in the entryway, watching her—"look, don't feel like you have to—"

"I don't." She shook the rattan place mats over the sink and straightened them in front of each chair with brisk movements. "So. What couldn't wait until I checked my voice mail?"

"I wanted to say that what happened last night wasn't okay. I know that. We never should've brought you guys out there."

"You knew he was going to do that to us."

"I hoped he wouldn't. I figured we might check the place out and leave. I didn't think, with Hadley there . . ." He saw Pearl reach for the broom, came over and touched her shoulder. "Stop. Okay? It doesn't matter."

Pearl barely resisted the impulse to shove his hand away, a

reaction that surprised even her. She took a breath and faced him. "When Tristan turned off his flashlight, you didn't hesitate. You say you're sorry, but what about then? Why didn't you do something?"

"That's not how it works with Tristan."

"You mean that's not how it works with *you* when you're with Tristan. You and Akil act like he's God or something. It's crazy. I mean, is that really what you guys do at night, cruise around finding new ways for him to torture you?" Bridges glanced away. "He tried the cave thing with you first, right? That's what he meant when he said, 'You managed to figure it out,' about following the sound of water to the chamber pool."

"He tried Akil first. Then they brought me." Bridges pulled out a chair and sat, tugging absently at a lock of hair over his ear. "It's not always like that. Sometimes it's fun. We go all over the place. The islands, wherever. Explore some of the waterfront estates in Bar Harbor."

"You mean trespass." Oh, the irony.

"I guess. One time, we borrowed this boat." He looked at her quickly. "The keys were in it. We didn't hurt it or anything, just took it out on the bay to see what it could do and brought it back. Tristan . . . he's not scared of anything. He doesn't worry. None of my friends back home would have the balls to try that stuff. They wouldn't even believe me if I told them about it. But it's like if Tristan decides nothing can touch him, nothing can."

She thought of Tristan's rapt expression as they'd danced, as he'd told her about midnight defining him, about forcing himself out onto the dark sidewalks and beaches to run. That didn't sound like somebody who was untouchable. Was it possible that the boys didn't know about any of it? "But sometimes it's more like last night, right? Like he's pushing to see how far you'll go for him." No backing down now; she was into the fray. "Quinn told me about a video that was posted online last summer. She said it happened at a party you guys had." She paused. "There was a girl."

He gave his hair a final tug and then pressed his hand flat against the table, as if willing himself to stop fidgeting. "There are always girls."

"I think this one was pretty memorable."

His gaze went to the far wall, to a calendar they'd gotten from the heating oil company, covered bridges of New England. "It's over now. Done. The video's down, nobody else can watch it."

"Decent of you."

His eyes cut to her. "I didn't say I did it. Seriously, you just assume it was me?" Pearl stared levelly back at him. "Did Quinn tell you that? Because she doesn't know what she's talking about. She wasn't even there that night." He sat forward. "Look, nobody made anybody do anything. And everybody was wasted. Tristan's parents were out of town with Joe, so we pretty much cleaned out the bar." Still she didn't speak. "I was with Hadley then, so I didn't—I'm not into that stuff, what happened upstairs."

"But you were there?" She watched him rub his mouth with his hand, pulling his thumb slowly beneath his lower lip. "In the room?"

"No, no. At the party. Some of the guys were sharing the video around at the end of the night. I don't know who posted it online."

Pearl's stomach did a slow slide, and she examined the pattern of the linoleum for a while until she felt like she could look at him again. "This girl knew somebody was filming her? And that people might see it?" Bridges hesitated. It was answer enough. "So now he's got blackmail on anyone who was in that video. Or anyone whose girlfriend might not be too happy that he watched what happened upstairs."

"Look, if we do something, it's all in. If Tristan told on us for this kind of stuff, he'd get busted, too. And anyway, he never would. It's more like . . . everything takes you deeper. You know? Even if one of us wanted to break away sometimes, or maybe say stop"—his gaze on her, almost pleading—"it's already too late, because of everything else we've done. Does that make any sense?"

"It makes sense why Tristan would want you to feel that way. Then he owns you." She didn't wait for Bridges to make another excuse. "Does this mean that the next time Tristan thinks it'll be fun to trick or trap me somewhere, you'll go along?"

"No. No way."

"Kind of hard to believe that after everything you just said."

"I swear to God. He's going through some dark stuff right now, and I get that, but I can't keep messing with people. That's his thing, not mine. College starts soon, and—I don't want to be that guy anymore." Bridges took a deep breath. "Are we okay? I don't want to screw things up with you, Pearl. I like you." He gave a half smile. "You don't let me off the hook for anything."

She waited, considering him. Then she put her hand out. "If we shake on it."

Bridges shook. "Cool. Thanks."

He left after that, he and Dad exchanging nods as Bridges got into the Jaguar, apparently one of his grandfather's lesser rides. Pearl stepped back from the screen door before Dad turned toward the house, feeling like a coward, knowing she should go out there now and face up to whatever he had to say. She couldn't; she felt drained, nothing left.

She curled up on the couch with her tablet until Dad came inside. She kept tabs on him from the corner of her eye, listening to him wash his hands at the kitchen sink. Had Bridges smelled alcohol coming from his pores after last night's six-pack, like she could? Or was Reese right, it was an acquired skill? Dad turned, leaning against the counter. "What's going on, Pearl?"

She sat up slowly, looking at him over the arm of the couch. "He's a friend."

"Since when do you have friends from the Row?" Dad didn't sound angry, exactly; his speech was slow, measured.

"I met him in the dining room. He comes in a lot." She waited to see if Dad knew who Bridges ran with, if he'd mention Tristan's name.

"I thought you were too busy working to be meeting boys." She flinched a little; he saw it, looked down, scuffed his thumb against his jeans. "What happened to Reese?"

"Nothing happened to him. He's around."

"Not like before. You're telling me that's got nothing to do with this Spencer kid?"

"I'm telling you that Bridges is a friend. He wanted to talk." She didn't know how much longer she could keep her voice steady when he wouldn't look at her, when this whole thing felt like losing Reese all over again, times ten. "Dad? Are you listening? I'm not—" *Switching sides. Turning on you. I haven't forgotten.* "Just please trust me. Okay?" He didn't answer. *"Okay?"*

It was such a lame note to end on, but exhausted tears were threatening now. He nodded a little, looking around the kitchen, maybe noting her hasty attempt at straightening up. "The Cat sold."

It took her a moment to understand. "What?" The word escaped on a breath. "When?"

"Yesterday. A guy pulled in, made me an offer after I got off work. I was going to tell you about it last night." The implication was clear, that she'd been out too late and he wasn't happy about it; like she was the one always gone, spending half her life at the Tavern. "He's coming by with a trailer tomorrow."

Pearl set her jaw, but it still trembled. "Oh." She took a short breath through her nose. "You're really going to—"

"Don't have a lot of choice, do I?" He left the counter and went out the door then, leaving her sitting there with no reason to stop the hot tears from tracing down her cheeks.

SEVENTEEN

THE NEXT DAY was humid, hot, sunlight flashing through trees as Pearl navigated the road into Winter Harbor. Reese sat beside her, texting, finally putting his phone down to look out the windshield. "Okay. Got directions. Indigo told her grandma that we're coming."

"So she'll definitely talk to us?"

"I don't know. But Indy told her we're on our way."

Pearl nodded, tapping her fingertips on the steering wheel, trying to keep her nervousness under wraps. It stung to need Indigo's help, but in this case, there didn't seem to be any way around it; Pearl trusted Reese not to tell the other girl any more than the bare minimum about why they were asking for this favor. That in itself—Indigo helping him out at the first word, without needing details—implied a closeness that Pearl didn't like to think about.

A couple of minutes later, as they approached a street sign reading *Gull Reach*, he said, "Turn here. It's a blue trailer on the left."

The trailer sat on a neat square of lawn with a mailbox that read *Whitley* in hand-painted script, the property yards away from a spit of sandy earth that fed into the bay, bordered by wild rosebushes. Pearl parked beside a gray sedan, wishing her mouth wasn't so dry.

Reese followed her, hands in his pockets, whistling faintly, tunelessly; it would've been maddening if she didn't know him so well, that he was holding silence, his natural enemy, at bay. She led the way up the steps and knocked. Through the glass panes in the door, she could see sunlight gleaming on bare countertops, the chrome of a sink. She shifted, knocked again.

Pearl didn't hear so much as sense the woman off to her right, watching them from the stretch of town between the trailer and a small storage shed. Marilyn Whitley looked much the way Pearl remembered from the few times she'd seen her, barely five feet tall, her graying hair chopped bluntly to her chin. She wore a faded blue gingham shirt and jeans and held a fitted bedsheet balled in her arms. Her gaze was sharp, and she wasn't smiling.

"Hi." Reese rocked back on his heels.

Pearl waited for him to say more. When he didn't, she cleared her throat and walked down a few steps. "I'm Pearl Haskins. I think you know my dad, Win?" The woman continued to watch her. "Indigo said she called you about us coming."

Marilyn's gaze shifted over Pearl's shoulder to Reese. "You I know. Indy brought you by back in the spring." It didn't necessarily sound like a vote of approval. She glanced back at their car. "She's not with you?"

"Not today."

The woman worked her lips over her dentures, then gave an almost imperceptible shrug. "I'm hanging laundry." She went back around the trailer. Pearl and Reese glanced at each other, then followed.

Marilyn pulled clothespins out of the bag suspended from the line, keeping her back to them. "You were wondering about the Garrisons. Is that right?" *Snap*, she shook out the sheet. "That don't really make you special. I've gotten enough phone calls about that since December. Haven't had anything to say yet."

Pearl swallowed, watching as the woman's hands continued in their task. "So you did clean for them?" No response. "I guess you know my dad worked for them, too. I just wondered . . . what you thought of them. How they seemed to you."

"Seemed?" She put the last pin on the sheet and bent to grab pillowcases.

"I mean, were you surprised when they were killed?" The chapped hands continued moving, but there was a listening quality to her movements now, a deliberateness. Pearl took a step closer. "I'm asking because I'm scared for my dad. He did everything he could to help them that night. He still lost all his caretaking clients. Nobody trusts him now."

A silence. "Wasn't his fault what happened." Marilyn tsked faintly. "What's he supposed to do against somebody with a gun, for chrissake?" When she spoke again, the gruffness was back. "I'm sorry to hear about your troubles."

Pearl pressed her lips together. She wasn't going to get anywhere with this woman by hedging. "I'm trying to find out who did it. If there's anything you can tell me, I'd appreciate it. So would my dad."

"Ain't that what the cops are for? Finding killers? I already answered all their questions."

"I haven't heard anything about them making an arrest, have you?" Pearl waited. "I know Tristan, a little bit."

Marilyn finished pinning a T-shirt, then smoothed her hand over the damp cotton slowly, letting her arm fall to her side. When she turned, her eyes had changed, gone distant. "If you're smart, you'll keep it at that. A little bit."

"Why? What do you mean?"

Glancing over at the neighbor's house, Marilyn wiped her

palms on her jeans, released a short burst of breath. "Better come inside."

The kitchen was spotless, silent except for the humming of the fridge. Lace curtains sucked and gusted with the breeze, and Marilyn watched them move. The three of them sat at the table, each with a glass of iced tea in front of them.

"I'm not trying to get into your business. I got no interest in that. But I raised girls of my own . . . and Win's a decent kind of guy." Marilyn watched her. "Does he know you're spending time with Tristan?"

Only a few minutes into their acquaintance, there was no lying to this woman: Pearl shook her head. Marilyn leaned back, folding her skinny, freckled arms. "I worked for them for three years. Gave the house a light turn twice a month in the off-season, and cleaned regular for them all summer." She turned her glass on the tabletop. "Not because it was a place I liked to be."

"I've heard things."

"Whatever you heard ain't likely to be the truth. I don't think anybody left alive knows the truth, except that boy." She glanced over at the wall, where gold-tone picture frames held photographs of a little blond girl who Pearl recognized after a moment as Indigo. Elementary school pictures, her hair in braids or cut painfully short, face full of tender openness, the kind of pictures you wouldn't want just anybody seeing.

"I've been making my living cleaning for nearly twenty years now." She flicked her hand at Pearl. "You know how it is with summer people. After a while, most of them stop seeing you, don't even notice when you run the vacuum through the room. I've seen some things maybe I wasn't meant to." Her gaze sharpened. "And you don't get recommendations by running your mouth."

"I'd never gossip about this. I swear. No one will ever know we were here today."

Marilyn raised her brows at Reese. "What about him?"

Reese held up three fingers. "Scout's honor. Or something."

"Still a smart-ass. Glad to see nothing's changed." Marilyn exhaled, examined them for a beat. "I guess Indigo wouldn't have asked if she didn't trust you two."

Pearl sat forward in her chair, gripping the edge of the seat.

"The reason I told you that I've raised girls is because I think most of us women got a gut instinct to mother. Some of us want to mother our men. You can throw your whole life away taking in strays, trying to fix the damage that some other woman did to him while he was still in diapers. Plain truth is, some men are just broken."

"Is Tristan broken?"

"I never got a handle on what he is. But there's a piece missing, all right. He might look like a big success, collecting trophies and degrees, but when it comes down to it, he ain't nothing but a little boy who didn't get what he needed from the people who were supposed to give it to him."

"David and Sloane."

"You hear about black sheep. That was Tristan. Cassidy and Joe, they acted close. Always sharing secrets, had heads for puzzles, games. I remember Cassidy used to plan these scavenger hunts for Joe, get him roaming all over the property and beach, looking for stuff she'd hidden. Tristan wasn't home much, but when he was, he was alone. I'd have to put off straightening his room until last because he was usually locked up in there. Them other two kids steered clear of him most of the time."

More otherness, more separation. "I've heard things were bad between him and David."

Marilyn shifted, glanced at the door, as if someone might be peering in through the panes, eavesdropping. "I can't say what was between them. But I saw David punch Tristan once."

Pearl stared at her, a little surprised by her body's sympathetic reaction: tightening stomach, clenching fists. "God. Really?"

"I was cleaning the third floor, the loft. Looked out the window to see Tristan leaving by the back door, David right behind him, carping on him about something. Tristan wouldn't stop, so his dad pulled him around by the shoulder, popped him one in the eye."

Reese spoke up. "What'd Tristan do?"

"Nothing. Took the punch. David sort of braced up, like he thought maybe they were finally going to have it out or something. Tristan was taller than his dad, too, old enough to stand up for himself. But he didn't. He got back through the partying, I guess. Tearing the place to pieces with them other rich kids whenever his parents went away for the night. I'd show up in the morning and find kids still passed out drunk, sleeping it off. Had to flush them out of the bedrooms sometimes. Sent Cassidy's boyfriend packing once last summer. Never seen a couple kids so embarrassed."

Pearl rested her elbows on the table, her gaze landing on another framed picture of Indigo sitting on a shelf. This one was a candid, Indigo wearing a lavender snowsuit and pompom hat, smiling beside a snowman with the trailer in the background. Pearl thought of what the boys had said about Indigo, how everybody knew her; did Marilyn know about that? "How did Cassidy act that last summer? Did she seem like she was scared at all? Or nervous?"

"She was nervous as a cat, but that wasn't anything new. Just how she was wired. High-strung."

"Did you ever see David hurt her?"

"No. Never saw him lay a hand on the other kids. Cassidy had the pressure on her because of her talent, but David seemed real soft on Joe. Maybe it was because Joe was the baby, but he was the only one allowed to be a regular kid. They'd let him bike all around town on his own, go swimming with his friends. I don't think Sloane cared much either way, anyhow. That woman was concerned with dolling herself up, running up her credit card bill, and parading Cassidy around." Marilyn took a small sip from her glass, pushed it away as if bitter. "Who knows what really goes on inside a family? All I know is the little I saw. But if you ask me, the real trouble was between David and Tristan, always had been. When the two of them were in a room together, they didn't hardly speak, but it was like lightning coming, all the time. You didn't want to be there."

Pearl leaned on her elbows. "Did you know they were planning on coming back for Christmas break this year?"

"Nope. Not until two weeks before. Sloane called me, asked if I could get the place spruced up, have somebody deliver a Christmas tree to the parlor."

"Do you have any idea why they decided to come back to Tenney's Harbor?"

"They didn't give me reasons, I didn't ask. Except when I was cleaning the first Sunday they were there, I got the feeling it was the girl's idea. David was going on about the fact they'd come all this way, so Cassidy better enjoy it while it lasted, something like that."

Cassidy's idea. Pearl turned this over in her mind, glancing up when Reese cleared his throat and said, "Do you think Tristan knows who killed them?"

"Couldn't say. But what you asked earlier, if I was surprised when I heard?" Marilyn shook her head. "Something
was going to happen. Sooner or later. I just never thought it'd
be anything so awful as that." She put her hand to her mouth
for a moment, then dropped it. "I never thought anybody'd
end up dead. Especially not them kids."

She walked them out and stood on the front step as they
crossed the yard. "Reese." He looked back. "When you see
that granddaughter of mine, tell her to get her butt out here
more often. Probably been a month since I've seen her."

"Will do." He and Pearl sat together in the car when
Reese said, "She raised her. Indigo."

Pearl looked up, watching as Marilyn went back around
the trailer to her laundry. "Where were her parents?"

"Her dad was never in the picture. Indy lived here with
her mom for a few years, with Marilyn helping them out.
I guess her mom decided she couldn't take it anymore, the
whole mothering thing. She split. Marilyn's been it for Indy
ever since."

Pearl tried to think of something to say to play off her
surprise, but nothing came, so she started the engine, gazing
out the windshield at a single dandelion that had escaped the
blades of the lawn mower. She knew what it was like when a
family split apart. She had no idea how it felt when neither of
your parents wanted you.

* * *

The miniature club was waiting inside the club when they arrived, sitting on a drop-leaf table in the lobby. It sat open on its hinges with the lights on, every tiny replica room flawless and still. The dining room was complete with tables and chairs, white linens, place settings, oil paintings, and potted plants. A miniature piano sat on the stage, the bench pulled out expectantly.

Reese stopped, leaning down to look in. "This is it, huh? Think anybody knows who made it yet?"

"Probably not." Pearl shook her head. "What's it still doing here? Somebody won it in the auction on Friday."

"Maybe they figured out it's haunted and gave it back. Could you sleep with that thing in your house?" Reese bumped her shoulder, his uniform stuffed under his arm as he walked toward the staff restrooms. "See you in there."

"Yeah." She lingered a moment, considering the dollhouse, all the places Cassidy's and Joseph's hands had touched. The tiny wall sconces flickered then, ever so slightly, and she stepped away as if touched by a spark.

Dinner shifts were highly coveted; higher prices on meals and more courses meant, in theory, bigger tips, and management tended to schedule the older servers for the dinner hours, giving the teens and college students breakfast and lunch. A few of those usual servers had requested some days off, so this was the first dinner shift Pearl had been given since

May; she'd almost forgotten the more formal air, and how to make lugging a fifteen-pound serving tray look effortless.

It was a busy night, multiple families dining together, most everyone discussing the ball, who'd worn it best, who'd had too much champagne. Pearl told herself she wasn't looking for him, but in her moments of downtime between delivering salmon Florentine or lemon sorbet, her thoughts were on Tristan. Tristan, an outcast among even his family. Being hit, being made to feel small. It was such a stark contrast to his role among the boys that she almost felt like she had to see him, try to imagine a mark on his face, for it to seem real.

Quinn's and Hadley's families came in together, their mothers chatting as the girls hung back, scanning the crowd much the way Pearl had done all night, searching for the boys. Even after they joined their parents at a table, Quinn's gaze was hot, seeking Pearl across the room and fixing there, accusatory.

While Pearl was filling her tray with drinks, Reese came up beside her. "Hey. Got the skinny on the freaky little house. I guess Mimi bid on it Friday night and then donated it back. Lucky clubsters."

"Oh God. She must've thought she was doing this nice thing."

Reese snorted, heading off in the opposite direction with a stack of menus. Things were like they were supposed to be again, the two of them having each other's backs all shift, checking in with a joke or an eye roll, and her relief was so huge that when she turned from the Stewarts' table to put in their order, she almost missed the person standing close to her, waiting.

Hadley stood in the corridor that led to the patio doors, her face somber, watchful. "Hi." Her voice was barely audible over the din of dining room and kitchen. "Can I talk to you?"

Pearl hesitated. "Just a sec." She pushed through the kitchen doors, put in the order, then stepped into the corridor with her. The question, "How are you feeling?" sounded inadequate after Friday night's ordeal, but it was the best she could come up with.

"Okay. I was pretty much over it by the time Bridges brought me home." Hadley smiled weakly, shrugged. "Once I figured out that I wasn't going to drown in there in the dark and all."

Pearl remembered Hadley's white, stricken face in the flashlight beam, blood streaming from her bare knee, and felt a fresh chill. Saturday morning, she'd had to hide her own sandals in the trash can so Dad wouldn't see them, the pink silk spotted and streaked with water damage and muck. "So, are you never going to speak to them again? Because they deserve it."

"I don't know. Bridges and I already talked a little online." She gave a soft, awkward laugh. "Quinn's the only person I've told. She's really mad." She rubbed her elbow slowly.

"I'm sorry for tweaking out on you. I should've stayed put."

"It's okay. I didn't know what to do, either. It was really scary."

"I don't like small spaces. Bridges knows that. He's known it since we used to go out. We went to the fair together last summer, and there was this fun house. I got scared." She held Pearl's gaze. "That's why I came over. Quinn thinks I'm being stupid, but . . . you should be careful. Bridges would never do something like that to me if Tristan didn't put him up to it. Sometimes I think that's why Tristan chose him as a friend in the first place."

"Because he could control him?"

"Yeah. At least some little part of him."

"Double that for Akil."

"Akil's a jerk. I guess I just wanted Bridges to . . . remember I was around. Stupid, I know. You don't have to tell me." She leaned against the wall so a server could squeeze by. "What I'm trying to say is—I've seen Tristan choose people before. It's like he handpicks them, you know? I think that was what Friday night was really about. You, Pearl. He wants you." From a nearby hidden speaker, Dean Martin began crooning "Memories Are Made of This." "I'm not saying it's a sex thing, because I don't really know. But he looks right through most people. He doesn't look through you." Hadley shrugged, then turned to leave, saying softly, "Watch out for yourself," as she went.

EIGHTEEN

THE CAT WAS gone when Pearl pulled into the driveway that night. Nothing left but a patch of dead grass where it had sat since spring.

Dad wasn't home. He hadn't left a light on for her—somehow, she couldn't believe he'd simply forgotten—and the house was black, a dead cell, making her think of Tristan's home on Narragansett Way.

She slid her hand over the wall until she found the switch, not stepping over the threshold until the familiar glow of the overhead lamp came on. It changed the game, Bridges knowing where she lived. That meant the other boys knew. The three of them might as well share a mind. *He wants you,*

Pearl. She thought of Tristan's jacket lying in a black pool on her floor, covering her ruined pink silk.

TV was no comfort, and she lay on the couch, checking her social media accounts, almost wishing a private message would pop up from Mom. Not tonight. Bridges seemed to be giving her space, and Reese was off-line, didn't respond to the *Hey* text she sent him. Which meant his phone was probably sitting on someone else's nightstand, ignored.

She went to bed, her body programmed to wake to the sounds of Dad coming home in three or four hours, as always.

She awoke a little after seven a.m. The house was silent. Dad's bed hadn't been slept in.

She drove to the Tavern first, which slumped gray and silent in morning fog. She'd thrown on some clothes, hadn't washed her face—she'd been too busy envisioning Dad's truck pinned against a tree, steam rising from the cleaved radiator—and now she sat rigidly in the driver's seat, gaze cutting from side to side, searching.

He wasn't parked in the Tavern lot. Yancey's house was two streets over, and she went there, bracing herself to knock on the door, then pry Dad off the couch in Yancey's house, which smelled of dog and cigar smoke. But the only vehicles in the driveway belonged to Yancey, his wife, and their son Evan, who'd moved back in with them after living in the Midwest for a few years. As she slowed down, she saw Evan sitting in a lawn chair by the side of the house, smoking and staring off, his biceps dark with tattoos.

No sign of Dad. Fear trickled in then, running drop by frozen drop down her spine until she was driving much too fast, going up and down every street, praying Dad was on his way home right now and they'd pass each other any moment.

Pearl checked every public lot, every store that Dad went to, but each was closed and quiet. He was nowhere. Why'd she ever let him get rid of his phone? Of the two of them, he was the one who needed a connection. When she pulled into North Beach, it was because she was out of ideas, and North was the only place she wanted to be until she could fight back her panic. And there was the truck, in the far corner spot, completely alone as it faced the bay.

She parked beside him, saw the vague dark shape of him through the glass. She was about to rap on the window when he looked over at her, blinking as if she'd wakened him, and straightened a little.

Pearl let herself in to sit on the bench seat beside him. The air in the cab was stale, used. "Why didn't you call me?"

Dad shifted, rubbed his eyes with one hand. "It was late. Easier for everybody if I pulled in here."

"I didn't know where you were. I thought something had happened."

He cleared his throat, rolled down the window, and spat. "Well, it didn't. So you can relax."

She worked her jaw, remembering Mom's words: *it's not your job, fixing Dad*. Beyond the windshield, the tide was going out, exposing rocks strung with black seaweed, spotted with lichen. She smelled whiskey, saw the glass bottle sheathed in a paper bag nestled beneath his elbow.

Defeat sucked everything away, all her defenses. At once she was so horribly tired that her voice broke when she said, "We can't keep going like this," not even fully sure what the words meant, just that it was something to say that he couldn't ignore.

Dad propped his elbow on the window casing, squeezing his forehead. "It was one night."

"It's every night. Either you're at the Tavern or drinking yourself to sleep at home, and I'm sick of it." She grabbed for the whiskey protected beneath his arm, succeeded in ripping the bag. "Like *this*. You're seriously drinking from the bottle before eight in the morning? Dad—" She shut her eyes for a moment, exhaling slowly. "What the hell?"

He swallowed, staring at the steering wheel. "I could ask you some questions, too. What the hell have you been doing this summer? You're hardly ever around, and when you are, you're shut up in your room. That Spencer kid comes by the house in his fancy-ass car looking for you, and then Dickie tells me that word is you were at that ball the other night. People saw you, all dressed up. You didn't think I'd find out?"

She closed her eyes, shook her head. "I'm trying to help you."

"How does you running around with some rich summer boy help me? Jesus, Pearl, I thought you were smarter than that. Don't you know this crap has been going on forever? They come up here, use what we got, and then they go home. You think because he tells you you're different, that makes it true?"

"Yeah, Dad, that's it. I'm this pathetic loser now who needs some guy to tell her she's good enough. You figured it out."

"I'm not calling you a loser."

"You're just mad because I brought up the drinking. Period. You never used to care when I went out at night, or who I was with."

"That was before."

Before and *After.* She was sick of the words, fed up with them both for letting their lives be divided that way for so long. "It wasn't your fault that they died, okay?" Her voice was loud, filling the cab. He'd never forgive her for bringing it up in the daylight, when he was mostly sober, but she couldn't stop now. "You didn't kill them. If the people in this town don't get that, then maybe it's time to find another town."

He snorted, looked out the driver's-side window at the deserted stretch of beach. "Right. With what money?"

"I don't *know*, Dad, we'll figure it out. God! It's not like

Tenney's Harbor is the whole world. And you're not the only one who can earn a paycheck, either. I've been doing pretty well for a while now."

"You're talking giving up college? Forget it."

"I'm talking about helping out so it's not all on you, just like I've been doing this whole time. But we can't keep"—frustration bound her tongue for a moment—"bitching about the summer people for things that they can't change, and not doing anything to change ourselves, either. You know? It's stupid, and I won't do it anymore."

Her words were the last sound in the cab for some time. An SUV pulled into the lot; the driver let her golden retriever out of the backseat, tossing a rope toy for it to chase.

When Dad spoke, his voice was hoarse. "I've screwed a lot of things up. I know that. With your mom, and you." His arm twitched by the bottle, fell still. "I don't . . . I'm not sure how . . ." He jerked his chin, blinking, a moistness in his eyes that she'd rarely seen. "Guess I need some help."

Pearl watched him for a moment; then, tentatively, she leaned over and rested her head against his shoulder. On the beach, the dog played in the surf, hunting the rope, which bobbed and rolled, disappearing and reappearing in the waves.

Dinner shift. Indigo was in Pearl's way. She placed slices of the same cheesecake the Davidsons had just ordered from Pearl onto plates, not seeming to notice Pearl's presence until she'd finished. Indigo gave her half a glance and stepped away from the fridge.

Pearl moved in, pulled the plastic wrap from the next cheesecake dish, wondering if she should say something. As if they were friends now because Indigo had made a two-minute phone call to her grandmother. Anything she'd done had been for Reese, who was now out there working the room while Pearl was in the kitchen, angsting about decorum. "Thanks," she finally blurted, keeping her gaze firmly on the pieces she was slicing, "for yesterday. With your grandmother and everything."

She could feel Indigo standing close, watching as Pearl parceled out servings. No mystery where the girl had learned that unreadable quality, the tough shell that deflected countless pickup lines and come-ons from middle-aged men in golfing getups throughout the course of the day. Like it or not, there was no going back to thinking of Indigo as bursting into spontaneous existence just to thwart her; thanks to Marilyn, Pearl knew better. "Reese said you're going after those guys," Indigo said.

It was the first time she'd heard it phrased that way. She stopped, still holding the pie server. "Yeah, I am."

Indigo picked up her tray, balanced it, and said, "Good," before heading back out the swinging kitchen doors, prep cooks and dishwashers nearly knocking heads as they turned to watch her leave.

★ ★ ★

At closing, Pearl went out to look at the little club again. Someone had added a display of photographs from the ball, and there was a filigreed sign on a stand advertising the upcoming charity golf tournament, the last hurrah of the centennial celebration before July faded into August.

Knowing Meriwether, she was keeping a keen eye on the club's latest prize, so Pearl leaned close but didn't touch, examining each room. The amount of money and time required to make such a thing, haunted or not, was boggling. The attic even had stacks of little cardboard storage boxes, large enough to hold maybe a cotton ball, and furniture odds and ends. All the drapes in the house looked handmade, and Pearl tried to imagine Cassidy's fingers making the tiny stitches, sinking the needle, tugging thread through cloth. Controlling a small world because her own had become uncontrollable. But why the club? Why not her own house, or something generic, where she could decide for herself how things should look?

Pearl's phone vibrated in her pocket, and she pulled it out without taking her eyes from the house, assuming it was Reese back in the dining room, sending her some ridiculous emoji. Instead, it was a text from a number she didn't recognize, caller unknown.

Do you run?

It took her a second to catch the meaning, to understand

who she was talking to. *Only when chased.*

That can be arranged.

Biting the inside of her cheek, she hurried back through the deserted dining room, chairs upturned on tables, floor damp from mopping. *Bridges must be handing out my number. Nice.*

A pause. *Ocean Ave in an hour. If you can keep up.*

Pearl looked around the kitchen, but Reese wasn't among the last of the kitchen help stripping off aprons or punching their time cards. She made it outside in time to see the passenger door of the Skylark closing, and the red flash of brake lights as Indigo headed off down the drive.

It was nine thirty when Pearl got home. Dad wasn't there, although this time he'd left a lamp on for her and a tinfoil-covered dinner plate in the fridge. After their talk this morning, she'd seen him off to work, shaky but fueled up on triple-strength coffee and what little breakfast she'd been able to push on him. There'd been no further discussion of laying off the drinking or steering clear of the Tavern; they were beyond that now. She was scared for him, and he didn't know how to stop. At least they knew where they stood.

Her body was restless, and she picked at her food, glancing over at her phone. Who knew what was really waiting for her on Ocean—another hazing, another test to see how far she'd go? She'd be crazy to show up. But he'd challenged her. And she had to know what he had planned.

She dressed in mesh shorts and a white T-shirt, hoping for some visibility in the headlights, then drove to Ocean. It was nearly ten o'clock, and the streets had quieted considerably. She was so busy looking for his car that she hardly registered the shape that ran by, dressed in dark clothing, unconcerned with being seen. Pearl parked and got out, watching as Tristan slowed and turned, jogging back to where she stood. "You ran here?" she said.

"It's not that far." He took a few backward steps. "Are you coming?"

"I don't know. Is this when Akil and Bridges throw a bag over my head and push me into traffic or something?"

"They're not here. I don't run with them."

"But you'll run with me. Why should I go anywhere with you? You put Hadley and me through hell Friday night."

"But you're here now. You came. Why not run?"

He was leaving now, and she followed, slowly at first, then picking up speed when she saw that he'd be gone in a minute if she didn't. Pearl rarely exercised on purpose, and her body was unaccustomed to the staccato pounding of her sneakers on pavement, the shock each step sent through her frame.

Tristan could've left her behind easily, but instead, he slowed his stride enough so that she could stay with him, while still having to push herself harder than she had in a long time. They crossed the street to Forest Drive and continued uphill, breathing together, running through pools of orange arc sodium streetlight glow.

Soon, she could focus on nothing but the fight to fill her lungs. As they reached Route 3 and left the sidewalk, her thighs burned. They ran in the breakdown lane with the guardrail to their right, cars passing close enough to whip their clothes with hot, forced air. The test was not to give in, not to beg for a break or even ask where they were going. To follow on faith.

Between passing cars, the darkness was almost complete. Only Tristan's footsteps and measured breathing assured her that she hadn't strayed into the northbound lane. A bank of streetlights appeared ahead: the scenic turnoff, where tourists could pull in and take pictures of Tenney's Harbor embroidering the edge of the bay below. Tristan jogged in. As soon as Pearl saw that he was really stopping, she dropped heavily onto one of the granite boulders lined up along the ledge.

He watched her gasp for a bit, said, "You shouldn't double over. You'll get cramps."

She leaned back, bracing herself on the heels of her palms. "At least . . . pretend to be tired."

Eventually, he sat on the rock beside her, waiting as she slowly got her breath back. "So, this is what you do," she said, looking at him. "Run up here. Even in the middle of the night."

"Sometimes. I have other places I go."

"It's got to be dangerous. Somebody could hit you."

Tristan said nothing. "Unless that's what you're hoping for."

He stood, stretching his quads, bouncing on the balls of his feet a few times, as if she'd never spoken. "We can take the shortcut down Pleasant Street on the way back."

She forced a laugh. "Going easy on me now?" Pearl watched as he took off across the highway without glancing in either direction, blending into the night before she'd even taken her first step.

This time, he didn't hold back. He put so much distance between them that Pearl lost sight of him completely, running down Pleasant Street alone, wondering how this was a shortcut, until she saw Narragansett Way ahead, the streetlamp globes gleaming whitely up the slope. She slowed to a walk, unsure what the next challenge was—go back to her car, dismissed for having the bad taste to point out his recklessness, or follow him. Ultimately, she followed, making her way to his front walk. She'd chosen well: tonight, the light was burning over the entrance.

She knocked. He opened the door, stepping away without a word. His hair was soaked with sweat, dark stains down the front and back of his T-shirt. Pearl took her sneakers off, aligning them on the mat next to his; it was the kind of place that demanded right angles and exactness. The kitchen had the look of a professionally cleaned space, recessed lighting gleaming off stainless steel and white tile. There was nothing on the walls, no decoration of any kind, only a row of stools along the granite-topped island to provide seating. Their equidistance from each other suggested they were never used.

He leaned into the fridge and tossed her a bottled water, drinking from his own as she looked around.

"I like your place." She wandered down the hall toward the living room, which was almost empty except for a wall-mounted flat-screen TV and a black leather recliner. She fiddled with the cap on her bottle. "I guess you didn't have much to move in."

"There was nothing left." He followed her at a distance, silhouetted by the kitchen light. "During the fire . . . the attic floor collapsed."

Pearl bit her lips together, picturing it, bedroom furniture and personal possessions dropping into the flames devouring the second floor, a pit where his loft used to be. She searched for another topic. "Hadley's doing okay now. In case you were wondering."

"I wasn't. But thanks for the update."

"What's your problem with her?"

"I don't have a problem. She isn't interesting enough to earn that." He finished his water and took the bottle to the counter, talking as he went. "Hadley is the kind of person whose entire existence is dependent on other people. She has that symbiotic friendship with Quinn. She was the same way with Bridges when they were together. Attached."

"Maybe she loved him. Ever think of that?" She watched

Tristan return in the distorted reflection of the flat-screen, his likeness stretched and skeletal, hers impossibly wide. "Maybe she and Quinn are close. Haven't you ever felt that way about anybody?"

After a moment, he said quietly, "Not really."

"You've never had a best friend?" Still he said nothing, and she turned to him. "A girl. One girl you cared about."

"I've managed to avoid it."

"Why?"

"I don't think I need to explain. I think you already know." His gaze moved to her face. "Sometimes . . . it's better not to engage. Cleaner. Isn't it?"

She swallowed, and her throat still felt dry, like there wasn't enough water to quench this. "Maybe. But sometimes you can't help it."

There was nothing, then, but the faint hum of appliances, the house living around them, and Tristan's dark eyes, intent, but not as piercing as she'd thought, not cold. Her voice seemed to come from deep down inside her, faint and hoarse. "If you wake up tonight, don't go for another run. It's too much. You're pushing yourself too hard."

"I don't know what else to do."

She had some idea what it cost him, admitting helplessness. She remembered the sounds of the traffic up on the highway, the blinding headlights. Her hands found the back of the chair, squeezing. "Don't go."

He was quiet, gazing at her. "Maybe, tonight, I won't need to." He crossed the room toward her. "Maybe, tonight, I won't wake up." His hip grazed hers as he passed, leaving her rigid, barely breathing, as she listened to his footsteps go into the next room. A few moments later, there came the sound of water pounding from a showerhead.

Gradually, her grip relaxed, leaving finger imprints in the leather. Her breathing was shallow. She didn't know what to do with herself in the quiet, so she went back to the kitchen, setting her water bottle on the counter, opening and closing her hands as she walked, thoughts moving at light speed, too fast for her to catch hold of.

The hallway around the corner was dark, and she hit the switch. His bedroom was down here—the house had a full second floor, but it didn't surprise her that he wanted to sleep on the ground level, close to a way out—and she stood, pulse throbbing as she looked at the king-size bed, nothing on the walls but one framed Ansel Adams print of a pine forest in the snow.

The room across the hall looked like it was meant to be used as a study or sitting room, but it had no furniture in it, only some cardboard cartons stacked along the wall. There was a faint, acrid smell here, one the housekeeper hadn't been able to erase, and Pearl went back to the kitchen, then the living room, where water still rained against the other side of the wall.

There was light, and she stepped closer. He'd left the bathroom door open.

She could see him in there, behind the translucent curtain. The shade of his skin, the darkness of his hair. Her body seemed to be nothing but heartbeat now.

His hands rose, smoothing through his hair, rinsing shampoo. In her mind's eye, she saw her feet crossing the tiles. Felt the steam gauzing moistly over her face, the plastic curtain in her fingers as she drew it back.

Something jarred her—a distant car horn, maybe, down on Ocean. She still stood in the doorway, six feet from the shower and the shape of him, the suggestion of the open door. He reached down and turned off the faucet.

Pearl left the house, shutting the front door gently behind her, breathing deeply of the night air. She walked back to Ocean, and her car. Tristan was right. It wasn't far.

NINETEEN

THE NEXT DAY, Reese met Pearl at the picnic table on their last fifteen-minute break, plunking down on the bench beside her, phone in hand. "Go. I want updates."

"I went to Tristan's place last night."

He stared. "No shit. Inside the lair. Did he have mirrors on the ceiling and a vampire harem?"

"Shut up, or I tell you nothing."

He made a *get on with it* gesture and she dove in, telling him everything but how the night had really ended, or of the feelings she could barely sort through herself.

She could've stayed. The invitation had been there, and it had kept her up much of the night, watching the clock as the midnight hour passed, wondering if, across town, Tristan had woken up yet. The knowledge that she could've been there, in that bed, acting as his anchor, left her hot, restless, kicking the sheets off and then tugging them back up again. She should feel one way about it—know her own mind—but confusion was the only constant that carried her through till morning. The whole thing seemed ludicrous now, in the daylight, with Reese here, like a fragment from a dream.

"But I realized what the smell was. Smoke"—she watched as Reese's thumbs moved over the screen; she could never tell if he was texting or gaming—"coming from those boxes in the spare room. There was some powerful mildew, too. Definitely more stuff from the house."

Reese's thumbs stopped. "He actually went inside?"

"He must've. Nothing stored in the garage would smell that strong."

"That is messed *up*. He's hanging out where his family got torched."

"Well . . . he lived there, too. Maybe he's looking for anything he can save. He said that the floor of his room collapsed and he lost everything."

"Right. Because who wouldn't want souvenirs from the Garrison family barbecue? Isn't this the same guy who auctioned off his folks' stuff?"

"Then maybe it's more like . . . he's looking for something specific. He didn't find it in the boxes in the garage, so he gave those things away." She thought back to the times she'd seen Tristan alone. On almost every occasion, he'd had a searching air about him. In the boathouse; combing through Joseph's beach playhouse.

"Maybe he's trying to find his one-of-a-kind mono-grammed cigarette lighter before the cops do."

Pearl let a snort of laughter escape. "You know he didn't do it. He was up at Sugarloaf. They proved it."

"Well, what, then? And if you say his baby pictures, I swear to God, I'm gonna heave."

She rested her chin on her folded arms. "I don't know what it is." She looked at Reese. "Do you think he's trying to figure out who killed them, too?"

"If he is, it sounds like he's got a pretty good idea where to start looking. And he's not sharing with the cops."

They sat, listening to sounds carrying over from the pool, splashing and children's laughter. Reese's phone chirped, and Pearl watched him navigate who knew how many browser windows at once. "So. How's the apartment hunt going?"

Reese didn't look up. "I've got a line on something."

"Here in town?"

"Yeah."

"Oh. Good." She tried not to show how relieved she was; there wasn't much in the way of year-round housing in Tenney's Harbor, where landlords could charge three times normal rates for a summer rental. "Sure you can afford it?"

He looked at her from under his brows, and she held up her hands. "Okay. You're the king of tips. All hail Reese."

"Damn straight." He stuck the phone in his pocket and stood, giving her a shot in the arm. "Time's up. Let's roll."

The boys came in later, sitting in the same formation they had on that first day: Tristan close to the lobby exit, Akil in the middle, Bridges with his back to the room. They were seated in the section nearest the patio doors, and Pearl was glad for the distance, keeping her head down, trying to kill the final ten minutes of her shift without having to face Tristan so soon after last night.

At one point, when she came out of the kitchen, she couldn't avoid Bridges's gaze. He smiled, waved a little; Akil continued sucking down his iced coffee, ignoring her. They didn't know about her visit to Tristan's house. Akil would be smirking and whispering, and Bridges—the guilt hit her, then, with unexpected force—would probably be too angry to look at her. Apparently, the flow of gossip only went one way in their group.

Tristan watched her for a moment, then went back to pushing the food around his plate. She couldn't guess at what he was feeling, but for her part, she was right back in that moment, faced with the open door again, the big bed in the dark, spartan room. And the choice still seemed impossible.

She punched out, left by the back way. Knowing she was

taking a chance, she texted Tristan. *Sorry about last night.* She hesitated. *It seemed like a good time to leave.*

There was a long pause; she was in her car with the engine running before his response popped up, maybe waiting for a moment when Akil wasn't right by his side: *I wish you'd stayed.*

The woods surrounding the Garrison house were thick with life, birdsong, the lush green overgrowth of summer.

Pearl had left her car parked on the Cove Road turnaround again and walked in, in case Tristan should show up. A squirrel chittered at her as she approached the fence and wrapped her hands around the bars, looking up at the house with its burn scars and socketed windows.

She walked aimlessly, lost in thought, running her fingers along the bars until she reached the front gate. It was massive, like the entrance to the Emerald City. Nobody else had security like this on Millionaires' Row—fences, yes, alarm systems, but not a fortress. What, or who, had the Garrisons been so worried about keeping out, right from the first day they moved to Tenney's Harbor?

Pearl rattled the gate on a whim. It moved, sliding a few inches forward over the grass. Surprised, she shoved harder, then walked the gate open wide enough to slip through.

Tristan had left it unlocked with the same half awareness that allowed him to leave keys in ignitions and hundred-thousand-dollar boats floating at deserted island docks. Knew he'd left it open, but couldn't be bothered to retrace his steps and remedy it. Even from here, she could see the big black combination lock hanging from the front door handle, the signs declaring private property.

She followed the walk, grass and weeds creeping up through the slate slabs. She imagined Bridges's and Akil's feet passing this way, sometimes Hadley's, sometimes Quinn's, when the house was still pristine New England white from foundation to eaves, the clapboards touched up by Dad's paint roller each spring. Imagined music pounding from inside and silhouettes passing by the silk drapes on the nights when Tristan had thrown his epic parties, inviting the rest of the summer kids to tear the place down.

Some of the blinds were missing from the kitchen windows, and she cupped her hands against the glass, peering in, a little apprehensive about what she might see. Cupboards, marble countertops, a stainless-steel fridge twice the width of their Kenmore at home. Cream-colored floor tiles smeared with ash, which someone had made a halfhearted attempt to sweep up. A few grim artifacts: a cup and bowl on the draining board, a cardigan hanging from a hook by the side door.

Pearl dragged over a planter to use as a step stool to see into the parlor. A Christmas tree stand lay on its side in the corner—of course, the ten-foot balsam would've been there, framed in the three-paned bay window, probably with white lights and carefully coordinated ornaments; no construction-paper-and-glitter creations from childhood like the kind Dad faithfully hung on their tree each year. There was a bald rectangle above the mantel and another on the floor, where a painting and throw rug had been removed. Through the doorway on the right, the base of the center stairway was visible. The steps were blackened, strewn with ash and chunks of plaster.

She climbed down and walked the circumference of the house, looking up at the bare second-story windows, most of them smoked dark, like the glass panel in a gas boiler. She remembered from the *Time* article diagram that Cassidy's room was adjacent to her parents', with an arched window that looked out over the backyard and woods.

The window was directly above her now, and Pearl stopped, looking up. Like the rest, the glass was cloudy and streaked, but she imagined it having lace curtains before, maybe a window seat beneath. She took a few steps, and sunlight bounced off the panes, vanished, flashed again. Like a signal. A beacon saying *look at me*.

She stood there, reminded of another flashing light, a flicker, really, one she'd pushed from her thoughts as residue from Reese's talk of hauntings. Another signal. Maybe.

Pearl went back around the house and replaced the planter, making sure she hadn't left any sign of her presence before dragging the gate shut behind her and heading for the trees, faster and faster, until she was running. She had her phone to her ear before she even made it back to the car, relieved when Reese picked up after only two rings.

"I think I know where to look."

TWENTY

"HOW MUCH TIME do you think you'll need?"

"I don't know. Probably not a whole hour?" Pearl saw the look on Reese's face and tossed her hands up. It was the next night, and the dining room and the start of their dinner shift waited beyond the kitchen doors, strains of Steve Mills singing "When Sunny Gets Blue" rising over the current of conversation. "Well, there are a lot of rooms. And I don't know what I'm looking for."

"But you'll know it when you see it, huh?" When she shrugged, he sighed, glancing over at the rear entrance to the kitchen. "How sure are you about this?"

"It's a feeling. I'm going to do it either way. You don't have to help."

"Haskins, I'm helping. You're the one who actually cares about keeping her job here." He took her shoulders and steered her ahead of him, massaging her like a fighter. "If Meriwether comes sniffing around, I'll give her an ankle to chew on until you're clear. Sound good?"

"Thanks, Reese. I mean it."

He split off from her, and the evening began, passing far too quickly, the hours slipping through her fingers as she greeted and served and cleared away, nervous energy propelling her toward what was easily one of the craziest things she'd ever done.

At nine o'clock closing time, Pearl wiped down her section, topped off the salt and pepper shakers, and made a pretense of counting her tips as the other servers prepared to go home. Then, grabbing her bag, she went to the staff restrooms, chose a stall, and climbed up on the toilet tank, where her feet couldn't be seen beneath the door.

The restroom had already been cleaned for the night, and everything was damp, smelling of bleach. She closed her eyes, listening to the distant sound of footsteps, the occasional laugh carrying from the kitchen. Overhead, the energy-saver sensor light turned off, leaving her in blackness.

Eventually, all sound stopped. Pearl shifted on the cold porcelain, checking the time on her phone. Nearly a quarter to ten. Everybody must be out by now. She slid down, making the light blink on again, and went to the door, peering out.

The sconces in the corridor were still on. She had no idea whose job it was to make sure all the lobby lights were off at night, but generally everybody who worked the front desk and office was gone by five o'clock. Except sometimes salaried employees, like Meriwether.

With that, there were footsteps, and Pearl jerked back through the doorway, forcing the slow-close door shut with her hip. Light, quick steps across the hardwood, joined by others, and Meriwether's voice rang out in the silence. "Mr. O'Shaughnessy? Can I help you?"

"Not unless you've got my car keys." Reese spoke in the usual bored monotone he used with the assistant manager. "Can't find them anywhere."

A short, tense sigh. "I haven't seen any keys. It's way past closing time, so I suggest you call someone for a ride."

"I can't just leave my car here. Look, they're around somewhere—I went to the bathroom during my break, so maybe—"

"No one is supposed to be back here." Pearl pictured the telltale vein standing out in Meriwether's brow. "You already have one write-up. It would be wise not to push it. If you don't have a phone handy, use the lobby line."

"Okay, okay." Reese muttered something more under his breath.

"What did you say?" The silence stretched on, so long that Pearl strained her ears, wondering what she was missing.

Then it hit her: the restroom was still bathed in light; the motion sensor hadn't timed out yet. Meriwether could be staring at the strip of light beneath the door right now.

Pearl shoved the manual switch over, sending the room into darkness again. The moment stretched on—then Meriwether said, "I asked you to repeat yourself."

"I said, yeah, I've got a phone. Right here, see?"

"Very impressive. Use it outside in the parking lot."

Pearl listened as their footsteps left together; there was no way Meriwether could resist seeing him to the door to make sure he obeyed. Sagging against the wall, Pearl waited. A few minutes later, Meriwether's footsteps passed by again, and the corridor light disappeared from the space beneath the restroom door.

She didn't poke her head out again until she absolutely couldn't stand it anymore. There was a faint reddish glow spilling over the floor from the lobby exit sign; everything else was dark and silent. Go time.

In the lobby, the little club was an angular shadow outlined by the streetlamp beyond the front windows. After some fumbling, she found the hidden switch behind the house that turned on the lights, wincing at the brightness. Somebody might see from the road—better work fast.

She moved the furniture around, looking under tables and chairs, taking down paintings, tipping over divans. Nothing behind the curtains, or inside the attic storage boxes.

Cupboards, drawers, hutches, all matches or near matches to the real thing, placed exactly so—she shook them, knocked them over in her haste.

Finally, Pearl sat back, gripping her knees, barely resisting the desire to trash the inside for the sheer satisfaction of it. She took the sides of the house in her hands—it was heavy, she could barely manage it—and tilted the entire thing back and forth, shaking it, looking for any confirmation of what she'd seen.

The lights flickered. She shook the house again; another flicker. There was a short somewhere. She reached around and followed the electrical wire that fed into the house; it disappeared under the floor of the ballroom. She leaned into the room as far as she could, running her fingertips over the floor and wall, searching for anything.

The seam in the wallpaper at the far-left corner of the room felt deep; she could fit her fingernails into it. The slice went all the way through the board behind the paper. She continued to pull, waiting to hear a crack, destruction that she'd never be able to repair—but the wall panel came away without much resistance.

She pulled it as far away from the outer wall of the house as she dared, providing a space of about three inches. The house had been hooked up using tape wiring, nearly microscopic brads holding it in place. She couldn't see well enough into the space to tell much, so she wriggled her fingers in, sliding them up and down the walls.

Something small and metallic lay in the space between. She flicked it, watched it skitter out onto the ballroom floor.

A set of keys. Two identical silver keys on a wire ring, the sort that might come with a padlock. Wedged in there for who knew how long, aggravating the junction splice, causing a short.

Breathless, Pearl grabbed them, stuffed them into her pocket, and began the painstaking task of setting things to rights.

Some of it she could do from memory—she knew the layout of the dining room and surrounding areas by heart, but there were two other floors that she never had any reason to go onto. She ended up putting tea tables and bookshelves back in any random place, anxious to get out of the silence and artificial glow of the little club. Maybe the desk staff would think somebody's kid got into it earlier in the day and moved things around.

She eased out the front exit, heard the lock click behind her, and ran for the staff parking lot. She was digging for her car keys when a set of headlights flashed on across from her, high, then low.

Her breath caught. The car's engine started, and it crawled into the spot beside her. Thank God. Reese's old clunker.

She got into the passenger seat, sighed, and rolled her neck, which felt like it had a couple of steel rods jammed up through it. "Who'd you think I was, the po-po?" he said around a mouthful of candy bar. "Looked like you were passing a stone out there."

"How'd you get around Meriwether?"

"*Pssh*. As soon as she knew I couldn't get back inside to steal the silver or whatever, she took off in her Mini Cooper. So? Find anything?"

She held up the keys, glinting in the dashboard light. "Behind one of the walls."

Reese swore. "You were right." A pause. "You think Cassidy put them there?"

"Or Joseph. If this is what Tristan was looking for, he missed the flickering lights. You couldn't even tell that the wall had been cut into. They must've used an X-Acto knife or something."

He took the keys from her. "Okay. Now riddle me this. What do they go to?"

"Good question. A small lock, obviously. A locker padlock? A diary?"

"Diaries come with locks?"

"Must be a girl thing." Pearl sat back. "This is too strange. It's like I was meant to find them." She shot a look at him. "I know how crazy that sounds."

Reese shook his head slowly. "I'm not laughing. I think this whole thing is freaky as hell."

From the corner of her eye, Pearl noticed more clutter in

the backseat than usual, and she turned to look at cardboard boxes full of Reese's things. "You're moving already?" She looked at him. "Why didn't you say anything? I didn't even know you'd signed a lease yet."

"Everything happened kind of fast." He crumpled the candy bar wrapper and stuck it in the cup holder, wiping his fingers on his work slacks. "Jovia isn't thrilled, but she's being cool about it. She's helping us hunt down some extra furniture and stuff."

"Us?"

Reese paused. "Indigo and me." He didn't hold her gaze long. "Her roommate's finally going to move in with her boyfriend. Indigo needs help with the rent, and I need a change. Makes sense."

Maybe she should've seen it coming. Hearing it spoken out loud still felt like falling way, way down into a place with no light. Pearl tried to get her bearings, but her voice sounded odd, unfamiliar, as she said, "I didn't think you guys were that serious."

He shrugged, half smiling. "We're going to give it a shot. Never know until you try, right?"

She was supposed to laugh here, to agree and turn the conversation onto lighter things, but she couldn't. Couldn't force another word from her mouth as she sat there, feeling sucker punched, tasting a memory of rum eggnog and humiliation, hearing the whisper *everything you hoped for, sweetie?* as her eyes burned with tears.

He still held the keys. Pearl took them back, grabbed her bag. "I better get home. Dad will be wondering." And now she'd just told a lie to Reese, who knew better and made a soft sound.

"Pearl, come on. Don't run off."

"I'm not. Thanks. For tonight." Her voice broke at the end, but she was halfway out the door and hoped he hadn't caught it. She got into her car, keeping her face averted as she started the engine. She was glad when he left first, so she could sit for a minute and let her vision blur, feel some release before making the drive home through the rows of quiet, sleeping houses.

TWENTY-ONE

IT WAS A relief when they weren't on the next afternoon,
Reese and Indigo. Pearl didn't mind the solitude in a crowd
this time, spending most of her shift in her head—so long as
she didn't have to see them together.

She'd lost him. No wonder Indigo had been so willing
to help with Marilyn, had even spoken a few words to Pearl
in the kitchen the other day. Not hard to be magnanimous
when you knew you'd won. Pearl had known frustration and
jealousy during this cold war, but never grief like this. It
dragged her around by the collar all day, catching her up,
jerking her back whenever her mind strayed too far from the
nagging ache that was Reese belonging to Indigo, no longer
being the person Pearl could call, day or night, no matter

what. Because he'd be sharing a bed, making a home.

There were the keys, of course. Pearl had those. She kept expecting Meriwether to call an emergency staff meeting and announce that there'd been a break-in and a case of doll-house molestation, but nothing happened. Apparently, the little club had become a part of the scenery already, and no one was looking closely at the rooms anymore.

On her lunch break, Pearl took the keys from where she'd stashed them—the coin purse in her wallet—and went through the lobby as though she were on official business, keeping her gaze trained away from the front desk in case Meriwether was lurking.

The fitness center was packed, the room filled with hard breathing, the sound of bodies pounding against machines. Pearl went past the desk with a smile at the attendant and headed straight for the women's locker room, hoping she looked like she knew what she was doing. They'd all gotten the lecture about using member facilities without a guest pass, so this had better be in-and-out—sooner or later, somebody would put a bug in management's ear, and Pearl would be the one getting a write-up.

The showers were all in use, women changing and stretching in the locker area, giving her a few glances as she picked a locker at random and, hoping the owner wasn't around to see, tried the key in the padlock hanging from the hasp. The key was too small, all the wrong shape. She looked down the line, saw a row of identical padlocks, standard Yales distributed by the club.

Next was the cabana house, poolside. She walked down the line of sunbathers, keeping her eyes on the concrete, hoping Quinn wouldn't appear and rip into her about the cave and Hadley, as if Pearl were the boys' keeper or something.

The cabana snack stand had a line around the corner, and Pearl ducked between members to get into the changing area, trying to see around the traffic coming and going from the stalls to where the lockers were. More Yale locks. Strike two.

Her phone vibrated as she let herself out into the sunshine. Incoming text: *I can c u.* Bridges.

She glanced around, spotted him sitting in a chaise lounge across the pool from her, shirtless, wearing board shorts and sunglasses. Akil sat beside him, eyes closed, earbuds in. She went over, aware that she was sweating through her uniform blouse, that every other girl nearby wore a bikini or a skimpy cover-up.

Bridges drew himself up, taking off his sunglasses. "I called you last night."

"I know. Sorry. I fell asleep really early." She'd stayed awake until one, eyes swollen and red, checking her phone now and then to see if a new text might pop up from Tristan. None had. "How's the water?"

"Awesome. Can you stay? It's too nice out to be stuck inside."

"You should tell my supervisor. I'm sure she'll go for it."

"Listen. When's your next day off?"

"Tomorrow."

"Come by the cottage. I can show you our beach, take you around the place. The estate's a lot bigger than it looks from the road."

"Okay. I'll be there." She could see a hint of a smirk playing around Akil's lips as he pretended not to listen, probably thinking that she was clueless about what it really meant for a girl to go to Bridges's cottage. At least Tristan had been up front with her about it; she wanted to ask where he was today, but she didn't trust her own poker face, didn't want Bridges reading too much into the question. It worried her, the thought of Tristan alone, nothing to distract him from whatever heat-warped film reel played in his head as night approached.

She walked across the golf course to meet Dad at the end of the day. They'd rode in together earlier, but this time she didn't have to hunt him down. He was with the other groundskeepers, locking up the outbuildings for the night. He squeezed her around the shoulders as she came up beside him.

They drove most of the way home in silence before she asked, "Have you thought any more about what I said?" Her gaze was on his hands. They were trembling slightly. "You know . . . about maybe moving off MDI?"

After the other morning, she thought he might bark at her, but all he did was turn the radio down. "I've thought about it. I don't know. I guess I thought you might not want to leave. This is your home, too."

Pearl thought of Reese, the backseat of his car packed with boxes, and the grief grabbed hold again. "I don't care," she said quietly, and Dad didn't ask any questions.

They ate, Dad having a cup of coffee with his meal, adjusting the mug on the place mat enough times that Pearl could practically feel the need burning in him, the willpower it took for him not to look at the fridge, where the better part of a six-pack waited. She was clearing away their plates when she finally worked up the nerve to say, "You don't have to stop on your own, you know."

His hand reached out, covered hers. "I'm not on my own."

"I went online. There's an AA group that meets in the basement of the Congregational Church every week. Maybe you could check it out."

"Maybe." Then his touch returned to the coffee mug, and she went to the sink, where late-day sunlight filtered in the window at eye level and she could see nothing of the outside.

It wasn't easy, deciding to go see Reese. She mulled it over for a couple of hours; what she really wanted to do was hang around her room feeling sorry for herself, but she kept remembering last night, how he'd asked her not to run off and she had anyway. Not much better than giving him the silent treatment. She didn't want to go back to that.

It was harder to leave Dad, who she knew must be fighting a battle not to go to the Tavern; it'd be easier for him if she was here. "I won't be late," she said, but he waved her off, settling back to watch the six o'clock news with yet another cup of coffee.

She drove to the carriage house, wondering how it would feel to find the place empty and dark, Reese already relocated to the second-story apartment downtown with bedsheets tacked up in the windows. She let herself in and went up the stairs, knocking once on the door out of habit, not expecting a response.

Footsteps crossed to the door, and Indigo stood there. She was barefoot, dressed in a paisley halter top and denim skirt, her earrings heavy silver hoops.

It took Pearl a moment to speak. "Can I talk to Reese?" Asking her permission was like forcing bits of broken glass up her throat.

"He isn't here. He's moving some stuff into the apartment." Indigo stepped back from the door, gesturing over her shoulder. "He should be back pretty soon."

Pearl hesitated in the doorway. Reese's mattress and his plastic drawers were still there; Indigo was emptying his clothes into a cardboard box. Pearl nearly turned and left then, but the thought of the keys in her wallet made her step over the threshold. Indigo didn't look back, but Pearl could sense the girl's awareness of her. "So, when did you guys decide to do this?"

"About a week ago."

Pearl looked around the room, realizing that she'd probably never have reason to come up here again after tonight. "Big change."

Indigo snorted softly, dropped a flannel shirt into the box. "He'll leave his toothbrush at my place now. That'll be different."

"I meant for me." But she hadn't intended to say it aloud. Showing her vulnerability to Indigo—that had to be setting the bar for stupidity.

The girl was quiet, didn't take her shot; too easy, probably. Pearl cleared her throat and took a chance. "The other day, when you asked me if I was going after those guys, you said 'good.' Can I ask what happened there?"

Indigo shook out a pair of Reese's jeans, refolded them. "I help my grandmother clean sometimes. I met them . . . started getting invites to the parties and stuff." She shrugged. "I know how they are, that's all."

"Doesn't sound like a glowing review."

Indigo looked back at her. "You're telling me you haven't gotten a taste of that yet?" Her eye shadow was bronze, drawn into faint Cleopatra tilts at the outer corners of the lids. "Those guys don't let a girl hang around unless they think they're going to get something out of it."

Almost word-for-word what Reese had said that first day at Dark Brew. "Any particular guy, or all three?" Indigo kept packing. Pearl tried again, her voice loud in the nearly empty room. "I've been trying to figure some things out. Like . . . I'll think I get how they operate—alpha and omega dog and everything—but then they'll do something that totally blows all that away."

"Tristan's not the only one with a mind of his own, if that's what you mean."

"I don't know. I guess I was hoping you could tell me."

Indigo taped the box top, breathing out. "Look. In the off-season, I work with Marilyn most mornings. Earn a little extra. I've been in all their houses—Spencers, Malhotras, Garrisons. I've seen enough to know that Tristan doesn't control everything."

"Were you there this December?" She nodded. "Was something weird going on?"

She laughed shortly. "No. Pretty typical. Screwing and lying."

"You mean Sloane and David?"

"I mean at the Spencers'." She crossed her arms, meeting Pearl's gaze. "We were cleaning the cottages. Nobody was supposed to be in the last one. No flags out front, right? But I thought I saw—I looked in the window." She stopped. "Cassidy was in there. Not with Akil." She glanced down. "If you want more than that, ask Bridges yourself. I'm done with them. I'm not getting in the middle."

"Bridges was in town at Christmastime?" Indigo stared back. A tingling numbness spread through Pearl, as if from a loss of circulation. "But—" But now the clues were there, standing out in red as the rest of the summer faded to sepia tone. Bridges, defending Cassidy for using Akil. *Lots of guys would've traded places.* How he'd described her that morning on Little Nicatou. *She needed somebody to look out for her.*

Pearl stepped back, the numbness now a stinging sensation, as if she'd been scrubbed raw and splashed with salt spray. She had to get out of here, hide her stupid stunned face. Indigo was still watching her, arms at her sides, and now, with her own vulnerability showing, Pearl could almost hear herself saying it—*those guys . . . they said everybody knows you from the parties*—asking the question that might finally let her see the truth in Indigo's eyes: if she was the nameless townie who'd been passed around the party and then the web, who'd become just another broken link once somebody finally had the decency to take her down. Even as the words formed themselves, Pearl knew she'd never ask them. Because the idea of having leverage over Indigo was an illusion. If she was the girl from the video, chances were, Reese already knew about it.

"Tell him I stopped by, okay?" Pearl turned away.

Indigo's voice stopped her at the door. "You've got nothing to worry about, you know." Pearl looked back, saw her sitting on the bed, hair hanging over one shoulder, her gaze cool again. "You and Reese. Nothing's going to change." A slight shrug. "You're his best friend."

TWENTY-TWO

THE WIND WAS high the next day, the sky pale blue, full of fast-moving clouds.

Pearl drove to the Spencer compound. She went down the road to the cottages, parking at the last one, the flags whipping and snapping on the pole. She didn't wait for a response to her knock before letting herself in.

Bridges was making breakfast. Granola and a pitcher of milk sat on the island; some housekeeper or other minion had delivered a fresh carafe of coffee. Most of him was hidden by the fridge door, and he straightened up, surprised. "Whoa. Is it ten thirty already?"

It was barely nine. After a night of fractured anxiety

dreams, and a restless morning of watching the clock after Dad left for work, she couldn't wait anymore. She wanted the words out of her, the weight of them gone. "Why didn't you tell me you were in town when the Garrisons were killed?"

He straightened slowly, his arm still resting across the top of the fridge door. He wore a white undershirt, blue plaid boxers. He set a little sterling silver pot of cream down beside the carafe. "What?"

"You were here. On the night before Christmas Eve."

Bridges didn't move. "Who told you that?"

"So you admit it."

He laughed, a strained sound, shoving his hair back from his face as he added cream to his mug, wiping a drop off the counter. "Well, it's not like it's a secret. I didn't lie to you."

She shut her eyes for a moment. "How could you not say anything?"

"Because. I didn't think it was important, I guess. My family visits Gramps for the holidays every other year. I talked to the cops when they interviewed everybody else on Cove Road. It's not like I'm a witness or something."

Pearl bit her lip. "Were you in love with her?" His gaze moved slowly, resting on her. "Or maybe she was in love with you and you let her be, because it got you what you wanted."

"What—"

"No, be quiet a second, I'm trying to figure this out. You're the reason they came back to Tenney's Harbor for Christmas, right? You got Cassidy to ask her parents, so the two of you could hook up."

His lips parted soundlessly; he cleared his throat, tried again. "That's not how it was."

"You were cheating on Hadley and Cassidy was cheating on Akil last summer. You're the reason Cassidy ended it with him."

Bridges rested one palm on the counter edge, the other on the island, studying the floor. "Do I get to say something now?" When she stayed silent, he looked up. "You're making it sound like this terrible thing. We didn't *plan* any of it."

"That makes it okay?"

"We figured out how we felt about each other last summer. She was around more because of Akil, and—it just happened, all right?" He exhaled heavily. "We used to meet at Little Nicatou. She told me she'd liked me for a long time, and I thought she was . . . amazing. But she was always practicing and performing, and I always had a girlfriend. Until last summer."

"You're calling Hadley a friend with benefits? Because I think she'd be surprised to hear that."

"I didn't like doing that to Had, okay? She's a nice girl. And I broke it off with her eventually. It's not like I kept leading her on. Cassidy was all wrong for Akil, anyway, everybody knew it. We did what we were supposed to do at the end of the summer."

"Except tell the truth. Because that would've been too messy, right?"

"Well . . . yeah." His expression was pained, indignant. "Akil was wrecked after she dumped him. If he'd known it was because of me, it would've ruined everything. This place, the summer. I mean, we were going to tell people about us when we all came back together in June. But until then, it seemed better to . . ." At once, his eyes were damp, and he turned away from her, looking down.

Pearl stood there, hands clenched, uncertain how to push forward. "Did you know about all the stuff she was dealing with? The panic attacks?"

He nodded, his voice slightly hoarse when he spoke next. "I was the only person she told. She was embarrassed. She didn't want everybody knowing about the pills. Some of it was performance pressure, but mostly it was her family. She said nobody knew how bad it was. I tried to get her to talk about it, but she didn't want to." He rubbed his eyes with one hand. "God. When Gramps got the call, saying there'd been a fire at their house . . ." He paused, then spoke so quietly she could barely hear him. "We were supposed to meet the next day."

Empathy flooded in, the last thing she wanted to be feeling right now. "And you never told anybody."

Bridges went to the table and sat, hands dangling between his knees. "The cops know. They found some of our texts and stuff when they went through Cassidy's accounts. But that's as far as it went. Nobody else knows. Not even Tristan." He didn't move for a long time. "She said I made her feel safe."

Pearl couldn't look at him for a moment after that, her righteous anger spent in an instant after a glimpse of his pallid, still face. She sat down across from him, speaking quietly. "Was that what this was all about? You and me? Why you came after me so hard. Because I'm the opposite of Cassidy Garrison, and you were trying to forget."

He stared at the tabletop. "I really like you, Pearl. I mean it. I never lied about that."

It was about as clear a yes as she was going to get. From concert pianist to townie waitress over the course of six months: talk about a downgrade. "You should've told me about you guys." Fists hammering on the other side of a door, ready to tear it off its hinges to get to Cassidy. "It was important."

"Why?" His tone was soft, incredulous.

"Because it might have something to do with what happened."

"You think somebody did *that* because of us?" He pushed back from the table, shaking his head hard. "No. No way. Nobody could care that much."

"How do you know? How do you know Akil never found

out? If I did, anybody could." She stood. "Maybe it was more about killing one of them. Like, just Cassidy. Maybe the rest of the family was collateral damage or something to cover it up."

"What are you going to do?" Bridges followed her. "Look, nobody has to know—it's not going to help anything. If there was some connection there, the cops would've found it—"

"I just need to go, Bridges, okay?"

"Pearl, don't tell. Please." He was on her heels right up to the door, where he caught it just before it struck him, standing at the threshold, watching her take the steps two at a time. "At least tell me who told you."

She yanked her car door open. "Somebody with a good reason."

For a time, she drove aimlessly, so distracted that she nearly cruised through a red light down on Ocean. She found herself heading to Narragansett Way, not sure what she was going to do even as she reached Tristan's driveway and found it empty.

She pulled in and parked, staring up at the house, replaying the conversation with Bridges in her head, punishing herself with the details. She thought of the little club, Cassidy's miniature world, the one she would've associated most with Bridges. Watching him at the pool, the tennis courts, crushing on him but too trapped by her own life to do anything about it. Pearl checked her phone; already two missed calls and two voice mails from Bridges. And one missed call from Reese.

That one she returned. "Hey. Indy said you stopped by yesterday." He sounded like he'd woken up not long ago. "Sorry I missed you."

"Me too." There was an almost reverent pause; all that had happened between them over the last forty-eight hours deserved that. "I really just wanted to say sorry. You were right. I ran out on you the other night."

"It's okay. It was a lot all at once." She could almost see him sitting there, slightly rumpled from sleep, treading as carefully as he knew how to try not to wound her. And again, she felt on the verge of tears. "We're cool now, right? You're not secretly pissed and plotting against me?"

She laughed, hoping he couldn't hear the lump in her throat. "We're good."

"Nothing's going to change, Haskins. You know that."

It was changing now, hearing Indigo's words filtered back through him, having to wonder if the two of them had sat together and discussed her last night. A few raindrops splattered the windshield, and she looked up to see a partially clouded sky, much of the blue now lost behind gray patchwork. "I wish we could have a do-over for this summer, you know? I wish I could erase . . . I just never meant for us to fight." She pinched the bridge of her nose, felt dampness at the corners of her eyes. "If I'd known how much it would bother you—seeing me hang out with those kind of people—I would've dropped the whole thing." She wished to God she had, now. She wished she'd never found out about Bridges and Cassidy, about cheating and lies and what lay beneath the glossy veneer of the summer kids' world.

Reese was quiet a moment. "You know, my dad's one of those people, Pearl." He laughed drily. "He doesn't have their money, but he spends like he does. Everything's got to be the best. Got to be seen in the right company, you know? At the same time, he's using cards to pay off cards, and leaving Jovia hanging for all the support money he owes her." He paused. "I hate cheap, rich bastards."

They laughed together, releasing a burst of tension; she'd never wanted him with her so badly. "Are you on tomorrow?"

"You know it."

"Then I'll see you." She waited for the disconnect. She didn't want to be the first one to say good-bye.

She checked her other accounts quickly, found a message waiting from Mom. *Just checking in. Call me when you get the chance.* Pearl brought up the keypad, started to respond, then closed out. Later. Tonight. She'd get back to her tonight for sure.

Tristan's car wasn't parked at the club. Pearl backtracked to the Row and drove up to the shell of the Garrison estate, but no

Bentley. She knew of only one other place worth checking.

An occasional raindrop splashed her skin as she walked the yacht club dock, pulling on the hoodie she'd left draped over the tennis racket in her backseat. Tristan's Rivelle bobbed in its slip, unoccupied. She stood for a moment, watching it, cupping her elbows, then remembered the Islander.

The yachts were moored at the end of the dock, row after row of cruising vessels, some she recognized from the day of the regatta. *Starchaser, Penobscot Princess.* The *Cassidy Claire* was one of the last, and it seemed abandoned until she reached the edge of the deck and saw Tristan crouching, his back to her, using a compound pad to wax the boat's hardware with detailer.

He heard her approach and straightened up in the wind, his polo shirt rippling around him.

She raised her voice. "I had to see you." She stood there, wondering how much damage she'd done by leaving him the other night, if he'd want to hear anything she had to say at this point. "It's about Bridges. And Cassidy."

After a moment, Tristan stepped back, watching her come aboard. Now that she had his ear, she could barely find the words. "He begged me not to tell anyone, but . . . I thought you should know."

By the time she was done, Tristan was standing back against the mast, gripping a line, his eyes narrowed against the wind. "The police already know about this?"

"Bridges said they did. But he could've been lying again. He's good at that." She shifted, refolded her arms. "We don't have to tell anyone else, if you don't want to. I mean, I understand if you don't want Akil to find out. And Hadley would be hurt. I just didn't want to be the only one who knew." There was Indigo, of course, but her name would never come into it, at least not from Pearl's lips. "Should we go to the cops?"

"Probably." He brushed his fingers across his brow, tossed the compound pad onto the deck beside the bottle of detailer and a dry bag of gear, and stared off at the bay. "I'll call them."

She stayed quiet, wandering around the deck, running her hand over the railing. "It really is a beautiful boat," she said absently.

Tristan glanced back, wiping his hands off on a rag. "Do you want to take it out?"

She squinted at the sky. "Do you know what it's supposed to be like later?"

"Scattered showers, some wind. Nothing serious. We'll bring her back in if it gets bad."

Leaving land behind sounded wonderful. Her only regret was that, eventually, she'd have to come back. She remembered his big bed in the darkened room, the pounding of shower spray against tiles; this time, she said yes.

TWENTY-THREE

THEY WENT OUT into the bay, sailing as they had done the day of the regatta: Pearl trimming the sails, Tristan at the helm. They didn't speak much. It was a relief, not having to do anything but read the changes in the wind and watch the water spread out before them.

They passed Little Nicatou. It was impossible not to imagine Bridges and Cassidy meeting there, maybe sitting on the lip of the boathouse as Pearl had done with him that morning. Telling each other how they felt, touching for the first time. Pearl thought of Bridges's white, agonized face this morning, pleading with her to keep his secret, not to ruin everything. Watching Tristan's back, she couldn't say if it was guilt bothering her, or maybe, deep down, a case of wounded pride. Was she that petty? Was she really upset because it turned out that Bridges had always controlled what they shared, using her to fill the hole left by a girl whose act Pearl could never hope to follow?

The wind pushed them northwest, into open water. The rain started to spit faster, speckling Pearl's face and lashes; she put up her hood. The sky had gone from patchwork to solid oyster gray.

Tristan locked the wheel into autopilot and came forward. "If you want a rain jacket, I've got some below." He paused. "We could have a drink. If you're interested."

She shifted, glancing up at the sails, the telltales fluttering. "We're okay to leave her for a second?"

"It'll be fine. Nothing out here but waves."

He held the cabin door for her, and she ducked under his arm, aware of their closeness as they started down together. Telling herself she wanted this, that uncertainty was all a part of it.

Pearl leaned against the galley as Tristan withdrew a bottle of port wine, something she'd never drunk and wasn't sure if she wanted to. But she was tired of holding glasses as props, setting things on coasters and hoping that nobody would notice. Tristan poured her a finger's worth and handed her the glass, saying, "You don't seem like much of drinker," as if her thoughts had been broadcast.

She found she'd lost her taste for lying. "No. My dad's got that covered."

Tristan took his own glass, sipped. "He's got a problem?" His eyes were calm, no judgment to be read in them.

"I guess so." She checked herself. "Yeah. He does. I didn't used to think so, but—" But Reese had always known and never pushed her on it. That got her thinking of their phone call, of Indigo's hands smoothing Reese's clothes. She wouldn't dwell on that, not this afternoon. "I think he's finally figuring out that he needs some help."

"You've been running things at home for a while, haven't you?" When she looked up, surprised, Tristan shrugged, finishing his drink. "It's your personality. Efficient. Responsible."

"Wow. I sound like a party waiting to happen, huh?"

Tristan gave a rare smile, tucked it away. "You're reliable. You know the Yeats quote, 'Things fall apart; the centre cannot hold.' You'd never let that happen, if you could help it. It's not a bad thing."

"Thank you. And thank you for assuming I know Yeats." Another twitch at the corner of his mouth. "Hey, two smiles in one day. I must be doing something right."

He looked at her. Then he leaned in, lowering his face to hers. She closed her eyes as he brushed his nose and lips over her temple, into her hair. He held his face there a long moment, breathing her scent, but he didn't kiss her, not yet.

His hand slid up her side, over her shoulder to stroke her neck, and then he pulled back, still close enough that she stood under the shadow of his bent head, the smell of port rich and sweet. "I'll go up top, make sure we're still on a good heading. Be right back." He went to a closet and pulled out two rain jackets, leaving one laid over the galley counter for her as he went up the stairs.

Pearl smoothed her hair where he'd touched her, exhaled shakily, then took her glass over to one of the settees. The port was heady and powerful, not bad at all, and she sipped as she waited for him, reaching out to brace herself as the boat gave an unexpected pitch. When she sat back, her gaze landed on a footlocker under the opposite settee and lingered there.

The lock was very small, the steel catching the gleam of the lamplight. Her hand lowered her glass slowly, mechanically, setting it on the chart table.

Her bag hung over a coat hook on the wall. Tristan's word—*reliable*—flitted through her mind, how she'd been considering telling him everything about Dad. *I don't know if you heard about the caretaker. . . .* But she was going for her wallet now, popping open the coin purse and shaking out the keys.

Pearl knelt and tried one of the keys in the lock. It fit. She dragged the footlocker out the rest of the way and opened the lid.

Not much inside. Some traveler's checks, registration papers proving ownership of the boat to one David Garrison. A small snub-nosed pistol and a box of cartridges, for protection, presumably. And a yellow-and-black digital camera in a waterproof case.

Pearl glanced at the cabin door, her heartbeat insistent against her chest; he'd be back any second. She picked up the camera, examining it. It didn't look like something that would've belonged to Cassidy. It had only a few simple buttons, and there was a sticker on the case from a cartoon popular with the middle school set. She remembered the video of Cassidy sneaking up on Joseph, him grabbing for her camera, Cassidy laughing—*Mom says you can't use it unless I say so.* Sometime between then and last August, Joseph had gotten his own camera.

She turned it on. It had both picture and video capability. The few pictures were of nothing, blurry selfies of Joseph and some friends, giving peace signs or hanging upside down from tree branches. A surprise-attack shot of Cassidy sitting in the grass with a book, smiling, her eyes closed.

Pearl didn't have to look any farther than the last video recorded. Water sounds, a close shot of a weathered board with a row of action figures straddling it. Joseph's voice, low, deepened for play: "We've found their hideout . . . follow me." His hand came into the shot, walking Captain America along the board, then diving him into a plastic crate of beach toys. This went on for some time, and Pearl forwarded through the scenes until the shot shifted.

Joseph had moved to the space between the boards, still filming, the camera badly off center. A cockeyed view of the Garrisons' private stretch of beach was visible, and so was Tristan, standing along the tree line, hands in his pockets, his back to where Joseph hid in the Roost. A man stood with him, dressed in a T-shirt and jeans, a cigarette in his hand. Pearl recognized him, though the sight of them together made no sense, had no place in the world as she understood it.

Tristan and Evan Sanford, Yancey's son, continued talking, whatever was said too far off to be caught by the microphone. After they parted without a handshake or much of a good-bye, Evan went up into the trees, following some unseen trail. Tristan turned and began making his way back, lifting his head. Catching sight of his brother, and the camera.

There was a scraping, fumbling sound as Joseph moved, his knees sliding over sand-covered planks, backing toward the ladder. The last thing the camera caught was a flash of Tristan coming toward him, walking faster, gaze locked on the Roost.

When Pearl looked back, the cabin door was open, and he was there, as she knew he'd be, his jacket beaded with rain. Holding his gaze, she slowly lowered the camera into the box.

Tristan came down the steps, pushing his hood back. He

stared at the footlocker for a long moment, considering what was inside. "You watched it."

"I wasn't . . ." She shook her head. "I didn't. I was only looking at it."

He walked over. "I never thought to check in there. I guess I just . . . stopped seeing it." His tone was slightly unbelieving, the idea of something not occurring to him so novel that he didn't even seem perturbed. "David kept those keys in the lockbox at the house in the off-season. They should've been burned. Where did you find them?"

She didn't answer, instead getting slowly to her feet. "We should go back now." Her words were like stones in her mouth. "It's raining harder."

A slow, chiding tilt of his head, and it was all laid bare between them, at least as much of it as she understood. Her legs faltered as she backed into the chart table; she grabbed the settee for support. "I don't even know"—now her words were dust, her tongue sticking to the roof of her mouth— "it's just a video. I—"

"Pearl." In a sigh. "You should not have watched that."

Panic trickled in, quickening, becoming a flood. Her gaze slid to the cabin door.

"It's okay. Really. I'm almost glad it was you." He stepped forward; she stepped back. "If somebody else had to find it first, you should be the one. I've been looking . . . for months. They didn't really know what they had, so it stood to reason that they hadn't hid it all that well." A slight lift of his shoulders. "I was wrong."

She opened her mouth, but a choked sound came out first, not words. "You did it." Horror, then, a sickening blow. "You had him do it."

"Hold still." She kept going. His eyes widened slightly. "Stop moving away from me."

Pearl dodged and ran, the steps and door twenty feet away, fifteen—he caught her around her waist and slung her back, slamming her into the edge of the galley counter. Then he was on her, shushing her, her cry smothered by his hand. "Stop it. Pearl? Stop it, or I won't let you breathe."

She thrashed against him, blows bouncing off his chest and shoulders. His hand moved to cover her nose, sealing off everything. She was still hitting, trying to bring her knee up to force him back, the roar of panic smothering everything, blurring the room in static and noise. He was still talking against her ear, nonsense sounds, until some instinct finally kicked in and she went prone, knowing only the heat of his palm and her starving lungs.

"*Shhh.* Like that." He sighed again, as if mildly put out, adjusting his grip so that one of her nostrils was free. She had to cough but couldn't, instead sucking at the pitiful stream of air. "I'm going to let go now. Can you control yourself?"

She nodded once. He released her, stepping back. Pearl gasped, stars bursting across her vision, edging down the counter away from him until she hit the wall and could go no farther. Her eyes were still watering, and she swiped at them. "You're pretty good at that." Her voice shook. "Get lots of experience with your sister?" He kept observing her, his eyes as still as polished obsidian, catching the lamplight. "She recorded you. Breaking down the door to get to her."

He lowered his head slightly, gaze traveling the row of liquor bottles. "That must've been the day she hid it." He moved away from Pearl, staring into the footlocker for a second before shutting the lid with the toe of his shoe and pushing it back underneath the settee. "She told Sloane that she was going to the Islander to make one of the videos for her site, but she must've brought both cameras. I followed. Too late, apparently." His tone was vague, musing. "Protecting the little brother."

Pearl watched him, not sure if this was shock, the numbness that spread through her, the feeling of detachment from this moment, this place. She saw the gate around the Garrison house. Not trying to keep someone out—trying to keep someone in. "Everybody thought it was David." Her voice was a husky whisper. "You let them think he was the monster, making everyone afraid. But it was you. You were the one."

Tristan absorbed this, slowly shaking his head. "He was the monster."

The boat gave another tilt; glass tumblers slid together

with a musical clink. Her gaze went to the cabin door; too far away, he'd be on her in a second. And she wasn't giving him any excuse to take her air again. She talked fast, words coming nearly on top of each other. "Your brother and sister were scared of you. Weren't they? You went after Joseph to get the camera back, but Cassidy helped him, hid it from you. They didn't need to know why it was so important. Just that you'd hurt them to get it."

"You're not trying to understand."

Gooseflesh, nausea, washed over her. "He killed them. He *burned* them."

"And I told you. I carry that with me, all the time."

A confession as they'd danced, mistaken for grief. "How awful for you." Eventually, more words came to her. "How did you even find him?"

"Offer enough money, you can find someone to do anything. Something like this . . . you can't leave a digital trail, bank transfers. The police will find it. You have to be meticulous. I can be that." He picked something up from the magazine rack—a tube of lip gloss with a sparkly label. Cassidy's. "He'd done time while he was living in Illinois. Manslaughter. I told him what I wanted. He should've been able to do it."

It took Pearl a second to find her voice again. "You must've let him in. While your family was at the club that night, before you left to go up north. He was already in the house." That was why Dad never saw any footprints by the fence, why the home protection system never went off until it detected smoke.

"He was supposed to kill the watchman. It was the best way to let the fire burn, to destroy everything. But he didn't."

Because Dad was Yancey's friend. He'd been coming around the Sanfords' house for years, since Evan was a kid. Whatever atrocities Evan had been willing to commit inside the house, when he'd recognized Dad, he hadn't pulled the trigger. Pearl shut her eyes for a moment, released a trembling breath. "God. They were your family."

Tristan stopped walking the lip gloss through his fingers, dropping it back among the *New Yorker*s and *Architectural Digest*s. "They weren't." He turned to her. "David and Sloane Garrison were self-serving hypocrites who treated their children like trophies. I was always the one David chose. To crush. To try to break down." He exhaled slowly, through a clenched jaw. "Cassidy was their automaton. Joseph was their pet. All I wanted was to be free of them."

A gust of wind slatted rain against the portholes. The stained-glass lamp swayed on its chain, casting red and yellow dapples of light across the teak paneling. "Are you free now?" He didn't answer her. She was sweating slightly, taking slow steps toward the cabin door. "That's not what I see. I think it's tearing you apart. I think that's the real reason you didn't leave town. You couldn't stand to leave what you did.

You're grieving." She shook her head, disbelieving. "You never expected to feel anything, did you?"

Tristan's fingers curled, released. He closed half the distance, tension spooling between them. "Stop moving. Don't make me hurt you more than I have to."

She hesitated, swallowing an acid taste. "You're going to have to."

Pearl ran. He was faster, agile, blocking the path to the door, making her wheel around—she shoved over a storage container, strewing the contents in his path. The only place left was the head.

She ran inside, slid the catch home, spun to face the tiny room, full of a sickening understanding of things already done, scenes played out. As if in slow motion, she went for the cupboards under the sink—there must be a weapon, something Cassidy hadn't thought of—then screamed as the door was slammed from the outside.

It took only two hard kicks. The gold catch—weakened from last time—exploded. Pearl lunged forward, going nowhere, only wanting to escape his hands. But he had her, grabbing her hair and shirt, heaving her forward into porcelain and a gradual, yielding darkness.

TWENTY-FOUR

THE RAIN WOKE her, pattering against the awning overhead. She blinked, gazed at a miasma of gray and shadow. Her
stomach rolled, and she turned her face against the ground,
waiting for the need to be sick to pass.

It did, though her mind was still clouded as she sat up.
Being upright expanded the ache, thrumming through her
head, sending bolts of pain down her neck into her shoulders.
Pearl dropped back on one hand, dazed.

Tristan was there, at the mast, the hood up on his raincoat.
He was refitting the sails, preparing to change course. She lay
on the deck of the cockpit, her bag tossed beside her. Spots of
blood, still tacky, splattered the front of her sweatshirt. She

reached up, found the throbbing, matted place where her head had connected with the shower stall. He must've carried her here. She thought again of her bag, the only belonging she'd brought on board. The only evidence. It seemed so clear: she was about to go overboard. Unconscious.

Heart pounding, Pearl dropped into a crawl, leaving the cockpit and making her way, elbow by knee, along the deck. The storm had darkened the day almost to night, rain coming down at an angle. The deck was slippery; there wasn't much to keep her from going over the edge. The metal railing had gaps wide enough for her body to easily slide through into the waves below, unseen, unheard. Lost.

She dropped onto her belly as she passed below where he worked at the mast, gritting her teeth as the nausea came back, the blurred vision. She didn't dare think any further than rounding the curve to the pulpit, reaching it, clinging onto the railing there. There must be a lifeboat somewhere on board—in fact, she was almost sure she'd seen one, bright yellow, the inflatable kind that folded into a storage valise—but where it was or how she'd get to it now was beyond her.

She heard him move, the squeak of rubber soles on the deck. Pearl lay her head down, squeezing her eyes shut, waiting for him to say he could see her. Nothing. He must be on his way back to the cockpit. He'd realize she was missing in a second. She crawled on, finally reaching the bow and clinging to the railing, spray striking her face.

"Pearl." His call carried on the wind. "There's nowhere to go. Come back." A pause. "You know I'll find you."

She stayed low, as far below his line of sight from the stern as she could get, wriggling her legs out through the railing so the top of her head didn't clear the cabin housing. The edge of the deck pressed into her solar plexus, and she struggled to hold on and keep her center of gravity balanced.

Cold spray soaked her legs. Her arms shook. She tried to hear his approach, but it was lost in the sound of waves. The boat pitched and yawed, rolling her to the side, and she clenched her teeth against a scream, finally dragging herself back up with her arm strength alone. Forehead pressed to the deck, she closed her eyes, waiting for discovery.

The next sound was one that she felt more than heard, a slight vibration up through the deck. Footsteps on the cabin stairs. He'd gone below to search. He must've looked down both sides of the deck and hadn't seen her.

Pearl crawled the rest of the way to her feet, catching a glimpse of the ocean below, terrifying in a way it had never been before, sharkskin gray and merciless. There was almost nowhere to hide in the cabin; he'd be back in a moment. She rounded the bow, searching the horizon for other boats, a sign of land. Nothing but fog and rain. Who knew how far out they were now?

She kicked something—the bottle of detailer. Tristan had left his stuff out, the dry bag with deck gear, some extra pins, compound pads.

When he came out of the cabin and walked around the awning, she was waiting for him by the mast. Trembling, drenched, rain dripping from her nose and chin. His face was mostly hidden by the hood, his hair clinging damply to the lining. He watched her, holding utterly still.

"Did you bring the gun?" She had to raise her voice over the falling rain.

"I don't need the gun."

He stepped toward her. She had to force herself to hold her ground. "Tristan. Don't do this."

"Nobody knows we came out here together. Nobody even knows you were looking for me earlier, do they? There was nobody for you to tell." Another step. "That's what I mean when I say I'm glad it was you who found out. We're alone. Both of us. You understand it."

"I'll never understand what you did."

He paused, gave the faintest gesture of dismissal, and came at her.

She dropped to her knees, grabbing the tool she'd taken from his bag and laid on the deck behind her—hydraulic rigging cutters. He grabbed her, and she lashed back with the cutters, off balance, catching him in the kneecap. He staggered with a muffled curse, nearly fell. She clambered to the preventer line, opened the cutters, and sliced.

It didn't take much; the tool was strong enough to cut through wire line. The preventer snapped. The boom swung across the deck, pulled by the gusting mainsail.

She scrambled back, cringed away, not watching to see where or how it struck him.

There was no cry, nothing to tell her what she'd see when she turned back. When she looked, Tristan was gone.

She sat where she was, staring at the place where he'd stood before the boom had caught him. Before he'd been swept over.

She went to the railing, seeing nothing below but the gray, hungry water, the surface alive with rain. She stared until her eyes burned, until she imagined a hundred shadowy shapes reaching from the waves, but nothing emerged. He might have been hit in the head. Unconscious now, sinking.

She untied the life ring and tossed it, watching it wash away in the *Cassidy Claire*'s wake.

Shaking, Pearl went to the cockpit, never taking her eye from the loose boom, which hovered toward starboard with the pull of the mainsail, bouncing ever so slightly, ready to sweep back.

The VHF marine radio was mounted on the wall in the cabin, the LCD screen glowing orange, full of readouts she didn't understand. She knew enough to flip down the red cover over the distress button and hit it, to press the channel sixteen button for hailing another vessel, to pick up the receiver and hold down the button. "Hello?" Her head was splitting; she rubbed her eyes, trying to remember Dad on the little radio in the Cat. Pull it together, for God's sake. Talk like a sailor. "Mayday, mayday, mayday. This is the *Cassidy*

Claire. I'm alone. I need help. I'm hurt . . . I was attacked. The preventer line is cut." She swallowed hard. "One man overboard. Send the coast guard. Over."

Static, hissing. In time, a voice came back: "*Cassidy Claire, Cassidy Claire, Cassidy Claire*, this is the Tenney's Harbor marina. Coast guard dispatched. Switch and listen channel sixty-six, over."

"Switching channel sixty-six, over."

The conversation went on for a few more minutes—they asked for the color of the boat hull and cabin housing, recommended she put a compress against her head and wait until help arrived.

"No. I'm going to try turning her around. Over."

She didn't wait for a response to that. Back up to the cockpit, then the mast, where clouds moved overhead in a brooding formation. She gripped the lines, always watching the boom, ready to dodge it if necessary. She could tack on her own, follow the starboard pull and see if she could execute a gradual turn, even with this much resistance. If she couldn't, the GPS in the radio was transmitting her exact location to the rescue authorities. They'd find her, sooner or later.

Once she'd done what she could with the sails, Pearl took the helm, gripping the metal wheel in both hands as she motored toward rescue lights, and people, and home.

TWENTY-FIVE

PEARL WASN'T THE only person on North Beach. The swimmers were some distance away, granting her privacy as she walked down the shore to the waterline with a box in her hand.

She knelt where ocean and sand began to mix, soft, clay-like, molding around her knees. It had been three weeks; the effects of the concussion had subsided, the nausea finally ebbing away along with the worst of the bad dreams. Still, Dad had driven her here, and now he lingered at the edge of the parking lot, keeping an eye on her without crowding.

The truth was known. The police had gotten a confession from Evan Sanford within forty-eight hours of Pearl's return to the harbor, extracted with the help of the video from Joseph's camera. The money Tristan had paid Evan—thousands of dollars in cash he'd agreed not to spend until one year after the crime—was found in a bag under the floorboards of his bedroom closet in Yancey's house.

Pearl removed the lid from the shoe box, looking down at the mass of sea glass and shells. Amazing that her entire collection fit in there; she'd spent years collecting these, dusting the mason jars she stored them in, keeping them carefully aligned on her windowsill so she could watch the sun pass through them morning, afternoon, evening.

Now she tossed a handful into the surf. She could still see the colors glinting through the foam. She threw a fistful, harder, until they were gone from sight. Gone, like the summer. Her freshman orientation at College of the Atlantic was next week. Gone, like Bridges. She'd received a final text from him a few days ago: *Going home tomorrow.* Then: *I'm sorry.* Pearl had looked at the message a long time, unsure what to say, if she wanted to say anything. Finally, she'd written, *Take care.* Silence since then.

Gone, like Tristan. The water had taken him completely, never providing a body despite the numerous coast guard searches. At Pearl's worst moments, her mind went there, to the idea of him, alone, adrift, fathoms deep, and she'd have to fight to drag herself back to the here and now.

She hurled another handful and another, until she was out

of breath, her shoulder sore, chest aching.

Dad came up behind her, hesitating a moment before speaking. "You okay?"

"Yeah." She stood, brushing off her knees, and looked up into Dad's watchful expression. "Cut it out."

"What?"

"Thinking you shouldn't have let Mom leave. She had to get back to work. And there's nothing she could do that you can't." Mom had taken a week off when she heard, staying in a local motel so she could be close while Pearl recovered. It had been awkward, the three of them stuck together for the first time in years, but weirdly nice, too. Like maybe not so much had changed after all. Pearl cleared her throat, picking up the box. "Did you hear back from Mimi yet?"

He nodded. "She says she'll give me a recommendation."

"Nice. And the Philbricks will, too, I bet. If you ask."

"Not a lot to jump-start a business with."

"It's something." Since the news broke, Dad hadn't exactly received a flood of apologies and job offers from Millionaires' Row; the silence was stunned, sickened, disbelieving. Maybe, in the eyes of Tenney's Harbor, some of that would always cling to Dad, deserved or not. But at least now he was talking about looking into caretaking jobs in Trenton, Ellsworth, Cherryfield. Seeing what was out there.

He nodded to what was left of the sea glass. "Took you a long time to find all that."

"Finding it was the fun part." She held out the box. "Want to throw some?"

He did, watching the pieces scatter into water tinged orange with sunset. Pearl's phone buzzed, announcing a text; she checked the screen and smiled. Reese.

Dad started down the beach, hands in pockets as he glanced back at her. "So, what're you going to do when you come to the beach now?"

"I don't know. Maybe start a new collection." She nudged him. "Strictly mainland glass."

He kissed the top of her head roughly. As they walked together, she let the last of the sea glass fall between her fingers, leaving a trail for the next beachcomber to find.